# The
# SURVIVALIST
## (Anarchy Rising)

# Books by Dr. Arthur T. Bradley

৵ ৶

Handbook to Practical Disaster Preparedness for the Family

The Prepper's Instruction Manual

Disaster Preparedness for EMP Attacks and Solar Storms

Process of Elimination: A Thriller

The Survivalist (Frontier Justice)

The Survivalist (Anarchy Rising)

The Survivalist (Judgment Day)

The Survivalist (Madness Rules)

The Survivalist (Battle Lines)

The Survivalist (Finest Hour)

৵ ৶

Available in print, ebook, and audiobook at all major resellers or at:
**http://disasterpreparer.com**

# The SURVIVALIST
## (Anarchy Rising)

Arthur T. Bradley, Ph.D.

# The Survivalist
## (Anarchy Rising)

Author:        Arthur T. Bradley, Ph.D.

Email:         arthur@disasterpreparer.com

Website:     http://disasterpreparer.com

Illustrations used throughout the book are privately owned and copyright protected. Special thanks are extended to Siobhan Gallagher for editing, Marites Bautista for print layout, and Nikola Nevenov for illustrations and cover design.

ISBN 10: 1492340626
ISBN 13: 978-1492340621

Printed in the United States of America

Anarchism is a political philosophy that sees the state as undesirable, unnecessary, and perhaps even harmful. Proponents often advocate the establishment of stateless societies whose organizations are based on voluntary participation. Democratic voting and the ownership of private property are viewed as unfair to the broader population. While not all anarchists advocate the use of violence to achieve their ends, it does resonate as a common thread among many groups.

Anarchy is generally held at bay for three reasons. First, those who hold political power provide important goods and services to the population, and are, therefore, viewed by many as necessary. The authorities also possess the military might to contain and suppress anti-government movements. To that end, many people fear the violent chaos that might ensue from a stateless society. Most are willing to suffer the imperfections of what is arguably an unfair system for the benefits that it provides. Finally, those who have established or inherited wealth see structured society as a means by which to protect their prosperity, and thus, are strongly opposed to a change in the status quo.

Should the world's societies suddenly be disrupted by a major disaster, such as an asteroid strike, deadly pandemic, or global financial collapse, many of these reasons would no longer hold true. History has proven that when governments can no longer maintain order or provide life-sustaining services, the larger population will rise up and overthrow them. When this happens, more often than not, the streets run red with blood.

ॐ ॐ

*"'I'm not afraid to die like a man fighting,*
*but I would not like to be killed*
*like a dog unarmed."*

William H. Bonney (a.k.a. Billy the Kid)
March 1879

ॐ ॐ

The cab of Mason Raines' black F150 pickup was quiet and empty, like a school bus that had just dropped off a load of noisy kindergarteners. In his case, however, it was not a welcome silence. Rather, it was the quiet resignation that a soldier feels when he leaves home to go to war. It was not the first time he had felt such loneliness; nor, he suspected, would it be the last. Such was the price he paid for walking a path directed by duty.

He glanced in the rearview mirror to take one last look at the town of Boone, North Carolina, as it slowly disappeared behind the foothills of the Blue Ridge Mountains. The image brought back memories of despair and hope, of life and death, of love and loss. Boone was where a few brave men and women had stood against an enemy bent on destroying any semblance of law and order. They were outnumbered and outgunned, but with his leadership, they had triumphed in the end.

Many convicts had died at Mason's hands, but none he felt who hadn't deserved it. He had made lifelong friends, including Father Paul, Chief Blue, and perhaps even Erik, Boone's leader of those infected by the Superpox-99 virus. While the townspeople still had a great deal of work to do, they had taken many important steps, including reestablishing water service, setting up a soup kitchen, and clearing the streets of bodies and abandoned cars so that some rudimentary commercial activity might eventually resume.

The reflection in the rearview mirror was momentarily blocked by Bowie's massive head as he peered in through the open window between the cab and the truck bed.

Mason smiled. "It's just you and me now, boy."

The one-hundred-and-forty-pound Irish wolfhound leaned in and licked his ear, coating it with a thick layer of slobber.

"Yeah, yeah. I hear you," he said. "It's all going to be fine. We'll be coming back this way soon enough, right?"

Bowie tried to lick him again, but Mason leaned forward to avoid the dog's enormous tongue.

Mason thought about his girlfriend, Ava, standing in the street waving goodbye. He forced himself to recreate her image in his mind . . . thick black hair, dark eyes, and a soft, warm body. He remembered the sound of her voice, the eagerness of her kiss, and the warm sensation of her breasts pressing against his chest. How long, he wondered, would he be able to recall the details with such clarity? A day? A week? Eventually, they would fade like the ink in a journal.

They had met under the direst of circumstances but had somehow managed to find comfort and even happiness in one another's arms. He didn't know if relationships crafted from hope and hardship were lasting or simply short-lived panaceas to ease the pain. Was she still watching his truck drive away like in the closing scene of a classic western? Or, had she already accepted that he was gone and was now waiting instead for the next gunslinger to roll into town?

"Enough," he said in a loud voice. "When did I get so damn soft?"

Bowie turned and looked at him through squinted eyes, unsure if he was talking to him.

Mason couldn't help but marvel at the dog's uncanny ability to understand him. Whether he told him to lead the way or guard a prisoner, Bowie rarely let him down. Where he had received such remarkable training remained a mystery, but Mason suspected that it was the result of being part of either a military or police K-9 unit. When he had found Bowie, the dog was lying at the feet of his previous owner as she slowly rotted away in the storeroom of a convenience store. The finality of the situation left Mason with more questions than answers about the dog's origins. Bowie was in many ways like every other dog, fun loving, constantly hungry, and loyal to a fault. But he was also unique, not only for his size and intelligence, but for his willingness to engage in a fight.

Mason leaned closer, and Bowie slowly extended his tongue as if he thought a sneak attack was the only way to hit his mark. When his master didn't pull away, the dog licked him again, this time with a gentleness that was as comforting as a close friend's embrace. He reached up and patted the side of Bowie's massive head. Everything was going to be okay. He had been leaving people behind his entire life. Sometimes he returned, and sometimes he didn't. But either way, Mason liked to think that the world he left behind was slightly better for his passing.

As for those who remained in Boone, they would do well enough. With the convicts soundly defeated and the town's major needs addressed, the survivors were well positioned to survive the coming months.

There were still uncertainties, of course. Not the least of which was Erik and the other victims of the virus, who were still living outside the mainstream community. When the Viral Defense Corp soldiers had arrived in Boone, the townspeople had offered no assistance in locating those who had survived the infection. Disfigured men and women had stepped up to fight Rommel and his brutal soldiers when the town was all but lost. Alliances, even if unspoken, had been made. Bonds like those, which had been forged in blood, were not easily broken. The question of whether Erik and the others would eventually pose a threat to the town, as Colonel Gacy had suggested, was still open. For now, the townspeople seemed to have found a balance where all could coexist in peace.

If things became too dangerous, Ava could seek refuge at Mason's cabin. However, he thought it highly unlikely that she would ever do so, no matter what the threat. Ava was the type of woman who would stick by the people of Boone even through their darkest hour, partly because they needed her skills as a doctor and partly because she needed them to provide structure to her shattered life.

When she and Mason had parted, Ava had told him that she loved him, and he had returned the words without hesitation. Every time he held her close and looked into her beautiful eyes, love was exactly what he felt. And why not? It was a new world where things like love could no longer be waited for; nor could they be tossed around like confetti at a wedding. Now, more than ever, powerful emotions were to be cherished as an important part of the human experience.

Mason hoped to return to Boone within a couple of weeks, but even as he and Ava kissed goodbye, neither asked for, nor made, any such promises. Nothing was certain anymore. Violence was everywhere, and the best laid plans were only a bullet away from being disrupted.

Looking for a distraction, he popped in a Rolling Stones CD and turned his attention to the road ahead. Mick Jagger's words were not only catchy; they espoused a cool, carefree philosophy that could comfort even the most worried soul. Before the song was even halfway through, Mason was singing along, tapping his palm on the steering wheel.

*You can't always get what you want*
*But if you try sometimes*
*You just might find*
*You get what you need*

੭ ੬

As a deputy marshal, Mason felt duty-bound to do what he could to reestablish order, not only in his corner of the world but all across the nation. The events in Boone had proven that such order sometimes required lining the streets with the bodies of those who preferred anarchy. Despite his recent success, he fully understood that he couldn't do it alone. Mason needed the Marshals as much as they needed him. The question was whether or not the Marshals even existed anymore. He concluded that the only way to really assess their strength and numbers was to travel to his assigned post at the Federal Law Enforcement Training Center, located in Glynco, Georgia.

The trip from Boone to Glynco was just over four hundred miles if traveled along the interstates. It would be quite a bit longer than that for Mason because he planned to navigate the majority of the journey on two-lane county roads. He figured that he could make it as far south as Gastonia, roughly eighty miles, before having to detour off Highway 321. An indirect route from there forward would allow him to skip Charlotte, which, like other large cities, was likely fraught with all manner of danger.

Mason only made it as far as the small town of Lenoir, about twenty miles south of Boone, before his first encounter. A procession of six vehicles drove slowly north, each following closely behind the other, like a column of army ants. They moved carefully even though the highway near Lenoir was sprinkled only with the occasional car parked on the shoulder.

As the convoy approached, Mason slowed and then stopped his truck on the far right shoulder. He unlatched the floor-mounted rack and retrieved his Colt M4 assault rifle. Bowie was already standing up in the back, peering over the top of the cab.

"This way," he said, sliding across the seat and exiting through the passenger side door.

Bowie leaned over the edge of the truck bed and dropped carefully to the ground beside him.

Mason stepped around to the front of the truck and set his M4 on the hood so as not to appear too threatening. In a world where violence was now a way of life, first impressions could make the difference between an encounter ending in a gunfight or a handshake. He stood on the opposite side of the engine compartment, figuring that the engine block might offer some protection from small arms fire.

The convoy of cars eased to a stop about thirty yards away. After a few seconds, a man and a woman climbed out of the rusted station wagon that was leading the procession. A girl, no older than six, peeked out through the back window. The man gripped an antique single-shot shotgun with both hands. He and the woman walked slowly toward Mason and Bowie, glancing back at the occupants of the other cars for encouragement.

Both wore filthy clothes, discolored from weeks of accumulating sweat stains and spilled soup. Even at a distance, their body odor was stiffer than a block of Limburger cheese. The woman's hair was a matted, stringy mess, and her face was smeared with more dirt than makeup. The man didn't look any better with a scruffy beard that extended along the underside of his neck and greasy hair that draped down in front of both eyes.

"What's your name, mister?" the man asked in a nasal voice that sounded a lot like Ernest T. Bass from the old *Andy Griffith* show.

Mason stepped around from behind the truck, leaving his assault rifle where it lay. His Wilson Combat Supergrade .45 pistol was holstered at his side. Bowie stood beside him, eyeing the strangers, a deep grumble sounding in his chest.

"I'm Deputy Marshal Mason Raines," he said, parting his jacket so they could see both his badge and his gun. Each conveyed an important message that he didn't want overlooked. "And you folks?"

The man looked over at the woman, and she shook her head, furrowing her eyebrows.

"Our names don't matter none." He looked over at Mason's truck. "You got any water in there?"

Mason shrugged. "A little."

"We need some real bad."

"How many of you are there?"

The man looked back at the convoy. A few people had gotten out to better see what was happening.

"Twenty seven, including the young'uns," he said. "So you got any water or not?"

"Not enough for twenty-seven thirsty people."

"How much you got?" He stared at Mason with suspicion, the shotgun slowly swinging toward him. It was a 20-gauge and likely loaded only with birdshot, but even so, it could ruin a person's day.

Mason couldn't help but play back his encounter with the two convicts, Red Beard and Teardrops, only a couple of weeks earlier. Like these people, they had needed supplies. And like these people, they seemed willing to take them by force. But Ernest T. and his wife weren't convicts, just desperate people trying to survive however they knew how. Mason wanted to believe there was a difference. He wanted to believe there was a way forward that didn't end with someone bleeding out on a deserted highway.

He put his hand on his Supergrade, and when he did, Bowie tensed as he prepared to leap forward.

"If you point that pop gun at me," said Mason, "I'll have to put you down. I don't think you want your wife and daughter to see that. Do you?"

Ernest T. sucked in a deep gulp of air between wide-spaced teeth as he turned once again to his wife for direction.

She reached out and put a hand on her husband's arm.

"We don't mean no harm, Marshal," she said with a deep drawl. "Just thirsty, that's all. Real thirsty." She licked her lips, which were just starting to split.

Mason thought long and hard before answering.

"I'll tell you what. Have each of your people bring forward a cup or bottle, and I'll fill them. That will be enough to get you down the road a ways."

His generosity would nearly empty one of his three, five-gallon, water cans, but he didn't see that he had any other choice. The decision to be generous or selfish was often dictated by circumstance. For now, he had plenty of supplies, and watching children suffer was not something he could justify.

The woman smiled, showing off a missing front tooth.

"God bless you, suh." Before he could say another word, she turned and hollered to the rest of the group. "The marshal's gonna give us some water. Come on!"

Before Mason knew it, two dozen people were swirling around his truck, poking into things they had no business in.

"Hey!" he shouted. "Move away from the truck."

Most of them didn't even hear him. The few that turned to look at him paused only for a moment and then went right back to rifling through his belongings.

Mason drew his Supergrade and fired a shot into the air. The sound echoed above their heads like the sharp crack of lightning.

People screamed and rushed back toward their cars, ducking their heads as they ran. Bowie chased after them, barking and circling like a sheepdog facing an unruly flock.

Ernest T. scrambled to pick up his shotgun, which he had leaned against one of the tires on Mason's truck.

"Don't," Mason said in a stern voice.

Seeing the marshal standing on one side and the dog approaching from the other, Ernest T. stepped away from the shotgun.

"Here's how this is going to work," said Mason. "You'll bring the cups and bottles a few at a time. Once I fill them, you'll take the water back to your people. Are we clear?"

He nodded. "Yes suh."

"If, at any point, I feel that my generosity is less than appreciated, the deal is off. Clear on that too?"

He nodded again.

Mason holstered his pistol and secured his M4 back in the cab. He went to the bed of the truck, slid aside a tarp, and hoisted out a blue jerry can filled with water. He carried it around front and set it on the hood a safe distance from his other supplies. Ernest T. was on his best behavior now, patiently waiting for Mason to begin pouring the water.

With the ground rules now in place, the distribution of water was completed without any additional fuss. Most of the people took their time drinking it, fearing that it might be the last water they would have for a while. When Ernest T. was done with his, he came back holding an old handkerchief with something wrapped inside. He held it out to Mason.

"It's the only thing I got of any value."

Mason reluctantly took it and unwrapped the cloth. Inside was a beautiful antique silver harmonica. The sides were inlaid with gold letters that read *Hohner Meisterklasse*. Mason didn't know much about harmonica brands, but it looked valuable.

He immediately started to hand it back to Ernest T. but then stopped himself. Who was he to refuse another man's gift?

"It's beautiful," he said. "Thank you."

"I pay my debts, Marshal. We appreciate that water. It was real good."

Mason wrapped the harmonica back up in the handkerchief and stuck it in the breast pocket of his jacket.

"Papa!" Ernest T.'s daughter was leaning out her window. "Mama says, come on!"

He nodded to Mason and turned to leave.

"Hold up a second." Mason quickly dug through his supplies and came back with three large Hershey chocolate bars. He handed them to Ernest T. "For the kids," he said.

"You got my word. Bless you, Marshal."

"I suggest you head toward Boone. It's about twenty miles that way." He pointed up Highway 321. "Go straight to the church and ask for Father Paul. If nothing else, he'll make sure that everyone gets food and water."

Ernest T. nodded again.

"Just understand that, if you hope to stick around Boone," warned Mason, "you'll have to pull your own weight. If you don't, I'll personally come back and toss you out on your ear."

"We're all hard workers, Marshal. Even the young'uns. You'll see."

Mason nodded. "Best be on your way then. And don't stop for anyone. No matter how little you have, there are people out there willing to take it."

Presided Rosalyn Glass sat at the head of a large mahogany table. Vice President Lincoln Pike was to her right, and the Secretary of Defense, Retired General Kent Carr, sat to her left. Leaders from nearly every remaining government agency took up positions around the conference room table. There was a cold sense of worry in the room that felt like someone had accidentally left the air conditioner running all night.

She held up a hand, and the chatter in the room quickly subsided.

"Let's get to it," she said, turning to General Carr and nodding. "General, tell us what you know."

The general was a tall, proud man who sat perfectly straight as he spoke. He was clean shaven except for a thin pencil mustache that had been out of fashion since the days of Vincent Price. With the collapse of so much of the nation's defense infrastructure, his role as the Secretary of Defense had recently been expanded to become a true commander's position.

"Yes, Madam President," he said. "Over the past six days, we've been receiving reports of a rapidly growing insurrection. Military bases have been attacked and ransacked, supplies taken, and soldiers killed or missing."

"Do we know who's behind it?"

"The attacks appear to be uncoordinated and lacking any kind of central authority or command structure. Based on what we know, it's more of a widespread civil uprising than an organized rebellion."

"Are you saying this is a national uprising?"

"It could be the early stages of one, yes."

"And you believe that this violence is a result of the lack of services? Food, water, electricity—that sort of thing?"

"That's certainly a large part of it. There's obviously been a great deal of suffering following the outbreak of Superpox-99. People are not only dealing with the death of loved ones but also the complete loss of services. Most people had grown completely dependent on our national infrastructures. Now, they find themselves foraging for their most basic necessities while dodging violence on every corner. All of this is breeding discontent."

"That's understandable," the president said. "We've all lost so much. Still, Americans love their country. There's got to be more to it than simple discontent and hardship."

"Indeed." He turned to the vice president. "Perhaps it would be better if you explained." The general made no effort to hide the contempt in his voice.

Vice President Pike openly sneered at him before turning to face President Glass.

"The executive order that you signed, Madam President, authorizing action against those infected by the virus is understandably unpopular."

"Lest you forget, I signed it at your insistence," she said, her lips pressing firmly together. The thought of the executive order issued against her own population sat in her gut like rancid peanut butter.

"And I still firmly believe that it remains necessary," he said. "While there is some resistance to it among the broader population—"

"That is an understatement," said General Carr.

She turned to look at the general.

"Tell me."

"By all accounts, the Viral Defense Corps is viewed as the brutal arm of a suppressive regime. No different than the Khmer Rouge or Battalion-316."

"We're a suppressive regime?"

"When a government sends out hit squads, one could see how the term might be seen as applicable."

She stared at him, surprised by the directness of his words.

He continued. "Madam President, exterminating people for any reason is a distasteful task, one that many of us find to go against our convictions and even the rule of law. I've been outspoken from the beginning that this executive order was a mistake." Several people at the table murmured in agreement.

"Yet, you offered no alternative," interjected the vice president.

President Glass turned back to face him.

"Look," he said, "despite the distastefulness of the task, it is truly necessary. We'll lose our nation if we don't stop the maniacal behavior of these . . . these . . ."

"People. They're people, Lincoln."

"Are they?" He shuffled through papers in a folder with the words *Top Secret* stamped across the front. "The latest CDC reports show that the infected are undergoing all sorts of physiological changes. Not only to their brains, which, let's face it, make Charles Manson look like Mahatma Gandhi, but also to their bodies. Here," he said, pulling out a page. "This one states that they're experiencing calcification of their bones as well as significant increase in their muscle mass. Christ, they're all but turning superhuman." He slapped the page. "Who knows where this ends."

She looked to General Carr for his response.

"What the vice president says is true. Some are becoming stronger and more violent, and that is indeed worrisome. However, he is conveniently leaving out the fact that many of the infected are not experiencing these changes. In fact, many have stabilized and are viewed as able to safely reintegrate with society."

"Let me get this straight," she said. "Are you saying that some of those infected are turning into monsters in every sense of the word, and the rest are basically staying human?" She looked to Vice President Pike and then to General Carr for their confirmation.

Both men nodded.

"The question," said the vice president, "is whether we want to be reactive or proactive. Are we going to wait until these crazies are banging on our front door before we take action? If we do, it's going to be too late."

"I don't think that's the question at all," argued the general. "The real question is whether we want to trade one form of violence for another. With your order, the government essentially declared war on a significant portion of our remaining population. Worse yet is that it also bred a sense of fear and hate in those who were not infected. Believe me when I say that, if we continue down this path, the government will be overthrown. Of that, I have no doubt."

After a long moment, President Glass said, "All right. Let's stop this madness."

"That would be a terrible mistake," said the vice president, leaning forward across the table. "If anything, we need more aggressive action. If we don't—"

President Glass held up her hand. "I mean it, Lincoln. By the end of the day, you will have a retraction of the executive order on my desk. Are we clear?"

He stared at her for a full five seconds before answering.

"Fine, for what good that will do."

She cocked her head.

"Explain yourself."

"The VDC rules of operation will prevent any interruption in their mission for many months."

"What are you talking about?" she said, her voice rising. "What rules of operation?"

"Madam President, surely you recall our discussing their need for operational autonomy."

She thought hard. "So?"

"The only way we could ensure that the VDC didn't get squeezed by political agendas was to have them operate in the black."

"What the hell does that mean?"

"It means," said General Carr, "that Vice President Pike issued orders in your name for the VDC to operate with zero base contact for a period of six months."

She spun to face the vice president.

"You did what!"

"We discussed this," he said in a calm voice.

"Like hell we did."

He shrugged. "I recall the conversation quite clearly."

She pressed both her hands against the table to keep from strangling him.

"You will leave this room immediately to draft the necessary paperwork to cancel the executive order."

He nodded with a smug grin.

"Of course, Madam President. I'm here to serve." He stood up and walked slowly from the room.

When Vice President Pike was gone, her face softened as she turned to face General Carr.

"Can you find a way reach the VDC soldiers?"

"The VDC consists of three hundred specialized teams dispatched all across the country. They are essentially sovereign forces. To track them down would require a force ten times their number. We no longer have that kind of manpower available. One by one, they'll eventually check in. And when they do, we'll deactivate them. Until then . . ." He shrugged.

She put her hand on his.

"General, do what you can. Even if it takes months to complete, let's stop this."

He nodded. "Yes, ma'am."

"Will that be enough to get us out of this mess?"

"No, ma'am. I wouldn't think so."

"What else then?"

"The level of discontent with the government is growing all across the nation. Ordinary people are killing one another for supplies and over-throwing any local authorities that still remain in power. Unless things change, social disintegration will only accelerate."

"The uprising you mentioned."

"Yes, ma'am."

"So how can we reverse this . . . disintegration?"

"I'm not sure that we can. Not only is the average citizen acting out of desperation, we also have a large population of convicts, paramilitary sur-vivalists, anarchists, and separatists. The only thing they have in common is that they either don't want, or no longer believe in, the United States of America. Madam President, our enemies are many."

She turned to Dr. Jack Fry, the Director of the Federal Emergency Management Agency. Jack had been a close friend and confidant for more than ten years. Just after President Glass took office, he had been in a car crash that left him unable to walk and confined to a wheel chair.

"Jack, can we accelerate our relief efforts?"

"On paper, yes. In practice, no. We have warehouses full of all sorts of supplies, MREs, bottled water, blankets, medicines, you name it. The problem is that there's no viable way to efficiently distribute them. The roads are congested with cars, making ground transportation difficult. Commercial airports are inoperable, making air transport even more dif-ficult. Distributing by train requires—"

"Okay, okay," she said, holding up her hands. "Who can we get supplies to?"

"The big cities are all but lost. We've tried to truck in supplies, but the shipments are either attacked by those infected by the virus or hijacked by violent opportunists."

"What about the smaller towns?"

"That's where we're beginning to focus our efforts."

"So things will improve then?"

"For some communities, yes."

"You don't sound optimistic."

He sighed. "I don't want to oversell this. The truth is that we're losing ground each and every day. People are dying of dehydration and starva-tion, and I'm not able to stop it." His voice broke slightly as he struggled to keep from getting emotional.

President Glass offered a heartfelt smile.

"Jack, if you save a single life, you're helping. Don't you give up on me, you old fool."

Tears welled in his eyes.

"No, ma'am," he said, swallowing. "Never."

She turned to General Carr.

"I need for you to help put a stop to the hijacking of relief supplies. Do whatever's necessary. Let's get the supply convoys to people who need them the most."

The general nodded. "Yes, ma'am. I'll make it a priority."

Next, she turned to Bill Baker, the Secretary of Energy. Bill was a big, jolly man whose proudest achievements had come while serving in the Peace Corps in Africa. With a few beers in him, he would often recount his time dodging armed rebels whom he claimed were only slightly less common than the blood-sucking tsetse flies. He had not been entirely successful in avoiding conflict, however, as one such encounter left him with a bayonet wound to his throat. While the wound had eventually healed, his vocal cords had been permanently damaged.

"Where are we with the nation's power grid?" she asked.

Bill answered in a slow, guttural voice that caused several people in the room to clear their throats.

"Experts are drawing up plans to get some systems back online. As you know, the electrical network is divided into several major and minor interconnections, or grids. The country is roughly divided in half along the Rocky Mountains by the two major interconnections. The minor interconnections cover parts of Texas and Alaska."

"And how many of those are back up?"

He looked surprised by the question.

"None."

"Okay, let me ask this differently. Which one will come online first, and when?"

"The Alaskan Interconnection is the only one likely to come online anytime soon. That system is isolated from the major Eastern and Western grids and is therefore easier to bring back up. Also, the people of Alaska were not hit as hard by the virus because they are geographically spread out. In fact, some rural Alaskan communities were not hit by the virus at all."

"Yes, yes, I know that. What I want to know is why we're not bringing up the major power grids now."

"Ma'am, the nation's power grid is made up of independently owned power stations, transmission lines, and distribution substations. There are literally hundreds of companies that own and maintain these facilities. We simply have no authority to bring them back up."

"Even so, can't we help what's left of these companies to get the lights back on?"

"Of course, and we're trying to do just that. Unfortunately, there are too few skilled technicians and engineers left alive. For every one we find, two more leave their posts to care for their families."

"So how long, Bill? Give me a number. A week?" She cringed when he didn't answer. "A month?"

"With the help of military personnel," he said, looking at General Carr, "we might be able to have one of the major interconnections up and running by this time next year."

President Glass nearly fell out of her chair.

"Excuse me? If you just said that we won't have power for a year, we all might as well say our prayers right now because they'll hang us from the Statue of Liberty well before then."

"Ma'am, there are more than five hundred power stations, including over one hundred nuclear power plants. Add to that the nearly two hundred thousand miles of transmission lines and countless thousands of distribution stations. To get an entire region online would be a huge undertaking, requiring many thousands of trained personnel. I'm sorry, but those people no longer exist. The truth is that a year is very optimistic."

She took a deep breath, struggling to compose herself.

"Do what you can, Bill."

He nodded. "Yes, ma'am."

She turned back to General Carr.

"General, it seems that relief is many months away. How bad are things likely to get between now and then?"

Everyone turned their attention to him, as his answer affected them all equally.

"The situation is already grave. As it stands, we've already lost control of most of the continental United States. For all practical purposes, the vast majority of the country has become a lawless wasteland. In the absence of a strong military presence, history dictates that it will eventually devolve into tribal regions, governed by violent warlords."

"Can't we bring the full military in on this? Certainly, we're not in any imminent danger from abroad. Everyone's struggling to pick up the pieces."

"That's true," he said. "Russia and China are in even worse shape than we are. However, even if we turn all eyes inward, we barely have enough military remaining to gain control of a few key bastions across the country. By and large, the states would no longer be united. It would, however, at least provide a way to save our democratic republic."

Several people around the table began to mumble to one another.

"Okay, okay," she said to everyone. "Let's not allow despair to get in the way of doing everything we can to save our nation." She turned back to the general. "If we had to consolidate people to these . . . bastions of civilization, where would you recommend that we start?"

"Several plans are already being drawn up, but they all revolve around recolonizing major cities a few at a time. The military would move in to clean them out and set up basic services. The end game would be to entice populations to return. It would be a very slow and arduous process, I assure you."

"Nation building from the ground up."

"Yes, ma'am."

"And how long would it take to reestablish say, ten major metropolitan areas?"

"I'm not sure."

"Years?"

"Yes, ma'am. It could be a decade or more."

"And in the meantime, what can be done about the violence?"

"Unfortunately, not much. We simply don't have the manpower to contain all the factions out to do harm. When we grow in strength, assuming that we do, we can take control one mile at a time. Until then, the great people of this nation will have to sort out their own rule of law."

Having served more than four years in Talladega's Federal Correctional Institution, Tanner Raines had learned to be a patient man. As a prisoner of the state, he had to wait to eat, to exercise, to receive mail, to do damn near everything. With that said, even a prisoner's patience can be tested.

The president's eleven-year-old daughter, Samantha Glass, sat behind the steering wheel of a four-door Jeep Wrangler. Tanner was on the seat beside her, making no attempt to hide his frustration.

"Are you planning on driving this thing or just warming the seat?"

She cut her eyes at him.

"I'm eleven."

"You keep reminding me. So?"

"So, eleven-year-olds shouldn't be driving. It's illegal . . . and dangerous."

He sighed. "We've been through this. You need to know how to drive. What if I get shot? Who's going to take me to the hospital?"

"There aren't any hospitals."

"But if there were."

"If there were, then I'd call an ambulance."

He shook his head.

"You're impossible."

She took a deep breath.

"Fine. I'll try. But when you fly through the windshield, don't crawl back with an attitude."

"I won't," he promised. "Now turn the key already, before I die of old age." Without drawing attention to his action, Tanner pulled the seat belt across his lap. Samantha's was already latched.

Samantha turned the key, and the engine came to life. She stomped the gas pedal, and the entire Jeep began to shake as if preparing for liftoff.

Tanner touched her shoulder and shouted over the roar of the engine.

"Easy on the gas, Mario!"

She eased her foot back on the pedal, and the engine quieted.

"That's better," he said. "Now press the brake, and put it in drive."

She did as instructed.

"Ease off the brake."

The Jeep started to roll slowly forward.

"That's good. Now just keep it at this speed for a while."

Samantha steered the Jeep across the large parking lot that Tanner had specifically selected for her training lesson. The closest car was easily fifty yards away. She drove across the lot a few times, making wide U-turns when she got to each end.

After a few minutes, she said, "This isn't so hard."

"I'm glad you think so. Now, take us out into the street."

She shook her head.

"I'll hit something."

"So, what if you do? At this speed, we'll be fine. And there's no shortage of cars if this one gets damaged."

She snorted, not buying into his logic. But she did as instructed, carefully steering the Jeep out of the parking lot and into the street.

As they exited the lot, a herd of small animals darted out from behind an overturned Greyhound bus. They were light brown in color, measured a few feet in height, and had long, ridged horns.

"Whoa!" she said, hitting the brakes.

They watched as more than a dozen of the animals dashed across the street with amazing speed, finally disappearing around a corner.

"What were those?" she asked. "Deer?"

He shrugged. "Gazelles, I think. They must have been released from the zoo."

"Why would anyone just set them free?"

"It was that or let them starve," he said, thinking of his own fortuitous rescue from a cage.

She nodded. "Well, I'm glad they let them go. They're pretty."

"Pretty good eating if that's what you mean," he said with a grin.

She frowned. "That's not what I meant at all."

"You say that now."

"I'll say that always. I would never want you to kill an innocent animal for us to eat."

"Uh-huh," he said with a knowing smile.

"Really, I mean it."

"Fine. Now, no more excuses. Let's get going already."

She looked back at the road. There was no straight path through the congestion of abandoned cars, so she began to carefully maneuver through the maze of wreckage. She kept the Jeep running at idle, and the car never got above ten miles an hour.

"You okay?" he asked.

"I'm bound to hit something. I told you I'm clumsy."

Tanner leaned his head against the window.

"I'm going to take a nap. Wake me when you crash or see a sign for I-85."

"You're crazy."

Tanner closed his eyes, and before long, he was snoring softly.

Samantha glanced over at him, unsure if he was faking it. She certainly wouldn't put it past him. Tanner had a weird sense of humor, and sometimes she had trouble telling when he was messing with her. The fact that he was putting his life in the hands of an eleven-year-old girl said a lot about his lack of common sense. She shook her head and turned her attention to the road. He really was crazy.

☙ ❧

Tanner didn't know how long he had slept, but it felt like he'd been lying in a grave. His neck hurt, and his mouth tasted like tuna fish. Samantha was pushing his shoulder, rocking him from side to side.

"Wake up." She sounded worried.

He sat up and took a quick look around. A sporty little two-door sedan was directly in front of them, steam pouring out from under the hood. The windshield, hood, and doors were all peppered with bullet holes. The trunk was open, and a suitcase with clothes spilled out was sitting behind the car.

"Where are we?" he asked.

"Just outside Atlanta."

"How long have you been driving?"

She looked at the clock on the car radio.

"Almost three hours. I'm tired."

He yawned. "You hit anything?"

"No," she answered, squinting at him while waiting for some retort.

He didn't offer any. Instead, he opened his door and set one foot on the asphalt.

"I saw a car heading that way." She pointed toward the tall buildings at the heart of Atlanta.

"Did anyone see you?"

"I don't think so. They were going pretty fast."

Tanner grabbed his Remington 870 Police Magnum shotgun and stepped from the Jeep. Before advancing, he took a long moment to study the area. Vehicles of all sorts littered the freeway, but none were moving, and he didn't see anyone alive either. Like other highways they had traveled, this once frantic medium for people rushing to and from work had become a graveyard filled with technology and decomposing corpses.

"If you spot them coming back, honk the horn."

She nodded, staring in the direction they had fled.

Tanner approached the bullet-ridden car from the passenger side. The door was ajar, but the seat was empty. The driver, a man in his thirties, lay slumped over, his chest riddled with bloody holes. A shiny gold police badge had been hastily pinned to his shirt, and an empty holster hung at his waist. Tanner noticed a distinctive white tan line on his left ring finger. He leaned down and put his hand on the man's neck. There wasn't a pulse, but the body was still warm. Whoever Samantha had seen racing away was likely responsible for his death.

Tanner slowly walked around the car, taking in the details of the scene. A woman's tennis shoe lay on the asphalt. He picked it up and gave it a once over. It was a cute little canvas slip-on, something a young woman might wear when going out for a day hike. He set the shoe on top of the car and continued his survey. Inside the trunk was an assortment of clothing and empty food packages. Whoever had done this had taken not only the man's wife but everything of value they could find.

He squatted down and examined a thin trail of fluid that led away from the car, like a fuse leading to a stick of dynamite. He rubbed it between his fingers and sniffed. Oil. The trail led in the direction that Samantha had pointed, right into the heart of Atlanta. He stood up and returned to the Jeep, his mind playing through how things had likely gone down.

Samantha looked at him expectantly.

"Well?"

"He's dead."

"I kind of figured that. It just happened, right?"

"It wasn't long," he mumbled, lost in thought.

"What is it?"

"Nothing."

"Not nothing."

"There was a woman too."

"Is she . . . dead?"

He shrugged. "Don't know. They took her."

She sat back against the seat.

"Should we go after her?"

He shook his head but said nothing.

They sat for nearly a minute without speaking.

Finally, she said, "What else?"

"How do you know there's something else?"

"You haven't told me to start the Jeep yet, so I figure there's more."

He sighed. "The man was a cop of some sort."

"Like your son."

"But not my son."

"No." She paused. "But it isn't right what they did to these people."

He looked at the tennis shoe lying on top of the car.

"No, it isn't right."

"We should do something about it."

"They're strangers, Sam. Not worth risking our lives over. We're going to Virginia, to your mom, remember?"

She nodded. "Virginia will still be there."

"You're assuming that we won't get ourselves killed."

"Technically, even if we do get killed, Virginia will still be there."

He sighed again. "I gave my word that I'd get you home safe."

"You're an escaped convict," she said with a laugh. "How good could your word be anyway?"

He growled at her.

She grinned. "I'm just saying that I'll understand if we don't go straight there." She touched his arm. "You'll get me home eventually."

"We shouldn't get detoured like this."

"No," she said, "we shouldn't."

"But we're going to, aren't we?"

She nodded. "I think so."

Tanner closed his eyes and saw the face of the dead police officer. He was right in what he had said. The man was not his son. But by God, he was someone's son.

"All right," he said. "We'll go after her."

Passing through the towns of Hickory and Lincolnton reminded Mason of his time traveling across war-ravaged regions of Iraq and Afghanistan. Festering bodies littered the streets. Dogs tore away pieces of the corpses, as did vultures and crows. Death had not arrived all at once, and the bodies were in different stages of decay. Some remained swollen from the gaseous pressures within. Others had burst, like over-filled water balloons, into pools of blood and bile, serving as grotesque reminders of man's noxious contents. Still others had started to dry into unrecognizable clumps of skin, hair, and bone. The only constant among the dead was the incessant wave of black blowflies that pushed violently against one another to better enjoy the macabre feast.

On nearly every corner, survivors scavenged through stores, homes, and cars, uncertain and afraid of what the next day would bring. Like prisoners of war, they stared out at him, wondering perhaps if he would render aid. Unwilling to stop and be drawn into their misery, Mason set his eyes on the road and continued ahead. Bowie, on the other hand, seemed unfazed by the carnage and suffering, barking enthusiastically as if to offer a warm hello to everyone they passed.

It was less than twenty miles from Lincolnton to Gastonia, but as he got closer, the roads again became congested and difficult to navigate. Gastonia was a city of nearly one hundred thousand people, large enough that, when bodies started piling up, its inhabitants had tried to get out. Like countless other cities, the roadways quickly became jammed with accidents and emergencies, stranding thousands of motorists, many of whom were already infected with the deadly virus. The result was pure chaos as desperate people tried to either squeeze or ram their way through the stalled traffic.

Mason had planned to drive through Gastonia like he had the smaller towns, but as he found himself struggling to work his way around the wreckage, he began to doubt that a direct path would even be possible. Frustrated by the slow progress, he finally pulled to the side of the road and opened an atlas with the hope of finding a suitable detour.

Bowie whined from the back of the truck, and Mason motioned for him to go and relieve himself. The dog quickly hopped out and wandered off through the abandoned vehicles, sniffing each of them in his never-ending quest for food. Like every dog Mason had ever owned, Bowie had an insatiable appetite. It didn't seem to matter if he had just consumed an entire pig, there was always room for a little more.

After studying the map, Mason concluded that the Dallas Cherryville Highway would probably get him around most of the traffic clogging Gastonia's roads. It forced him to make a wide circle around the city to the west, but the added distance was a small price to pay. As he finished scribbling a few notes on the map, he heard Bowie barking in the distance. It didn't sound like an angry bark, more of an announcement, like, "Timmy's fallen into that damn well again."

Mason climbed out of the truck and walked slowly through the abandoned vehicles toward the sound of Bowie's incessant call. Many of the cars still had people inside, clutching one another or lying prone on the seat as they had waited for their inevitable doom. He considered searching through some of the cars for additional supplies, but clouds of flies banging against the windows warned him off.

He found Bowie less than fifty yards away, pacing back and forth in front of an overturned BMW.

"What is it, boy?"

Bowie barked at the car, looked back at Mason, and then barked again.

"Yeah, yeah, I get it. You found something interesting."

Putting his hand on his Supergrade, Mason squatted down and peered into the overturned vehicle.

Inside, a middle-aged man dangled from his seat belt like a trapeze artist who had lost his balance. The skin on his face had shriveled into deep creases, making it look like his bones were slowly dissolving from within. Both eyes had sunken in, leaving deep black voids where blood had pooled in their sockets. His lips were split and peeling, and his swollen tongue puffed out of his mouth like a pink sponge. A dark brown urine stain had spread across the crotch of what were once bleached white trousers. The amazing part of it was that he was still alive.

"Hang on," said Mason. "We'll get you out of there."

Glassy eyes stared out at him.

Mason reached around and tried to unlatch the man's seatbelt. The mechanism was mangled and refused to release. Using his hunting knife, he carefully cut the shoulder strap. Before he could catch him, the man tumbled forward and fell to the roof of the car. Mason grabbed him under the arms and dragged him out onto the asphalt. He was conscious but just barely so.

Mason turned to Bowie.

"Watch him while I get some water."

Bowie circled once, sniffing his trousers, and then flopped down next to the man as if trying to keep him warm. The scene reminded Mason of when he had first found the dog lying beside its dead master's chair. Bowie was no stranger to suffering, and despite his eagerness to enter a fight, he seemed to have a soft spot for those in need.

Mason hurried back to his truck and grabbed a bottle of water. By the time he returned, the man had scooted over and was propping his head on Bowie's body. The dog looked at the stranger with genuine curiosity, occasionally leaning down to lick the side of his shriveled face. Mason couldn't help but smile. His ferocious companion had become a four-legged nursemaid whose only treatment was a good tongue bath.

Mason squatted down and held the bottle to the man's lips.

Gagging and coughing, he struggled to get the water down. When half of it was gone, he pushed the bottle away with his swollen tongue.

"Let that sit a minute," said Mason.

The man blinked a few times, staring up at him, and then tried to speak. What came out were unintelligible rasps of air.

"Just take it easy," Mason said, patting him on the shoulder.

The man lifted his arm and pointed at Mason's holstered pistol. He blinked twice trying to communicate his message.

"You hang in there. I've got water, and we can get you through this."

He pointed at the pistol again, grunting softly.

Mason started to reassure him again, but the pleading in the man's eyes would not be appeased by any words a stranger could offer.

"Don't you have family? Someone who wants to see you make it home?"

He shook his head, and the tiniest tears formed in the corners of his eyes.

Mason looked down at the man and saw only suffering and despair. His will to live had been gone for some time, perhaps even before becoming trapped in the car.

"You're all done, aren't you?"

He nodded and closed his eyes, relieved that his rescuer understood his request.

"Stay here. I'll be back."

Mason stood up and returned to his truck. From his glove box, he removed the snub-nosed revolver that he had taken off Red Beard's body a couple of weeks earlier. Carrying it with both hands in front of him like a parting gift, he walked slowly back to the man. He considered what he was about to do. Two months ago, such an action would not only have been morally wrong, it would have landed him behind bars. But the world was different now. Rules were different. Maybe even right and wrong had to be recalibrated. He saw the man ahead, lying helpless and utterly alone in the world. His eyes were closed, and he seemed peaceful resting against Bowie.

Mason motioned for the dog to go back to the truck. After hesitating for a moment, Bowie reluctantly got up and left them alone. Mason squatted down beside the man.

"Do you want another drink?"

The man opened his eyes and nodded.

Mason held up the bottle and let him drink the rest of the water.

"More?"

He shook his head.

"Are you sure about this?"

He nodded again.

Mason checked the revolver, inspecting the first round to make sure that the primer and casing were both good. They were. The chance of a misfire with properly manufactured ammunition was very low. It would take a lot of guts to squeeze the trigger, and he didn't want the man to have to work through that kind of anguish more than once.

He carefully placed the revolver in the man's hand.

"I'll wait until I hear it go off."

The man blinked slowly and tried to speak. Words failed him again.

Mason wanted to believe that he was offering thanks, but it could just have easily been profanity against God for his most recent handiwork. With the decision made, he stood up and walked away. Before he had even reached his truck, a sharp boom sounded, followed by the metallic thud of the revolver hitting the pavement.

Tanner knelt beside the road, studying the dark trail of fluid like an Indian tracker.

"Well?" Samantha asked, looking over his shoulder.

"They're leaking oil."

"That's good, right? If they break down, we'll catch up to them."

He shook his head.

"No, if they break down, they'll switch vehicles, and we'll lose them for good."

"Oh, right. We should hurry then."

"They're headed straight into the city. Are you sure about this?"

She looked at the large buildings off in the distance.

"How bad can it be? Most everyone's probably dead."

He stood up. "It's going to be bad."

They loaded back into the Jeep, with Tanner behind the wheel this time.

"You've got better eyes than me," he said. "Don't let me lose their trail."

"Me Tonto. You Lone Ranger," she said in a deep voice.

"Just watch the road."

They drove for nearly four miles, following the trail of leaking oil down Atlanta's side streets. Every few hundred yards, they lost sight of it and had to get out and hunt around to pick back up the trail. With every mile deeper into Atlanta, the chaos around them became more complete. The major roads were essentially parking lots, filled with thousands of vehicles and thus, completely impassable. The side streets were better, but not by much. Whoever they were chasing, however, was familiar enough with the condition of the roads to know which ones still allowed passage.

As they steered through a small alleyway that cut between streets, Tanner saw an unmistakable shadow pass over them from above. He stopped the Jeep and leaned out the window, looking up.

"What is it?" she asked.

Tanner shoved the Jeep into park and killed the engine.

"Helicopter," he said. "Grab your pack. We're on foot for a while."

Samantha snatched up her pack with one hand and opened the door with the other.

"Where are we going?" she asked.

"Where they can't see us. Come on."

They ran back down the alley, turning left when they got to the street. The sidewalk was cluttered with debris, overturned garbage cans, bicycles, pizza boxes, shopping carts, and bodies—so many bodies. A Sonic Drive-In diner was to their right, and a CiCi's pizza to the left. Across the street was a huge Bass Pro Outdoor World.

Although the helicopter was not yet visible, the heavy *thwup thwup thwup* of its blades buffeted against the walls of the alley.

"There!" Tanner yelled, pointing at the sporting goods store.

They ran, dodging between cars and jumping over decomposing corpses. About half-way across the street, Samantha stumbled over the bloated leg of a dead woman and fell to the ground. Flies immediately swarmed her, eager to lay claim to a fresh meal.

She screamed and blindly batted the air with her hands. Tanner reached down and scooped her up, holding her against his chest with one arm as he continued running at full speed for the store.

The front of Outdoor World had been designed to look like a rustic lodge. Huge logs framed the entire structure, stone chimneys poked out the top, and a thick canopy of artificial moss and leaves covered the forest-green roof. An enormous wood carving of a buffalo head hung precariously above the four entryway doors, all of which had been ripped from their hinges.

Tanner raced into the building, leaping over blister-covered bodies that were piled in the doorway. Entering the store was like stepping into a scene from Lewis and Clark's historic expedition. Elaborate motifs of animals roaming through yet uncharted wilds stretched from corner to corner. The closest had four mountain goats perched on a huge boulder surrounded by patches of sagebrush. Someone with a questionable sense of humor had defiled the beasts by painting smiley faces on their bone white fur using hunter's orange spray paint.

Further into the store, an open pond was surrounded by jagged cliffs on three sides. On the fourth side was a small staircase that crossed over the water to an overhanging viewing platform. At one time, water had flowed down the face of the cliff, but without electricity, the pool had become green and stagnant.

Overturned racks of hats, shirts, waders, books, and every imaginable piece of camping gear stretched across the enormous store. Most of it had been ransacked, and what remained of the equipment and clothing was now strewn across the warehouse floor.

Not far inside the entrance was the body of a large black man wearing camouflage clothing. An empty pump-action shotgun lay at his side, the stock split in half from having been wielded as a club. Twenty or more spent plastic casings were scattered on the floor. The body itself was a mess, hacked so badly that pieces of flesh and bone had splattered fifteen feet in every direction. He looked as if he had been caught in a boat propeller and then dumped in a blender for good measure. Samantha had her face buried against Tanner's chest and was thankfully spared from having to see the grotesque brutality. The pungent smell of decomposition, however, could not be escaped.

Tanner raced across the large room, knocking aside anything that stood in his way. He vaulted the viewing platform stairs two at a time until he was standing above the pool of slimy green water. With his hands under Samantha's arms, he hung her over the side, leaning over as far as he dared. From the bottom of her feet to the water was only about three feet.

"Get ready," he said. "You're about to get wet."

"What?" she cried, opening her eyes.

He dropped her.

Samantha instinctively tucked into a ball at the last second, hitting the water like she was doing a cannonball. She went under a couple of feet but quickly bobbed back to the surface. Mosquitoes by the thousands buzzed around her as punishment for disturbing their watery abode.

Tanner tossed his shotgun in ahead of him and then swung both feet over the side. He tipped forward as he fell, hitting the side of his face on a small rock cropping just before plunging into the water. When he came up, Samantha was wiping green slime from her face while waving off the cloud of mosquitoes.

"Gross," she said.

Tanner bent at the knees and felt around for his shotgun. The water was too cloudy to see the bottom, and he quickly gave up his search. He grabbed Samantha by the back of her shirt and began dragging her toward the rear of the pool.

"Lie on your back and keep your arms underwater," he said.

Before she could answer, a deafening boom sounded from the front of the store.

Samantha looked at him, fear in her eyes.

"Flashbang grenade," he said. "They're coming."

"You're bleeding," she said, instinctively touching the side of her own face.

He brought his free hand up and it came away covered in bright red blood.

"I'm fine."

He pulled her to the back of the pool where the rock wall hid a small alcove. Elevated a couple of feet above the water was a green metal service door. He reached up and pulled on a heavy metal ring. The door didn't budge. With nowhere else to run, he pressed into the alcove and held Samantha tight against his chest.

"Keep the arm with the radio tracker under the water as deep as possible," he whispered.

"Will it stop the signal?"

He didn't answer.

"Will it?"

"I don't know."

# CHAPTER
## 6

Vice President Pike wasn't terribly surprised by the outcome of the president's meeting. He had always known that President Glass would eventually try to reverse her decision regarding the Viral Defense Corps. It was the reason he had set them up in such a way that they couldn't easily be disbanded. They were what he called "Currahee," which, in Cherokee, meant self-contained. He had liked that word ever since he had heard it used to describe the 506th Infantry Regiment, famous for their exploits during World War II. The VDC was his army, out doing his bidding and, by God, no one was going to get in the way of that.

The telephone rang with an annoying buzz, and he snatched it up on the first ring, knowing full well who was on the other end.

"Tell me you have her."

"Not yet, but we're getting close." The voice was that of General Hood, currently the head of Special Operations Warfare, and a staunch ally.

"General, I shouldn't have to tell you how important this is."

"I'm aware of the importance, sir."

"What do you mean when you say you're getting close?"

"We should have her in custody within minutes."

"You've found her?"

"Yes. We're currently in pursuit."

"Don't let her get away again." The vice president could barely contain his frustration.

"I assure you that Agent Sparks is one of our best. There was no way he could have known that the girl would team up with someone so capable."

"Even so, I don't understand why it's taken him so long to find her."

"The range of the girl's transponder signal is limited to a few hundred yards. Not to mention that we've had to keep our search activities from drawing attention. If it hadn't been for the other military operations underway, it would have been even harder."

"What other operations?" Vice President Pike didn't like coincidences.

"A truck-load of FEMA supplies was taken from one of their distribution convoys. The Army has a few gunships in the area trying to pick up the payload signals."

"RF signals?"

"Yes. Most large shipments have embedded trackers. Their operations made it very easy to blend in our own search activity."

"Before long, we'll be tagging every single soldier on the battlefield."

"It's been proposed."

"Don't let this supply recovery mission get in our way. Find the prize, and do it quickly."

The general paused, obviously uncertain of what tone to take.

"It's a shame we had to shoot down her helicopter in the first place," he said slowly. "As you recall, that wasn't the original plan. It was to be a simple extraction."

"I'm aware of the plan, General. It was, after all, my plan." Vice President Pike's voice was rising. "If you recall, however, her bodyguard was supposed to do that snatch for us. How was I to know that he would suddenly grow a conscience? We had no choice but to take that bird down. If we hadn't, we'd both be standing in front of a firing squad by now."

"Yes, sir. Still, it's unfortunate that she survived the crash. We've had nothing but bad luck since this operation began."

"On the contrary, General. Her survival gives us a second chance to get the leverage we need. If we can get our hands on Samantha Glass, we can control the president."

"And if we don't?"

"If we don't, then we'll have to take more drastic measures."

It took an equally strange sight to clear the image of the suicidal man from Mason's mind. As he turned onto the Dallas Cherryville Highway, he saw a white Brinks armored truck flipped on its side, about twenty feet below the overpass. The thick concrete barrier had crumbled where the truck had smashed through it before falling nose first onto the freeway below. A Hulk-green Camaro was parked beside the armored truck, its trunk propped open.

Mason stopped his truck and took a quick look down off the overpass ledge. No one moved below, but he heard the unmistakable echo of a man's voice. He motioned for Bowie to stay put and keep an eye on the truck while he went down to take a better look.

Carefully hiking down the steep grassy embankment, he swung around to approach from the front of the Camaro. As he circled around the car, he saw that the trunk contained several canvas money satchels, all stuffed so full that tight bundles of hundred-dollar bills poked out of the top.

He continued around to the back of the armored truck where he heard the sound of a man's voice. The tremendous impact from the fall had crumpled the rear doors, and one had subsequently been pried open wide enough for someone to crawl inside. A man knelt down at the back of the truck, talking to someone inside through the makeshift hole in the door. His face was covered with a thick salt-and-pepper beard that matched his receding hairline. He had a big tight belly poking out from under a white t-shirt, and the waist of his pants was so tight that it was lost between folds of skin. Massive arms showed off tattoos of a blacksmith's hammer on one bicep and a matching anvil on the other.

"Get that cooler-looking thing in the corner," he said through the hole. "That's it. Now, slide it out to me." He reached in and pulled out a padded blue box about a foot square in size. "Jeezus, this one's heavy," he said, setting it beside a three-foot long metal pry bar lying on the ground.

As he turned around, Blacksmith spotted Mason standing about ten feet away. Startled, he jerked upright, smashing his shoulder into the corner of the armored truck's bumper.

"Shit!" he spat, wincing from the pain.

Mason stood, quietly watching him.

"What are you looking at, numbnuts?" he said, rubbing his sore shoulder.

Mason grinned. "I don't know. Part walrus, part gorilla?"

Blacksmith put his hands together and folded them back, cracking his knuckles like a Roman wrestler.

"Congratulations. You just earned yourself a first-class beating."

Mason slid his coat open to reveal his badge. He left his hand resting on the butt of the Supergrade.

"Consider your next move carefully."

"Ain't no cop gonna shoot an unarmed man," he said with a sneer. "And by the time you feel my hands around your neck, it'll be too late."

Mason took in a deep breath and let it out slowly. Blacksmith was only halfway right. It might indeed be too late if he let a man of his size get hands on him. But assuming that he was unwilling to shoot him was a grave miscalculation. At a full ten feet apart, the odds were not in the big man's favor.

"How about we start again?" suggested Mason. "I'm Marshal Raines."

Staring at Mason's hand resting on his pistol, the man shrugged.

"This ain't no business of yours, Marshal," he said. "We got as much right to this money as anyone."

"I couldn't care less what you take from the truck. My guess is that for all your hard work, you'll end up using the bills as toilet paper."

Blacksmith looked down at the blue crate that he'd pulled out, imagining piles of bearer bonds or other precious currency.

"Money is money," he said. But his tone was not at all convincing.

Mason shrugged. "If you say so."

Blacksmith thought about it a little more, rubbing his thick beard.

"Shit," he muttered. He leaned down and shouted through the hole in the armored truck. "Cletus, get out here. Ain't a damn thing in there we need."

A man's feet, legs, and then body slowly slid out of the small gap. Cletus was a tall, thin man with greasy red hair and a face covered in a thick layer of acne.

When he saw Mason, he said, "Who's he?"

"Some kind of a nosey cop."

Cletus leaned forward trying to read Mason's badge.

"It says that I'm a US Marshal."

"What's that mean to us?" Cletus asked his partner.

"Not a damn thing."

Cletus turned back to face Mason.

"You gonna arrest us, Marshal?"

"I hadn't planned on it."

"Come on," Blacksmith said, grabbing their crowbar. "He ain't gonna do jack."

They walked a wide circle around Mason, closed the trunk on the green Camaro, and climbed in. With Cletus behind the steering wheel, Blacksmith made it a point to flip Mason off as they drove away.

Mason shook his head. The quality of the planet's survivors left something to be desired. Evolution had its work cut out for it.

As he turned to leave, he spotted the blue case that Blacksmith had pulled from the truck. Curious, he went over, unzipped the top, and opened it up. Inside was a large plastic box with a red lid, the words *United States Mint* clearly visible on top. White straps held the lid to the box.

Using his hunting knife, he cut the straps and carefully pried off the lid. Inside was a collection of small white tubes, each about three inches long and topped with plastic red lids. He lifted one out. It was heavier than it looked. When he popped off the lid and saw what was inside, a grin spread from ear to ear.

Inside were twenty American Eagle gold coins, each containing exactly one ounce of pure gold. He tipped the tube and dropped one of the coins onto his palm. It felt warm, the way that only gold feels when it touches human skin. He rubbed it between his fingers, like a prospector examining a riverbed find. He had never actually held a gold coin before, and it was a little intoxicating.

He dropped the coin into his front pocket and put the tube back in the plastic box. A quick count revealed that there were twenty-five identical white tubes. Assuming that each tube contained twenty American Eagles, it put the total at five hundred gold coins. While he was confident that five hundred ounces of gold would have constituted a king's ransom before the pandemic, he wasn't sure what, if any, value the coins held now. People couldn't eat gold, and it wouldn't keep them warm at night. On the other hand, gold had been valuable since mankind's earliest civilizations. Even when food, water, and medicine were at the top of everyone's lists of needs, he suspected that someone would be willing to trade for the shiny coins.

He reassembled the plastic box, zipped up the blue case, and hauled it up the hill to his truck. As he set the case on the front seat, the green

Camaro came squealing down the highway. When it got to within about twenty yards, Cletus locked up the brakes and sent the car sliding to a stop.

Mason calmly closed the door and walked to the rear of his truck. Bowie moved to the back of the truck bed, propping its front feet on the edge of the tail gate. The dog's tail was tucked, and his ears were folded back. He looked to Mason for some indication of whether or not the men posed a threat.

Cletus and Blacksmith both jumped out of the car. Blacksmith was carrying the large crowbar in both hands, and Cletus had nothing but an uncertain look on his face. They approached quickly, one breaking off to the right, the other to the left.

"You tricked us, you son of a bitch!" shouted Blacksmith, cocking the crowbar back like a baseball bat.

Two things happened at once. Bowie leaped off the bed of the truck, landing on Cletus and sending them both tumbling to the ground. At that same instant, Mason drew his Supergrade and shot Blacksmith in the thigh. The impact punched his leg backward, and he fell like he had slipped on a patch of ice.

"Shit! Shit! *SHIT!*" he shrieked, dropping the crowbar to clutch his leg.

Mason swung around to check on Bowie. The dog had pinned Cletus against one of the Camaro's tires, its teeth sinking into the man's forearm.

"Get him off me!"

Mason whistled, and the dog reluctantly withdrew. A large urine stain seeped across the man's dirty trousers, and blood ran down his arm.

Using his pistol, Mason motioned for Cletus to move over near Blacksmith.

Nursing his injured arm, he scooted along the ground to sit beside his partner.

"I swear to God I'm gonna kill you!" Blacksmith shouted, trying to stop the flow of blood with his hands.

Mason turned to Bowie.

"Watch them."

The dog started toward them, growling.

"Hey," he said.

Bowie paused and looked back.

"I said watch them. Don't eat them."

The dog turned back and eyed the two injured men. To their relief, he stopped his advance.

Mason dug through the supplies on his truck and pulled out a thick white bandage. He tossed it over to Blacksmith.

"From the looks of it, I didn't hit the femoral artery. That's good news for you. Keep some pressure on it, and the bleeding should stop before long." He turned to Cletus. "And you better keep that bite clean if you don't want to lose the arm to infection."

"You're a dead man," Blacksmith said through clenched teeth. "You're so goddamned dead—"

"Save it," Mason said, holstering his pistol. "I let you off easy this time. If there's ever a next time, I won't be so kind."

Blacksmith continued to mumble threats as he tore open the bandage and began to wrap it around his leg. Cletus had nothing to say as he shook the fabric of his trousers with his good arm, hoping to help them dry a little faster.

Watching the big man work to stem the flow of blood, Mason wondered if he had made the right decision. Leaving an enemy behind who might be inclined to follow was never a good idea. On the other hand, killing in cold blood wasn't something he could do either. He had opted to shoot for the leg, and he would have to live with that decision.

Resigned to leave things the way they were, he lowered the tailgate and motioned for Bowie to get back into the truck. Once the dog was settled in, he went around and swung open his own door. Before he climbed in, Blacksmith issued one last threat.

"This ain't over, lawman. I promise you that."

Mason nodded.

Shifting the gold to the floorboard, he climbed in and started back down the highway. Glancing down at the blue case, he couldn't help but consider how many people had been killed throughout history for the shiny metal. Whether it had all started with the Spanish ransacking of the Incan empire, or many thousands of years before that, gold and blood were never far apart.

He caught a final glimpse in the mirror of Blacksmith and Cletus struggling to get to their feet and decided that carrying around such a large cache of gold coins would only invite more violence. He would need to hide his newfound treasure.

☙ ❧

Mason traveled down a small county road that weaved through Kings Mountain State Park. Tall oak trees towered above him, shadowing the single-lane road as the sun slowly began its descent to the west. The park was barely ten minutes out of his way, and it appeared uninhabited, save for the wild turkeys and occasional deer. It seemed an ideal location to bury the gold because it offered the right compromise between isolation and convenience. Certainly, the park was better than an urban area, which would all but invite discovery with the widespread scavenging underway.

He followed the road until it came to a dead end directly in front of Lake Crawford. Based on the tall grass and potholed road, the lake had not been a big attraction even before the world's demise. Its only parking was a small gravel lot that allowed would-be fisherman to try their luck.

Mason parked his truck and carried the box of gold and a length of paracord with him down to the lake. He wasn't exactly sure how or where to hide the gold, but he thought that something would probably present itself. Bowie ran ahead, barking, his ears flapping in the wind. The dog never complained about riding in the truck, but it was easy enough to see that Bowie was happiest when running free, rolling in the grass, and smelling the planet's most unusual odors.

Lake Crawford measured about two hundred feet across and perhaps four times that in length, making it small enough that most people would probably have called it a pond. The Clark Fork stream ran off each end to eventually connect to larger lakes in the state park. Grass and trees grew very close to the edge of the lake, except in one area where enough foot traffic had made a muddy boat ramp. A flat-bottomed aluminum jon boat lay upside down, tied to a small metal stake in the ground.

Seeing the boat secured to the bank gave Mason an idea. He went over, untied the rope, and pulled up the stake. Taking the stake with him, he called on Bowie to lead the way around the lake, hoping that the dog might detect and scare away any snakes enjoying an afternoon sunbath.

Mason walked slowly and deliberately, carefully counting his steps. When he reached exactly one hundred steps, he stopped and secured the paracord to the handles on either side of the case. Stepping out on a small dirt ledge, he leaned over and slowly lowered the entire blue case into the water. Weighing over thirty pounds, it quickly settled to the bottom, about four feet below the surface. No bubbles rose up, which told Mason that the combination of plastic cases was waterproof. Even if water did leak through to the gold, the metal would not rust. Gold had been pulled from the bottom of the ocean after sitting for a thousand years, and with a little cleaning, was made as shiny as the day it had been lost.

He tied the other end of the paracord to the metal stake and drove it into the muddy soil a few inches out into the water. With the weight of the case, he doubted that the anchor was even necessary. But when it came to gold, he figured that one could not be too careful. He stepped back and observed his handiwork. The water was cloudy enough that both the case and anchor were completely invisible to anyone on the bank. Even from a boat, someone would be hard pressed to see the box as anything more than a rock.

Mason smiled. His treasure was officially buried.

L
ess than two hundred miles away, Tanner and Samantha stood sub-
merged from the neck down in the pool of mosquito-infested water. To make it easier on her, Tanner squatted down and held her
against his chest so that she could push her arm as far under the water as
possible. Both of them strained to hear what was happening above them
in the sporting goods store.

Voices shouted, glass crunched, and racks were knocked over as men
advanced.

"Clear!"

"Clear!"

"Clear!" The last voice was very close, likely from a man standing on
the viewing platform overlooking the pool. It was followed by the sounds
of several people approaching.

"They came in here. I'm sure of it." The voice was that of Agent John
Sparks, a man who claimed to be on an official government mission to
retrieve Samantha, but whose intentions had never been made completely
clear. When she had refused to go with him, pleasantries had been dis-
pensed with, and he left empty-handed, spitting blood.

"They probably slipped out the back through the loading dock," said a
gruff voice.

"Nothing on the tracker?"

A pause. "No, sir. It's clear. With these buildings, though, they could be
as close as a few hundred yards."

There was another pause as actions were considered.

"Fine, go!" said Agent Sparks. "But remember, put the big guy down
first thing—no hesitation. Three to the chest. Got it?"

"Yes, sir. And the girl?"

"My orders are to bring her back alive. But if it looks like she's going to
get away again, do what you need to. Better dead than on the loose."

The soldier cleared his throat.

"Yes, sir."

The sound of boots stomping through the store slowly faded as the men retreated. After a few minutes, Samantha relaxed her grip on Tanner's arm.

"They're gone," she whispered.

He touched his fingers to her lips. After another couple of minutes, there was the sound of a single set of shoes leaving the viewing platform and walking slowly through the store. It, too, eventually faded away. When there was no sign of their pursuers for a full ten minutes, Tanner took his hand away from her mouth.

"I think we're clear," he said quietly, standing up.

"Good, because I'm freezing."

He let her go and slid forward a few feet to peek around the rocky alcove. The stairs and platform were both clear.

"Come on," he said. "Let's get out of this water."

He walked back around to stand in front of the platform and lifted Samantha into the air. He held her there until she was able to get a handhold on the rocks. She quickly climbed over the railing and back onto the platform. Before climbing up himself, Tanner used his feet to feel around the bottom of the pool. When he finally found the shotgun, he bent over and came up with it in his hands. Green slime poured from the barrel as he tipped it over.

"That's a mess," she said, looking down at him.

"Can you catch it if I toss it up?"

"As long as you don't hit me with it."

"I'm not going to hurl it like a javelin. Just hold your hands out and grab it before it falls on my head."

She shrugged. "I'll try."

He lobbed the shotgun up, and she caught it on the first try.

As he climbed up the ledge, she asked, "Will it work, being this wet and slimy?"

"I doubt it," he said, hopping over the railing. "Water will have gotten into the shells."

"Without a gun, what will we do if they come back?"

"We'll figure something out. Right now, let's worry about getting out of these wet clothes."

ତ୭ ଈଞ

They were forced to scrap their wet backpacks, as well as most of the gear inside. Fortunately, even after being looted, Outdoor World contained a wide assortment of clothes and supplies.

"This feels a bit like shopping," Samantha said, picking up a small plastic eating utensil that doubled as both a fork and a spoon.

"Do you know the difference between shopping and stealing?" asked Tanner with a sly grin.

"No . . . what?"

"About thirty days in the county jail."

She tried to suppress a smile, but it eventually forced its way out.

"I suppose that's convict humor."

"Darlin', if I've learned anything over the years, it's that whatever makes you smile is good."

"If you say so." She held up a white cotton shirt. "Hey, what do you think of this one?"

"It looks about your size."

Samantha draped it over one shoulder and continued sifting through the piles of clothes. When they were finished, they had changed into sturdy hiking pants, shirts, and boots, and had stuffed day packs with long underwear and lightweight jackets to keep off the evening chill. They also found several packages of freeze-dried meals, as well as nuts and dehydrated fruit. Headlamps and batteries were easy enough to find, as was a compass and several plastic Nalgene water bottles. They took everything they could fit in their packs. What they didn't find was water.

Samantha approached with a clean, white cotton bandana wadded up in her hands and a small bottle of iodine.

"Let me clean the cut on your head."

He touched the side of his brow. The bleeding had stopped, and a small scab was already starting to form.

"I'll be okay," he said. "I heal fast."

She opened up the bottle and poured some iodine on the bandana.

"If it becomes infected, you'll get all sweaty and weak. You're too big for me to move, so I'll have to leave you to die. Are you sure you don't want me to clean it?"

"You can be pretty convincing," he said, sitting down on a stuffed warthog that had been on display in the hunting section. "Go ahead."

She used the cloth to scrub off the scab and coat the entire area with iodine. Blood started trickling down his cheek.

"Jesus, Mary, are you trying to treat me or kill me?"

"My mom always says that you have to start with a clean wound to ensure that the scab forms properly."

"Was she a doctor?"

"No."

"Then how do you know she knew what she was talking about?"

"Did I mention that she's the President of the United States? She's obviously very smart."

Once again, he couldn't find fault with her logic.

"Fine."

She pressed the cloth tightly against his head for a full minute before pulling it away slowly to inspect the wound.

"And?" he asked.

"You're not getting any prettier, that's for sure," she said, setting aside the bloody cloth.

Tanner scoffed and stood up.

"Give me the iodine and a couple of those water bottles," he said as he tore open a pack of black shoelaces.

She handed them to him, obviously curious about what he was about to do.

"Keep an open mind," he said, walking back over to the pool of green water.

"If you think I'm going to drink that slime, you're even crazier than I thought."

He wrapped the shoestring around the lip of the bottle and cinched the knot tight.

"Did you see how I tied that?" he asked, sliding the knot up and back along the cord. "This knot lets you snug things tight. Think you can tie it?"

"I don't know. Maybe."

He untied the shoestring from the bottle and handed both to her.

She wrapped the string around the bottle and struggled to get the knot right. He talked her through the process until it was tied correctly.

"I've got it now," she said.

He untied it again.

"Prove it."

This time she wrapped the shoestring around the bottle and quickly secured the knot.

"Told you."

He nodded, satisfied.

"Does the knot have a name?" she asked.

"Every knot has a name. This one's the taut-line hitch."

"What are you, some kind of Jedi Master of knots?" she asked, laughing.

"When you're cooped up in a cell for twenty hours a day, you find ways to entertain yourself."

"Taut-line hitch," she said, trying out the words. She handed him back the bottle and cord. "That's kind of cool."

Tanner leaned over and lowered the bottle into the water below. It dipped down deep enough for him to get the liter-sized bottle about three quarters of the way full before hoisting it back up. The water was indeed green, although the smoky shade of the plastic made it look more like a muddy brown. He opened the iodine, filled the built-in eyedropper, and dripped eight drops into the water. Then he put the lid on and shook the bottle a few times. When he was satisfied, he repeated the process with the second bottle.

"What's the iodine do?" she asked. "Kill the germs?"

"That's right."

"I'm still not going to drink it."

"Me neither."

"Then why in the world did you fill the bottles?"

"Because, if we don't find water by tomorrow, we'll both change our minds." He put one of the bottles in a pouch on the side of her pack and the other in his own. "Enough about water. Let's see if we can find some cleaning supplies and fresh rounds for the shotgun."

"Right."

They searched the hunting section of the store, finding several jars of bore cleaner, a bottle of CLP lubricant, and a cleaning brush. Even after a careful search, however, they didn't find even a single shotgun shell. The ammunition shelves were completely bare, and the only bullets in the store were a handful of .22LR bullets scattered on the floor. Tanner gathered them up and put them in his pocket.

"Take a look around for a weapon of some sort while I clean the shotgun."

Samantha nodded, continuing her search.

As he finished field stripping and cleaning the shotgun, she came back holding a rifle.

"What about this?" she asked, handing it to him.

Tanner looked it over. It was a brand new Savage .22 Varmint rifle, fed by a small five-round magazine. He would have preferred something with more stopping power, but a .22 would still throw lead. Not to mention the fact that he had a pocketful of bullets.

"It's a fine rifle," he said.

Samantha watched him load the rifle and frowned.

"Are those even real bullets?"

"Don't insult our rifle. It will most likely save our lives."

"Most likely?"

"Too optimistic?"

She sighed and shook her head.

They spent the next few minutes making sure they hadn't left behind anything that could prove useful. Then they carried their packs to the front of the store and peered out into the street. The soldiers were nowhere in sight.

"Where to now?" she asked.

"We need to get water and ammunition from the Jeep."

She took a step toward the door, but he reached across and blocked her path.

"Agent Sparks is probably still too close for us to be out in the open. Let's wait until dark."

"Oh, great," she murmured.

"What? Now you're afraid of the dark?"

"Of course not."

"What then?"

"I'm afraid of what comes out in the dark."

Mason was getting tired. Traveling across a wasteland filled with abandoned cars and rotting corpses forever kept him on edge. Mix in the needy travelers, violent convicts, and a box of gold coins, and it had been nothing short of an exhausting day. He had moved Bowie up front, hoping that a little companionship might help to keep him alert. Unfortunately, after only a few minutes, the dog had flopped down on the seat and was now curled into a ball, snoring like he had taken a double dose of Ambien.

They were approaching the outskirts of York, South Carolina, from the north, along Highway 161. According to the map, the town was very small, perhaps only a mile or two across. With nightfall only a few hours away, it looked like as good a place as any to rest for the evening.

As he came around a sharp bend, Mason saw a large dump truck parked sideways across both lanes. On the side of the truck, the word "Stop!" was scrawled in red spray paint. Four men armed with identical Bushmaster AR-15 semi-automatic rifles stood in front of the dump truck. By the time Mason saw the roadblock, he was too close to reverse or turn around without becoming target practice for wannabe Marines.

The only thing he could think to do was ease off the gas and coast up to the barricade as peacefully as possible. He rolled down both windows as he came to a full stop. Then he placed both hands on top of the steering wheel where they could easily be seen.

Two men stepped in front of the truck while the other two split and came up along each side.

"Out of the truck!" commanded a burly man, wearing dirty denim coveralls.

Bowie sat up and growled.

"Easy, boy," Mason said, patting him on his side. "Stay in the truck."

Bowie whined and pressed his head to the windshield as Mason stepped from the vehicle with his hands raised.

Coveralls spun Mason around and searched him. He pulled the Supergrade from its holster and stuck it in the front of his own waistband.

Then he slipped the hunting knife out of its sheath and tossed the heavy blade into the bed of Mason's truck. When he came across his Marshal's badge, he seemed to lose a little of his unabashed confidence.

"You're a lawman?"

Mason nodded. "Deputy US Marshal."

He thought about it a few seconds.

"Well, not around here, you're not. We're the law."

"Okay. And who are you exactly?"

"We're members of the Free Militia," the man said with an air of pride.

Mason kept his tone calm and friendly. He considered Coveralls and his men to be extremely dangerous. After having stood for days on end on a deserted county road, they were undoubtedly looking for any excuse to try out their new Bushmaster toys. He had seen similar aggression in young soldiers who found themselves bored and looking for a little excitement to test their training. The best thing he could do was to try to appear nonthreatening without being so weak that it invited sadistic brutality.

"Do you men have a leader?"

"He's talking about Alex," said one of the men.

Coveralls tipped his head and looked over at him.

"What am I, a dumbass?"

"No, boss."

"Then shut your pie hole, and let me do the talking."

The man looked down at his feet.

"Yes, boss."

Coveralls turned back to Mason.

"If you give me trouble, it's within my right to shoot you." He leaned over and looked into the cab. "That goes for your dog, too. We clear?"

Mason nodded.

Coveralls made a motion for one of the men to get the dog out of the truck. As he approached, Bowie started barking ferociously, daring him to stick his hand in the open window. The man raised his rifle.

"With your permission," Mason said, stepping toward the man, "I'll get him out. He's a good dog, but he gets a bit nervous around strangers."

The man thought about it a moment, then shrugged.

"If he bites me, I'll shoot him sure as shit."

Mason slowly opened the driver's-side door. He glanced at the glove box. In a couple of seconds, he could have the Glock 17 in his hands. But a semi-automatic 9 mm pistol against four men with semi-automatic rifles was not a fight he would likely win. Besides, he was hopeful that the situation might yet be resolved with words.

Bowie leaned his head out and growled at the strangers.

Mason patted him again.

"It's okay, boy," he said in a reassuring voice. He leaned down and let Bowie lick his face. He did this for two reasons. The first was to calm Bowie, and the second was to show Coveralls and the other guards that the dog wasn't a threat.

Bowie eventually quieted, trusting his master's judgment.

Gripping his collar, Mason carefully led him out of the truck.

Coveralls stepped forward and put a heavy hand on Mason's shoulder.

"You're coming with us."

"Okay," he said. "Where are we going?"

"To see what Alex wants to do with you."

"And my truck?"

Coveralls nodded to the man who had threatened to shoot Bowie.

"He'll bring your truck. You and the dog will ride with us."

"Any idea how long this is going to take?"

Coveralls shoved him toward a faded blue station wagon.

"Just get in. You ask too damn many questions."

&#8494; &#8485;

Unlike the other towns Mason had passed through, York was bustling with activity. People hurried along the streets, many of which had been cleared of abandoned cars and dead bodies. A white bakery truck drove slowly through town, the driver stopping at nearly every corner to hand out loaves of freshly baked bread. They passed a shopkeeper, who was using a bucket of water to wash blood and body parts off the sidewalk. On the other side of the street, a woman and her teenage son hung fuel-burning lanterns from historic lamp posts.

Coveralls and two other men escorted Mason to the town's courthouse, a two-story yellow brick building with large Victorian columns out front. An old man was already out front, waiting to lead Bowie away. Mason considered protesting but feared that anything he did would only make the situation worse. The man was easily seventy years old and seemed to have experience handling animals. Not only did he pet Bowie as he led him away, he also spoke to him, which Mason took to be a good sign that the dog wouldn't end up on someone's dinner plate.

The guards led him up a single flight of stone stairs to an office that had the word "Magistrate" etched on the glass door. After about ten minutes of waiting, an attractive woman entered the office. She looked to be in her mid-thirties, had long brown hair pulled back in a ponytail, and was wearing blue jeans, a tight-fitting white cotton shirt, and a pair of leather work gloves.

She pulled off the gloves and extended her hand to Mason.

"Marshal, it's a pleasure."

Mason shook her hand, surprised by the strength of her grip.

"Are you the magistrate?"

"The magistrate, the mayor, and the supreme leader of these degenerates," she said, looking over at Coveralls with a reassuring smile.

"Alex?"

"Alexus," she said with a nod of her head. "What can I say? My father wanted another jarhead, but he had to settle for me instead." She extended her hands, showcasing her body, which in Mason's eyes looked pretty fantastic.

"If you don't mind my saying, you look better than any jarhead I've ever seen. And believe me, I've served with plenty."

"Thank you," she said with a cute little wink. "You've got a rugged handsomeness yourself." This time she didn't offer a consolatory smile to Coveralls.

Mason nodded his appreciation.

"You're probably wondering why my men brought you here."

"I assume they were making sure I wasn't a threat to your town."

"That's right."

"And am I?"

"To be honest, I don't know yet." She moved close to the window and stared out. "When the pandemic hit, our town fell apart. People were literally dying in the street. Those were dark times."

"For everyone," added Mason.

She turned back at him.

"Yes, for everyone. Someone had to pick up the pieces. And that's what I did." She walked over to Coveralls and patted him on the shoulder. "I truly believe that I was born for one reason—to lead the citizens of York through the most difficult times we've ever faced. We all have our destinies, right?"

Mason shrugged. "So I've been told."

"When my townspeople were dying and afraid, I stepped up and provided a little order. My men, a few of whom you've met, enforce that order."

Mason looked over and saw Coveralls beaming from her attention.

"Makes sense," he said. "There are a lot of convicts on the loose right now."

"Right again. Not to mention the blister faces."

"The what?"

She grinned. "That's what we're calling the people who were infected with the virus. They're as ugly as sin, and the name just seemed to stick. One of the first things we did was roll up our sleeves and drive them out like roaches from a kitchen."

"Why'd you do that?" Mason thought about his encounter with Erik back in the town of Boone. If anything, he felt only pity for the man.

"Are you kidding? York is being rebuilt from the ground up. We don't care about race so much, but by God, we have to draw the line somewhere. Before you know it, those nasty creatures would be making babies, and York would become some kind of carnival freak show."

Mason knew enough history to appreciate that similar arguments had been made in the past. Whether it was Nazis, Bolshevists, or Hutus, countless leaders before her had found reasons to expel or murder those whom they felt didn't belong in their society.

"Do you know what the country needs right now more than anything else?" she asked.

He shook his head, allowing her to go on with a speech that he was sure she had given many times.

"Leaders," she said. "People who are able to step up and make difficult decisions. That's a rarity right now." Without giving him a chance to reply, she continued. "As you can imagine, people were initially reluctant to follow a woman. For some reason, they mistakenly assumed that women are weak. They forgot about Cleopatra, Margaret Thatcher, Joan of Arc, and countless other women who led armies to victory."

"Is that what you're doing? Leading an army?"

"You bet I am. We're facing all kinds of threats, not the least of which is an impotent federal government."

"Impotent?" He raised his eyebrows. "Interesting choice of words."

She grinned. "My point is that we're on our own. Like you, Marshal, we're working without a safety net."

He glanced out the window.

"It looks like you're doing okay."

She moved close and took his arm.

"Come on," she said. "I want to show you our town. A man like you will appreciate what we've done here."

Mason noted that she didn't ask him if he was interested in seeing the town; she told him.

Alexus led him out onto Liberty Street, the main thoroughfare that passed directly in front of the courthouse. Coveralls and the other two guards followed closely behind.

"Two weeks ago," she said, "people were literally decomposing on these very sidewalks. No one would move them for fear of contracting the virus. Now look at it." She spread her arms like the ringleader at a circus.

Mason looked around. The street was peaceful, and while it still had some signs of damage and neglect, it was free of bodies. An elderly couple walked down the sidewalk picking up debris. A woman and several young boys were on the opposite side of the street, washing store windows. Other than the men pointing rifles at him, Mason didn't have any particular objection to what she had done. York was certainly in better shape than the other towns he had passed through.

"It looks like you're keeping people busy."

"Everyone does their part. It's one of our rules."

"What happens to those who don't go along with your master plan?"

"A fair question," she said. "Let me show you."

She led him east on Liberty Street, past a small cemetery. In front of the graveyard stood a tall metal arch with the words "Rose Hill" stamped across the top. A white cloth banner had been hung below the arch, which read: *Punishment Yard*. At the center of the cemetery was a small wooden stage, on which several four-by-six beams had been used to erect a primitive gallows. A man hung from the noose, swaying from side to side like the pendulum of a grandfather clock.

"Does that answer your question?" she asked, waiting for his reaction.

He nodded, not at all surprised by what he was seeing.

"Our laws are kept very simple," she said. "And we post all decrees so that no one can hide behind the excuse that they didn't know what was allowed."

"Why the noose?"

"I know that it must seem a bit barbaric, but public hangings are very symbolic of justice."

"And does it work to keep order?"

She smiled. "You'd be surprised."

"What was his crime?" Mason asked, pointing to the dead man.

"I don't remember." She looked to Coveralls, who shrugged. "Whatever it was," she said, "he had it coming."

They walked down the street another quarter mile to a large outdoor strip mall. The buildings remained closed, with many of them boarded up, but an open-air market had been set up in the parking lot. A hundred or more people milled about under large revival tents, bartering for food and other supplies.

"You see?" she said. "We've even set up our own free market. While the town provides the bare necessities, the townspeople are encouraged to trade amongst themselves. Most of it is stuff they stole from other people's homes before we took over, but I don't hold that against them."

"Impressive." Mason thought that in many ways, York was Boone's twin sister—the vain one who insisted that you tell her how beautiful she was.

They turned and started back in the direction of the courthouse. As they did, a man suddenly broke away from the crowd and sprinted into the street. Several people shouted for him to stop.

Alexus swung around and motioned for Coveralls to take action. To Mason's surprise, her lieutenant was surprisingly fast. He broke into a full run, catching the man before he had even reached the far side of the street. He swept the thief's legs out from under him, causing him to go down hard on the pavement. The man rolled to his back, staring up at Coveralls, and more important, the rifle in his hands.

Alexus led Mason and the two remaining guards through the crowd. As they pushed into the makeshift market, everyone retreated to clear a path. The woman who seemed to be the center of attention looked around nervously, trying to decide what was expected of her.

"What did he take?" asked Alexus.

"My late husband's gold watch," the woman said softly, lowering her head. "But I didn't mean for this to happen. There's no need for violence."

Alexus put her hand on the woman's shoulder.

"That's for me to decide."

"Yes, ma'am."

"Did he hurt you?"

She rubbed her wrist, hiding it like a child might hide a toy he had taken from his older brother.

"Not really."

"Let me see."

The woman reluctantly held out her hand. There was a red welt around her wrist and a small bruise forming on her palm.

"He did hurt you."

"Really, I'm okay."

"You know the rules."

The woman looked down.

"I'm okay," she repeated softly.

Alexus motioned to Coveralls by pointing to her hand.

He said something to the man on the ground, who immediately began to protest. Shaking his head, Coveralls aimed his rifle at him. For a moment, Mason thought that he might shoot the unarmed man. After a few seconds, the man rolled over and slowly placed his hand, palm down, on the pavement.

Coveralls raised his boot and stomped as hard as he could. Only those closest to them heard the snapping of bones. Everyone heard the agonizing scream. Coveralls reached down and snatched the stolen watch from the man's wrist. Then he walked back to the woman in the crowd and handed it to her.

Alexus turned to Mason.

"Are you familiar with Hammurabi's Code?"

"An eye for an eye, and a tooth for a tooth."

She smiled. "What could be fairer than that?"

"Perhaps, but it must be administered in a just way."

"And was this just?"

Mason looked at the man lying in in the gutter, cupping his broken hand like a kitten that had just been run over.

"It seemed more about making a point."

She touched him gently on the arm.

"Exactly. We were telling everyone who witnessed this that there are consequences for their actions."

Mason shrugged. The man would live, and there seemed no point in pressing any sort of self-righteousness. Lord knows, he had certainly administered his own brand of justice on more than one occasion.

They turned and walked slowly back toward the courthouse. Alexus moved close and slid her arm through his.

"Why are you here, Marshal?" she asked.

"Like I said, I'm just passing through."

"To where, if I might ask?"

Mason considered how much to tell her. He didn't see any harm in her knowing his plans since they in no way impacted her town.

"I'm headed to the law enforcement center in Glynco, Georgia."

"To see if you can help?"

"Yes."

"That's noble. Really, I'm impressed."

"It's my job."

She laughed. "There are no jobs anymore, Marshal. Just things we do to survive."

"Is that why you set up the Free Militia? To survive?"

"That's one reason, yes. I suspect there are similar militias forming all over the country. The Free Militia is small, barely forty men and women. We're starting with the simple goal of establishing an orderly society here in York. That's not something to be feared, is it?"

"I've fought for similar causes," he said, thinking back to Boone.

"I thought as much," she said, squeezing his arm. "The truth is that you and I are not so different."

"Strong and good-looking?" he teased, trying to lighten the mood.

"Driven by purpose."

He nodded. "Where are we going now?"

"You need some rest."

Again he noticed that she told him rather than asked him. In this case, however, she was right. It was already dusk, and he was growing more exhausted with every hour that passed.

"I could use a bit of down time."

"Let's start by getting you fed. Then we'll find you a warm bed for the night. We southerners are known for our hospitality."

As nightfall approached, Samantha grew more anxious. She stared at the broken doors leading from Outdoor World to the street beyond as if expecting a horde of undead to stagger in at any moment. Given the pile of blistered bodies already lining the floor, it didn't strike her as an unreasonable concern.

Tanner sat with his back to a small pillar, the Savage .22 rifle in his hands. The empty shotgun lay beside him, currently about as useful as sock full of quarters.

"Relax," he said. "As soon as it gets dark, we'll head out."

"And then?"

"We'll go to the Jeep for supplies and ammunition."

"And after that?"

"After that, we'll find a safe place to crash for the night. It's too risky to stick around here, in case your Secret Service friend decides to show back up."

"You heard what he said. He's willing to kill me too."

Tanner thought about it for a moment.

"I wonder what he's up to. Do you have any enemies?"

"I'm eleven."

"Right. What about your mom?"

"She's the president. Of course, she has enemies." Samantha stared off into space for a moment, thinking. "Wait a minute. I remember her talking about a very dangerous guy named Al."

"Al?"

"Al Kayduh. I think he's a terrorist."

"Ah," Tanner said, smiling. "All right. So, let's assume this has to do with your mom. You're probably just leverage to get to her."

"They should know I won't do anything to help them."

"Just having you in their hands would be enough. They could make all sorts of threats. And from what we've seen, they'd be more than willing to follow through with them if needed."

"Evil people are just so . . . evil."

"Can't argue with that one."

Samantha stood up and paced the floor. She couldn't help but look at the man who had been butchered inside the front doors. Her eyes weren't drawn to the bloody gore, but rather to a small white piece of paper sticking out of his front pocket. She glanced back at Tanner, but his eyes were closed as he rested his head against the pillar. Careful not to step in the thick pool of dried blood, she tiptoed over to the man's body and slid the paper from his pocket. It was a single sheet of plain white paper, folded into quarters. She carefully made her way back to Tanner, studying the paper, unsure if she should even unfold it.

When she looked up, he was staring at her.

"What'd you find?"

She held up the paper.

"It was in his pocket."

"So, what's it say?"

"I wasn't sure if I should read it."

"He wouldn't have put it in his pocket if he didn't want it read. Go ahead."

She carefully unfolded the paper and began to read aloud in a slow narrator's voice.

*If you're reading this note, it means that I'm dead. I've never had much luck in this world, so my end probably wasn't quick or painless. I have no right, but I'm going to ask a favor of you. In my left boot, you'll find a photo of my daughter, Isa. Our address is written on the back. I was away on business when the virus hit, and I've been trying to get home ever since. I wonder if you'd be so kind as to deliver a message for me. Tell my baby girl that daddy did everything he could to make it home and that I'll watch over her from heaven. Please tell her what I couldn't, so that I can rest in peace.*

*Forever grateful, Booker Hill*

Tears trickled down Samantha's face as she choked out the last few words.

"That's . . . that's awful," she said, refolding the paper.

Tanner looked over at what remained of the man. Booker was right about one thing. His end hadn't been quick or painless.

"There are lots of sad stories out there," he said. "Don't forget that's what led us to where we are right now."

"I know," she said, wiping away the tears. She looked back over at the dead man.

"Let me guess. You want to get the photo from his boot." It was a statement, not a question.

"We're his last chance."

He sighed. "So get it."

Samantha tiptoed back over to the man's body and untied the left boot. When she gave it a tug, it didn't budge.

"It's stuck."

"That's probably because he's started to swell."

"Aren't you going to help me?"

"Nope."

She pulled on it again, leaning back with everything she had. The boot started to slide off.

"I'm getting it," she said with a tone of excitement.

"Goodie."

The boot finally came off, and like the man had promised, there was a small color photo inside. It showed a smiling little girl blowing out five candles on a birthday cake. Samantha flipped the picture over. On the back side, an address was written in blue ink.

"She lives in Salamanca, New York."

He shook his head in disbelief.

"What? You know where that is?"

"You could say that."

She raised her eyebrows waiting for more.

"My ex-wife lives on a farm less than ten miles from there."

"Hmm," she said, leaving the rest of her sentence unspoken.

"Life's full of coincidences."

"Yeah, but ten miles?"

"Just put it in your pocket, Saint Jude."

"Who?"

"Patron saint of lost causes."

Samantha looked at the photo one last time and then slid it and the note into her back pocket. She walked back to Tanner and sat down next to him.

"My mom says that we should listen to the little voice in our head."

"I suppose."

"What's yours saying right now?"

He thought about it a moment.

"It's saying that I should get you home before we're both killed like that poor fool."

"Right," she said, hardly hearing him. "Do you want to know what mine's saying?"

"No."

"It's saying that we're going to be together for a while longer."

"Fine, but we're not going to New York."

"Okay."

"I mean it."

"Okay." A shadow of something in the street passed in front of the doorway. "Someone's out there," she said, nudging him.

"Just people looking for supplies. No different than us."

"Then why are they out at night?"

"I don't know. Afraid of a sunburn?"

She didn't laugh.

"I wish you had your shotgun," she said, sliding a little closer. She pointed to the 12-gauge. "That's a good gun."

"What are you complaining about? This is a fine rifle." Tanner held up the Savage. "It could probably hit a fly at fifty yards."

"I'm not worried about flies." She paused. "Not unless they're gigantic flies looking to vomit on our heads."

"What?"

"Flies throw up on what they want to eat. It helps to turn their food into liquid so they can slurp it up through their snouts."

"I swear you make up half of what you say just to freak me out."

"It's true," she said. "I learned it in science class. You know, you should have gone to school. You learn a lot there."

"Hey," he said, bumping her lightly with his shoulder. "What if I told you I used to be a college professor?"

She looked up at him, searching his face for clues. His grin was all she needed.

"Where'd you teach?" she asked. "At the College of Convicted Felons?"

They both laughed, putting aside for the moment their worries about virus-infected monsters, murderous agents, and giant head-slurping flies to simply enjoy one another's company.

☙ ❧

Tanner and Samantha sat in the store until it was so dark that they could barely see one another's face. When he was confident they wouldn't easily be spotted on the street, Tanner stepped up to the broken doors and peered out. A thick fog had rolled in, and only the shine of a full moon offered any illumination. Samantha had been right. There were a few shadowed forms moving along the streets, but no one seemed to notice them standing in the doorway. He motioned for her to follow him.

As they stepped out of the store, Tanner suddenly realized that finding their way back to the Jeep was going to be more difficult than he had first thought. They had run only a few blocks, but that was in the daytime. Now, with darkness and fog shrouding everything, the small street looked more like the road to Mordor. Streetlamps stood like towering tree Ents, and hunched scavengers sneaked around like Nazgul in search of their beloved ring.

"We came from that way, right?"

"I think so." She paused, looking around. "Maybe it was that way."

"Come on," he said. "I'm pretty sure this is right."

No sooner had they stepped from the curb than he bumped into a Honda Accord that had a wheel missing and one corner propped up on a jack. The horn suddenly started honking, and its lights began to flash weakly. Samantha nearly jumped into his arms, and the people who were scavenging up the street spun to face them. The strangers weren't close enough for Tanner to decide if they were ordinary people or insane victims of the virus, but either way, he instinctively knew there was going to be trouble.

"Keep moving," he said, pulling her by the arm.

One of the scavengers shouted something unintelligible, and several others took it as their cue to investigate the noisemakers. Rather than run upright, they bent their heads forward and shuffled clumsily, as if it pained them to bend their limbs too far.

Tanner had seen that kind of stiffness before when he was fighting a group of the infected. The virus apparently caused severe arthritis, along with a host of other physiological and psychological changes. Their clumsy movements and hideous appearance were partly to blame for Samantha's labeling them zombies. And, while Tanner was quick to point out that they were just people who had been altered by the virus, he accepted that such semantics made little difference when they were gnawing on his neck.

With the infected approaching from both sides, Tanner and Samantha did the only thing they could. They ran. They made it as far as the alley before being caught by the first one. Tanner heard him approaching from behind, panting with excitement. Without looking, he kicked backward like a mule. His heel caught the man in the gut, doubling him over. Without looking back, they raced ahead.

Turning up the alley, Tanner and Samantha were both relieved to see the faint reflection of moonlight coming off the tail lights of the Jeep. It was only about fifty yards ahead. Unfortunately, they also heard several more of the infected closing in from behind. Tanner knew they would never make it to the Jeep in time to escape.

"Run and hide," he said, dropping his pack to the ground.

"Where?"

"Underneath the Jeep. Go, Sam!" He shoved the empty shotgun in her hands and pushed her ahead.

She broke into a run, quickly disappearing in the dark soup surrounding them.

Tanner turned in time to see three figures round the corner to the alley, two men and a woman. He immediately brought the rifle up and shot the largest man in the eye. The tiny lead slug sliced through his brain until it lodged in the back of his skull. Momentum caused him to fall forward, and the other two stumbled over him, giving Tanner time for another shot.

The second bullet hit the smaller man in the neck, but he didn't even slow down. Tanner made no attempt at a third shot as they were now within melee range. Instead, he whipped the butt of the rifle sideways, the heavy stock crunching the man's cheekbone like a fossilized eggshell. Fragments of bone and teeth collapsed inward, as the momentum of the blow sent him spinning into the ground. He made no attempt to get back up.

The woman swung a small axe handle, catching Tanner on the side of the head and ripping open the wound that Samantha had doctored earlier. Once again, a steady flow of warm blood began trickling down his face.

Tanner stabbed forward with the muzzle of the rifle, catching her in the solar plexus. As she doubled over, he squeezed the trigger and popped a .22 round into her gut. She screamed and lurched for him. With the rifle still flush against her, he squeezed the trigger twice more. With the third round, she finally fell to the ground, moaning loudly. He quickly stepped forward and kicked her in the head until she quieted.

Pausing to catch his breath while staring down at the three bodies, Tanner was reminded of the second of the Four Noble Truths of Buddhism. *Suffering is caused by desire and ignorance.* In this case, he thought, their suffering was due to an uncontrolled desire to inflict harm on a man twice their size and meaner than a honey badger.

He squatted down next to the woman. Dried blisters covered her face and hands. Her eyes shone in the night, a web of black ink streaking down her face like mascara at a pool party. Tanner wondered if the change to their eyes was the reason the infected seemed to prefer the dark. Certainly, every time—

Something smashed into him from behind, knocking the rifle from his hands and sending it skittering away in the dark. He stumbled forward, barely managing to keep from falling. Blindly spinning around and pivoting off his back foot, he shot an elbow up at the attacker's jaw. The man's teeth smashed together, and his head whipped back. Stumbling back, his attacker began to wobble from side to side as he struggled to stay conscious. Tanner immediately swept his legs out and followed him to the ground with a series of brutal punches to the face.

Before Tanner could stand back up, another of the infected jumped on his back, pulling a blistered forearm across his throat. He twisted his hips and flipped the man over his shoulder, slamming him into the pavement. As Tanner stepped in to finish him, four more of the infected swarmed around the corner. He glanced back to see if Samantha was within sight. She wasn't.

Facing a seemingly endless stream of berserkers, Tanner decided to lead them away. He screamed and charged directly into the oncoming group, barreling through them like a linebacker going for the quarterback. Hoping to draw their full attention, he paused long enough to add insult to injury by shouting a colorful expletive about their mothers having fornicated with a wheel of cheddar cheese. They screamed and tore out after him.

The chase was on.

ॐ ॐ

Samantha lay flat on her back, staring up at the grimy undercarriage of a 2008 four-door Jeep Wrangler. She had no trouble fitting underneath, because, as she often told people, she was small for her age. The night was black and the fog thick, and she couldn't see much of anything, except for the engine block above her. She lay there, breathing heavily, as she listened to Tanner fight the zombies. Footsteps. The pop of a gunshot. Then a second. More scuffling. Three more gunshots in quick succession. The sound of a foot stomping something solid and wet. Then nothing. She wondered if it was over. Before she could make up her mind, there were sounds of more fighting. Then Tanner screamed something about cheese and there were sounds of footsteps racing away. Then nothing.

She waited. Were they still nearby? Did they know where she was? Had they killed Tanner? No, of course not, she thought. He was meaner and tougher than anyone she had ever met. Her bodyguard, Oscar, had been big and strong, and was probably some kind of kung fu master. But he was nothing compared to Tanner. Tanner was like a donut without the jelly filling—just hard through and through.

She waited for a few more minutes, listening. The only sounds were her breathing and the steady drip of water from a nearby drain pipe. Then she heard something else. A soft weighty pat of someone, or something, walking without shoes. It reminded Samantha of how her own footsteps had sounded when she wore moccasins at summer camp. And there was an odor too, a powerful musky stink that was so pungent that it seemed to soil the air.

It must be some kind of animal, she thought. Maybe it was one of the gazelles? The smell grew so strong that her stomach heaved. Certainly, something as cute as a gazelle couldn't smell so awful. Images of monsters of every size and shape came to mind. Werewolf? Maybe. They stink, right? Maybe a troll. Surely, they don't bathe regularly. She closed her eyes, telling herself that there were no monsters. Other than zombies, of course. Maybe it was just a dog, like the ones they had encountered on the highway. Yeah, that was probably it. She felt better. It was just a dog. A really stinky one.

A long deep growl sounded. It was so loud and so incredibly powerful that she knew with certainty that whatever made it was much larger than any dog. And it was close.

She held her breath as small beads of sweat started to form on her brow.

The heavy footsteps slowly circled the Jeep. She could just barely see the creature's four legs moving in the dark. They were big and covered in a thick, smooth fur. The creature moved cautiously, as if unsure of exactly what it had discovered.

A massive head pushed under the edge of the Jeep, sniffing loudly. Samantha's heart pounded so violently that she was sure that the creature could hear it. Tears formed in the corner of her eyes as fear threatened to overwhelm her.

She clutched the shotgun that Tanner had given her. This was his fault. He had done this to her. How could he have sent her off into the dark

filled with all kinds of evil creatures, armed with nothing more than an unloaded gun? She felt anger growing in her belly. She decided that she wasn't going to trust him anymore, and she would tell him so too. As soon as they were back together, she would give him an earful all right.

The terrifying growl sounded again, resonating through the entire frame of the Jeep. Samantha was now convinced of one thing. Whatever stalked her was not of this world. Tanner had told her that there were no such things as monsters, but that was simply untrue. What other explanation could there be?

The creature stopped and sniffed under the car again as it tried to make sense of her scent. Confused or maybe just disinterested, it stood back upright. Then it peed. A stream of dark urine sprayed onto the side of the Jeep, pooling into a huge steamy puddle.

Samantha covered her nose and mouth with one hand to keep from vomiting. The smell was so strong that even breathing through her mouth offered little relief. Her eyes watered, and her tongue tasted as if she had dipped it in a bottle of ammonia. She finally retched, holding the vomit in her mouth, afraid to let it spill out. This forced her to breathe through her nose, and for a moment, she thought she might vomit again. Samantha closed her eyes and prayed.

*Momma said I should call on You only when it's really important. I know You're probably busy telling the Pope what to do, but I hope You can spare a minute to help me. I'm not asking for much. Just make this monster go away. I'm too small to fight it, and the protector You gave me isn't here. God, please . . . please help me.*

Tears streamed down her face, but she stayed completely still, waiting for her small miracle to happen.

The massive creature circled the Jeep again, this time slow and deliberate, as if weighing its options. When it came back around, it gave another deep growl before leaning down to sniff the pool of urine. Apparently satisfied with its wet deposit, it wandered slowly off into the night.

Mason sat on a queen-sized bed covered with a handmade paisley bedspread. The decorative quilt looked like something a grandmother would make as a keepsake for her children. For all he knew, that was exactly why it had been made. Whether that grandmother or her kids were still alive was anyone's guess. Alexus had put him up in her own home, which was centrally located in the center of York. Despite her overt hospitality, she continued to keep him under armed guard. He could hear the two goons sitting outside the bedroom door, talking about how their chances of playing for the NFL had significantly improved, now that all of the professional players were dead.

He went to the window and looked out. The main strip through town was lit by the fuel-burning lanterns that he had seen being hung earlier. A few people still moved along the street, taking care of any last minute business. Mason was genuinely impressed with what Alexus and her militia had accomplished in just a few short weeks. While the world was busy dying, she had established a small outpost that was now well positioned to survive and carry on. Admittedly, she was a ruthless dictator who enforced her will using a hangman's noose, but, still, Mason gave credit where credit was due.

He checked the window and found that there was no locking mechanism. To open it, he simply rotated a small handle. When the window was fully extended, he leaned out a few inches to make sure that his chest would fit through the opening. Directly beneath the window was an awning, and below that was the front door. He didn't think it would be terribly difficult to lower down and drop to the ground. While he didn't appreciate being taken prisoner, at least he had been confined to the minimum security ward.

Mason weighed his options. He could stay put and see how things played out. Given what he had seen so far, though, his gut told him that doing so would not end well. Admittedly, he didn't know what Alexus had in mind for him, but she didn't seem inclined to send him on his merry way. For a reason he didn't fully understand, she felt the need to exercise control over him. Whether it was pure ego or part of her militant agenda, he didn't know or care. The only thing that mattered was that she had taken his freedom.

His only other option was to try to escape. When everyone was asleep, he could slip out the window, find Bowie, his truck, and, if possible, his Supergrade. Once he had what he needed, he could just drive away into the night. No harm, no foul. She hadn't yet crossed a line that couldn't be forgiven.

The challenges with that plan were many. Even though York was a small town, he had no idea where they were keeping Bowie. That meant he would have to convince someone to reveal the dog's location. As for his Supergrade, that required finding Coveralls, something that might prove even more difficult unless the big man was still on patrol. Fortunately, his truck would be the easiest of the three. The last time he had seen it, it was parked directly across from the town's cemetery, not three blocks from where he now stood.

Mason heard Alexus's voice coming from outside the bedroom door. He quickly closed the window, stripped off his shoes and shirt, and flopped down on the bed with his hands folded behind his head. Within seconds, she opened the door and slipped inside. The two NFL wannabes peeked in after her with obvious concern. She motioned to them that she would be okay as she pushed the door closed.

"They're worried you're going to attack me," she said with a probing smile.

"I don't beat on women."

"I know that." Alexus was wearing a long white cotton nightshirt that hung down to her knees. And, from the looks of the soft curves protruding from underneath, that was all she was wearing. "Comfortable?" she asked.

Mason patted the bed.

"It's fine. Once I get a little shuteye, I'll be back to my normal self." He faked a yawn.

She walked over to the window and looked out, as if knowing exactly what he had been doing before she came in.

"Nice night. Calm and quiet. And the full moon's beautiful. It's a night to be enjoyed, don't you think?"

He wasn't sure what she was getting at but thought he saw an opportunity.

"Maybe we could go out for a stroll," he suggested. If he could get her out on the street, not only might he find an opportunity to escape, he might also extract information about where Bowie was being kept.

She turned to face him, the unmistakable look of desire in her eyes.

"That's not what I had in mind."

She sauntered toward him like a runway model, letting his eyes feast on the delicate curves of her body as the nightgown slid across them. When she got to the bed, she sat on the opposite side and gently leaned back against the pillows. The nightgown slid up her thighs, showing rich creamy skin beneath.

"Tell me a little about you, Marshal," she said.

He rolled onto his side and studied her. Alexus was a stunningly beautiful woman, long brown hair, full tender lips, and a voluptuous body begging to be explored. Of course, all that was on the surface. He felt certain that something darker lay beneath.

"Not much to tell, really," he said, working to keep his composure. "I've been a marshal for seven years. Before that, I was a soldier."

"Did you see any action?"

He thought of his time in the Army's 75th Ranger Regiment, of the faces of people who had fallen on both sides.

"Some."

She reached over and put a hand on his. It was warm and soft, like she'd just finished rubbing down with coconut butter after a hot shower.

"When I look in your eyes," she said, "I see a strength that's rare in what's left of this world. Truth is, it was rare even before everyone died. You're someone who could give orders, a man who others would follow. That's a problem I have around here."

"What's that?"

"We have a very limited pool of men in York. Of those who remain, none have charisma or any sense of leadership. They're sheep waiting for someone to tell them what to do." She squeezed his hand. "I sense you're not that kind of man."

He shook his head, a hard look coming over his face.

"No," he said. "I'm not."

She leaned in and kissed him on the lips. It was soft and tentative, as if she just wanted a quick taste of his mouth.

"What kind of man are you?" she said, pulling back a few inches to look in his eyes.

Mason did what was expected of him. He leaned in and kissed her passionately, feeling the warm press of her lips and the electric touch of her tongue. His mind raced with possibilities. His first thought was that she was dangerous. If he offended her, she would have him swinging from the gallows by morning. Of that, he had no doubt. If he bored her, it might be even sooner.

Ava, his girlfriend in Boone, also came to mind. He did not want to betray her, even if it was to save his own skin. Women just didn't understand that sort of self-preserving logic when it came to sex.

In his years of fighting other people's wars, Mason had found himself in a number of tough scrapes. He credited his survival to a keen ability to read situations and react accordingly. There were times when bullets needed to fly and others when a few choice words had pulled his butt from the fire. In this particular case, Alexus was accustomed to getting what she wanted, and having her accept any kind of rejection would be a trick for Houdini himself. Mason thought he saw a way, but it was certainly not without risk. If she didn't react as he expected, things would quickly go sideways. There was an even greater risk that he would be unable to see it through. Sometimes treating fire with fire worked. Other times, it just caused things to get really hot.

He reached out and grabbed her by the small of the back, pulling her body against his. She moaned, surprised by his sudden aggression. He continued to kiss her, probing her mouth with his tongue. He moved over to nibble her ear and then started biting the soft flesh of her neck.

"Yes, yes," she breathed heavily.

He slipped his hand up her gown and began exploring her soft, sensuous body. For several minutes, he fondled her with a mix of finesse and unrelenting aggression, like a master fencer wielding a broadsword. She winced from the rough handling but never stopped squirming under his touch.

He slapped her bare butt, and she squealed in pain and delight.

"You bastard!" she exclaimed, biting his lip so hard that it started to bleed.

Then Mason did the unexpected. He suddenly rolled away and sat up on the edge of the bed.

Alexus was confused, her breathing shallow and rapid.

"Wh-what is it?" she asked, the lust heavy in her throat.

"Not tonight," he said, looking off toward the window, as if suddenly disinterested.

*"What?"* She sat up and put her hand on his shoulder, pulling at him. "What are you talking about? We were—"

"Maybe tomorrow. I'm tired tonight."

She jerked her hand away.

"What the hell is wrong with you?" she spat, scrambling off the bed and pulling down her nightgown.

He stood up too, towering a good eight inches over her, his body strong and lean.

"Come to me tomorrow, and I'll satisfy your hunger."

She swung at his face, not a slap, but a full-fisted punch.

He caught it by the wrist and squeezed hard. She winced from the pain. He pulled her close to him, their bodies once again touching like two electric wires. Leaning down, he kissed her hard on the lips. When he pulled back, the blood from where she'd bitten his lip was smeared across hers.

"I'll see you tomorrow night. And don't for a minute pretend you're not coming." He looked her up and down, grinning, as if admiring the lines of a new sports car.

Alexus pressed her lips together as she struggled to reconcile anger with lust. Her heart pounded like a jackhammer on Sunday morning. She was uncertain and off balance, and that was exactly how he wanted her. Without another word, she spun around and stomped out of the room, slamming and locking the door behind her.

Mason lowered himself to the bed and let out a heavy sigh. He looked down and saw that his hands were trembling. Over the years, he had faced off with all manner of violence, but manipulating a hellcat in the bedroom was outside of his comfort zone. Way outside.

"The things we do for love," he said with a nervous grin.

One thing was now for certain. He had to escape. When Alexus returned the following evening for unfinished business, she wasn't going to take no for an answer.

Even though Tanner was a big man, he had always been a capable runner. As he vaulted over cars, jumped garbage cans, and kicked aside anything that got in his way, he couldn't help but feel like he was competing in a life and death game of parkour. Unfortunately, despite his agility, his pursuers only seemed to be growing in number. How many there were now, he couldn't say, but it felt like the entire Confederate Army was hot on his heels, every one of which seemed absolutely determined to get a piece of him—literally.

The almost impenetrable darkness was both a blessing and a curse. It made Tanner harder to see, but it also hid all sorts of debris for him to stumble over. He figured the only way to escape his pursuers was to get enough distance between him and them, and then find a cubby hole in which to hide. As far as he knew, the virus didn't bestow the infected with a supernatural tracking ability rivaling that of a bloodhound. It did, however, seem to enhance their night vision. He suspected that might have something to do with their pupils being permanently dilated. As for the disgusting black ooze leaking out of their eyes, that was for doctors with stronger stomachs than his to diagnose.

As he whipped around a street corner, he thought he saw his opening. To his right was a small first aid clinic—a "doc in a box," as he had called them in the past. The glass door was smashed and hanging on the frame by only a single hinge. He bent over and carefully stepped in through the broken door. It smelled like a slaughterhouse in summer. The stench was so awful that it nearly shoved him right back out the door. Determined that this was his best, and perhaps only, chance, he covered his nose and pressed ahead.

The waiting area was littered with small metal chairs that had once lined the walls. The unmistakable shapes of three human corpses were slowly decomposing onto the white tile. While it was too dark to make out their details, he heard the incessant buzz of blowflies as they swarmed back and forth between the dead bodies. Tanner couldn't help but consider that, if he died here, the flies would soon enjoy his flesh as well.

"Over my dead body," he mumbled.

The flies didn't seem to appreciate his humor, continuing to feast without so much as a single chuckle.

Tanner burst through a heavy interior door and found a hallway with examination rooms on one side and a long built-in service counter on the other. The doors to all but one of the rooms were open. The body of a nurse wearing light green scrubs and a face mask sat on the floor in the hallway. She leaned to one side with her head propped against a small rolling cart. Her legs were splayed out in front of her, like a doll that had been hastily dropped.

He raced from room to room, searching the building for a weapon. The best he could find was a Brooklyn Crusher baseball bat. At twenty-nine inches and just over two pounds, it could do some damage, for sure. Best of all, it was made of hardened polypropylene, a material that was nearly indestructible. While it wasn't a twelve-gauge with triple-aught buck, it was better than bare fists. What a baseball bat was doing in a first aid clinic was anyone's guess. Perhaps a Little Leaguer had come in with a sprained ankle and forgotten to take it home. None of that mattered to Tanner. When fate gave him a baseball bat, he held on tight and swung for the fences.

He also found an assortment of medical supplies scattered on the floor, as well as several more bodies. While the entire facility stunk of human decay, the body count wasn't nearly as bad as the smell suggested. His last stop was to check the room with the door closed. He kept his fingers crossed that maybe the room had doubled as the armory for the town's National Guard.

When he swung the door open, hundreds of thousands of flies swarmed out, smashing into him with the force of an ocean gale. He squinted his eyes and waved them away, choking and gagging on the unrelenting insects. When they finally thinned, he saw that one side of the examination room was filled with a massive pile of bodies. How many people lay dead in the room, he couldn't say, but it reminded him of the mass graves he had seen in Holocaust documentaries. Even holding his breath, his eyes began watering from the gases released from the decaying corpses.

Garbled voices suddenly sounded from outside the medical center. Tanner whipped left and right, surveying the building for somewhere to hide. He could duck behind the counter or into one of the other exam rooms, but he would almost certainly be found. And, while he was eager to see how well the Brooklyn Crusher stood up to its name, he didn't

think it would be nearly enough to successfully stand against such overwhelming odds.

He looked back through the doorway to hell. Surely, there was another way.

The voices grew louder. They were in the building. When they came through the interior door, they would see him, and hiding would no longer be an option.

Tanner pushed through the flies and eased the door closed behind him. The room was so black that it seemed to be sucking photons from adjacent galaxies. He stumbled forward, feeling blindly in the darkness. Everywhere he touched, his hands felt something sticky and wet, bodies slowly melting into puddles of guts and goo. Eyeballs, intestines, organs, huge flaps of loose skin, skulls, everything one needed to set up the scariest haunted house ever made.

Ignoring every instinct to flee from the horror, he scrambled to the top of the bodies and slid down the back side. No sooner had he settled against the corpse of a bloated woman than the door swung open.

After a moment, a garbled voice said, "He's not here, either."

Another man screamed in anger and struck something heavy against the wall.

"Find him!"

The door slammed shut. Tanner waited in dark silence, the Brooklyn Crusher gripped tightly in his hands like a string of rosary beads. The only sounds that remained were the soft rasp of his labored breathing and the occasional *pfffft* of bodies releasing their putrid gases.

಄ ⚭

Samantha stayed under the Jeep for a good twenty minutes after the creature left. The night around her remained quiet, and she eventually felt safe enough to crawl out. She scanned the alley left and right. Nothing moved. Tired and afraid, she quietly opened the door to the Jeep and climbed inside. The back seat was packed with a variety of supplies, including bottled water, blankets, and food. While she was confident that Tanner would eventually return, there was no guarantee that it would be before something hungry managed to find her. She needed a weapon.

Digging through the pile of gear, she found an unopened box of shotgun shells. She was surprised at how heavy it was as she lifted it to the front seat. She opened the box, withdrew a shell, and studied it. One end had a brass cap with a small bead in the middle. The plastic on the other end was knurled inward to keep the shell's contents in place. She guessed that inside the shell there must be bullets as well as some gunpowder to project them.

Samantha had seen Tanner load the shotgun a few times, so she had a general idea of how it was done. She lined up a shell against the collapsible metal flap on the bottom of the gun and pushed it forward. The slide folded up and the shell pushed up and in, almost like it went into the barrel. That's weird, she thought. If all the shells go into the barrel, how does it know which one to fire? She studied it a little more. Upon closer inspection, she saw that there was a round metal ammunition tube below the barrel. She grinned, proud of her discovery.

"I can do this," she whispered.

She pushed a second shell in behind the first. It was a little harder to push in. She pushed in a third shell and then a fourth. Each shell was successively harder to insert as she compressed a spring in the magazine tube. She tried to get a fifth shell into the tube, but her fingers weren't strong enough. That's okay, she thought. Four will be enough.

She looked at the shotgun. Was it ready to shoot? There was a button at the base of the trigger guard. Even in the dark, she could see a small orange band showing on one side. She clicked the button both directions. One way showed the orange band, the other showed all black. She thought about it for a moment. Hunters wear orange for safety. So, logically, if orange is showing, the weapon is safe. She smiled again. This really wasn't so hard. She was ready to protect herself.

She dumped the rest of the box of shells into her backpack. Then she grabbed a bottle of water from the back and drank nearly the whole thing. She nibbled on a granola bar but found that she was too nervous to eat. In case she got hungry later, she stuck several more in her pack.

"Now what?" she wondered aloud.

She checked, and sure enough, the keys were still in the ignition. If it became necessary, she could drive out of the city. She felt a pang of guilt at having balked at Tanner's insistence that she learn to drive. The problem was that, even with the headlights on, it would be nearly impossible to navigate the dark streets, especially with the dense fog. It would be better to wait until morning, she thought. Besides, that would give Tanner time to come back.

But what if he didn't come back? Her gut twisted at the thought.

"I'll give him until the sun starts coming up," she said. "If he's alive, he'll be here by then."

With her decision firmly made, Samantha clutched the shotgun and curled up on the seat, determined to wait a few more hours.

☙ ❧

Tanner looked and smelled like the lowliest of grave robbers. His clothes, hair, and hands were sticky with blood, bile, and piss. He stood at the entrance to the first aid clinic, staring out into the street. Everything was quiet. His pursuers had either moved on to look elsewhere or had simply abandoned their search. Why the infected had such a hard-on for him was a mystery for another day. This wasn't his first violent encounter with them, and it surely wouldn't be his last.

Hugging the buildings, he began working his way back toward the alley. Tanner figured that he had run about a mile, so it was going to take him a good thirty minutes to get back. His thoughts went to Samantha. Had they captured her? Killed her? He forced brutal images from his mind. She was okay. He could feel it. Helping her to get home was the first really unselfish thing he had done in years, and, by God, nothing was going to get in the way of his redemption.

There was a gap in the buildings that left him exposed, so he knelt down and began shuffling from car to car. When he got close to a white Toyota 4Runner, he noticed that heat was radiating from the engine compartment. He put his hand on the hood. It was still a little warm. The engine had definitely been run in the past few hours.

A thought suddenly occurred to him. He shuffled around to the rear of the vehicle and found a large jerry can strapped to the rear hatch with several bungee cords. He tapped the side of it. Nearly full. Shifting his position so that he didn't block the moonlight, he bent down until his face was only inches from the blacktop. Tilting his head from side to side, he saw the light reflecting off a thin trail of oil on the pavement. He could hardly believe his luck. Either the universe was throwing him a whopper of a coincidence, or this was the car they had been pursuing.

He studied the buildings on both sides of the street. All of them were dark. Where had the killers gone? It didn't make sense that they would park any appreciable distance from where they were headed. And, if they had abandoned the car, they would have taken their spare fuel.

Tanner moved from door to door, listening. Nothing. He spotted a trail of white smoke rising from a vent on the roof of an Army recruiting station. The brick building looked old enough to have been used to recruit troops for the beaches of Normandy. An antique "Uncle Sam Wants You" poster was plastered to the front window, as were several more modern "Army Strong" banners.

He peeked in through the large window, which, surprisingly, had survived the apocalypse. Nothing moved, and there was no light coming from inside. Whatever was generating the smoke was housed deeper within the structure. He stepped through the broken door, crunching the glass under his boots. He stopped and listened to see if the noise caused any sort of reaction. It didn't.

He took a moment to walk around and survey the recruiter's station. The entry led into the main office area, where hands had been shaken and commitments signed. Three battleship gray metal desks remained upright. Just outside the main office were men's and women's bathrooms. Beyond them was a small storage room, filled with boxes of color brochures and pamphlets. There was also a small service door at the rear of the building.

He opened it barely enough to peek through a small slit between the frame and the door. Like the rest of the building, it was dark on the other side. He swung it open and stepped through. It led to an open-air courtyard that looked like it might have once been part of an alleyway, but was now completely boxed in by two-story brick walls.

Tanner looked up and saw millions of twinkling stars overhead. He took a moment to enjoy the sight. If there was one positive outcome of the virus, it was that, without electric lighting, people could once again marvel at the universe. A small consolation perhaps for the billions who had died, but he was willing to take what he could get.

A round table and two metal lawn chairs sat undisturbed in the small outdoor space. What had once been a delivery entrance was now an outdoor break area for recruiters to enjoy a cigarette. He noticed two other things. The first was a large metal hatch on the ground, and the second was a woman's tennis shoe. He walked over and picked up the shoe, turning it in his hands as he studied the details. It was a match for the one he had found at the scene of the shooting.

He turned his attention to the hatch. It was military grade, made from steel and hardened hinges. Tanner grabbed the handle and gave it a light tug. No surprise; it was locked tight from the inside. He surmised that it must be an old bomb shelter from the 1950s, a time when governments and individuals alike worried over the growing atomic threat. Kneeling down, he listened at the worn metal door. The faintest sounds of voices came from within. He had found his quarry.

The question now was how to overcome armed assailants locked in an underground vault, with nothing more than a baseball bat. He could beat on the door all night long and do little more than add a few dents. Even if he were lucky enough to somehow get the door open, they would shoot him before he could get close enough to swing the Brooklyn Crusher. There was only one way to have a fighting chance. He had to get them to come out.

After Alexus stormed out, Mason searched the bedroom for any-thing that might help with his escape. The only things he found were a can of black shoe polish and a roll of electrical tape. When he was satisfied there was nothing left to find, he lay down on the bed to rest for a few hours.

As a soldier, he had discovered that guards tend to become much less aware in the middle of the night. Perhaps it was their internal clocks shut-ting down, or maybe their minds tended to wander about the next day's activities. Either way, there were a few hours when an alert individual had a significant advantage over those just passing the hours.

He lay quietly until a few minutes after one in the morning. Then he carefully dressed, tucking the laces into his boots to prevent them from snagging, and using the electrical tape to make sure that nothing was loose or flapping. He smeared a little shoe polish on anything metal as well as his cheek bones, chin, and forehead. When he was buttoned up tight, he opened the bedroom window and peered out. To his surprise, no one stood guard outside the front door.

He slid both legs out the window, sitting precariously on the ledge. It was about seven feet to the metal awning below. Rather than jump, he spun around, grabbed with both hands, and lowered himself down. His feet touched the awning even before he was fully extended. Without letting go of the window sill, he allowed more and more of his weight to rest on the awning. When his weight was fully supported, he let go of the sill, ready to make a grab for it, in case something went wrong. It didn't. The awning felt sturdy enough to hold Andre the Giant.

Mason sat down and slid his legs over the edge. He then repeated the hang-and-drop process to the ground. In this case, however, the awning was a little high, and he was forced to fall about two feet. He landed, surefooted, and immediately stepped into the shadows lining the edge of the building.

He stood quietly doing nothing for about thirty seconds, giving his eyes time to adjust to the night. The oil lanterns cast small puddles of flickering yellow light in a sea of darkness, and the bright white moon hung overhead like a lucky silver dollar. He spotted two men patrolling west on Liberty Street. Based on their distance, he estimated that they had passed Alexus's house less than a minute before his stealthy exit.

Staying close to the buildings, Mason headed east in the direction of the cemetery. It was only two blocks away, and it took him less than five minutes. He was relieved to find his black F150 parked across from the cemetery, exactly where he had seen it earlier in the day. A lone man stood on the sidewalk with an over-and-under shotgun propped on his shoulder, broken open like he was returning from a day of duck hunting. He leaned against the truck, smoking a long, thin cigar. The unmistakable odor of Cavendish tobacco spread through the air.

Mason planned his approach. The truck was on the other side of the street, so the safest route was probably to come parallel to it and then cross over. He crouched down and shuffled forward, hiding behind a line of cars. Each time he came to a gap between cars, he rushed forward to the next one. He made it all the way to the car parked directly across from his pickup without being discovered. The riskiest part, however, still lay ahead. He looked left and right. All clear. It was now or never.

Rather than trying to hurry across the street hunched over, Mason straightened up and sprinted across the two-lane road. When he got to the truck, he ducked down by the rear driver's side wheel and waited. Nothing happened. He heard the man take a final drag on his cigar and flick it away.

Mason stood and peeked over the top of the truck bed. Stogie was leaning against the passenger door, less than six feet from him. Mason was pretty sure he could sneak around the front of the truck without the man hearing him. Then it would come down to a quick, violent struggle. Assuming that the fight went in his favor, he could interrogate the guard about the whereabouts of Bowie and Coveralls.

He shuffled forward to peek into the cab. Unfortunately, the M4 was no longer in its rack. He was disappointed but not terribly surprised. Mason liked the weapon but accepted that he would leave it if necessary. He wondered if the Glock 17 was still in the glove box. It was a far cry from an assault rifle but was still much better than being unarmed. Many of his fellow lawmen had labeled the Glock their "business gun" because of its outstanding reliability on the street. While Mason had always preferred a 1911-style handgun, the Glock would put him one step closer to being back on the right side of things.

He glanced into the truck bed and quickly surveyed its contents. His supplies had clearly been rummaged through, but the only things he immediately noticed missing were the two ammo cans containing .45 and 5.56 mm ammunition. He didn't keep a firearm in the back, but he noticed his hunting knife wedged between two large cans of beans. Coveralls had thrown it in the truck when they were at the roadblock, probably thinking that the vehicle would later be scavenged. While Mason had no intention of killing Stogie, a sharp blade might help to loosen his tongue.

Leaning over the edge of the truck bed, he inched toward the knife. An instant before he could get it in hand, Stogie casually glanced back his direction. Mason froze. He wasn't sure if a slight sound had tipped him off, or whether it had been nothing more than a bit of bad luck. Either way, the man stared at Mason like he was an apparition that had materialized in the night.

Stogie was tired, not to mention surprised, and it took him a full two seconds to process what he was seeing. In those two seconds, Mason leaped into the truck bed and dove headfirst at him. The impact knocked the shotgun out of Stogie's hands and sent the two men tumbling to the pavement. Mason ended up on top, and Stogie bucked violently, trying to throw him off.

Not knowing how else to quiet him, Mason leaned in and placed his forearm across the man's throat.

"Just calm down," he whispered. "I'm not going to hurt you."

Stogie managed to get a leg between them and kicked upward, flipping Mason over the top. As he felt himself being launched into the air, Mason latched onto Stogie's right wrist with both hands. He landed flat on his back and immediately pushed out with his legs, stretching Stogie's arm out straight. Then he bowed upward from the waist and locked the man's elbow. The guard screamed in pain as his elbow bent the wrong direction. Rather than breaking Stogie's arm, Mason dropped the heel of his boot onto the man's face. By the third kick, Stogie was bloody and unconscious.

He released Stogie's arm and rolled to his feet. He was disappointed that things had gone so poorly. Not only was the confrontation far noisier than he would have liked, it also made it impossible to ask the man any questions. Besides, he didn't relish hurting someone whose only crime had been drawing the short straw when it came to midnight guard duty.

Two men were already running in his direction from the east end of Liberty Street, each carrying a semi-automatic rifle. Mason looked left and right, considering his options. None of them seemed particularly good. He could quickly search his truck in hopes of finding a weapon, or he could run off into the night, unarmed in a town full of hostiles. In the end, he did neither. He simply put his hands on top of his head and dropped to his knees beside the fallen guard.

Within minutes, six armed men surrounded him like a posse cornering a notorious outlaw. Not having been trained as soldiers or lawmen, they stood with rifles pointed, waiting for someone to tell them what to do. Mason considered trying to negotiate his way out of the mess, but accepted that he had little with which to bargain. Instead, he did what any smart prisoner does when caught. He sat quietly and kept his mouth shut.

Alexus and Coveralls showed up at the same time but from different directions. Neither looked pleased to see him. Stogie was waking up too. Blood covered his face and shirt, and he seemed a bit disoriented. He struggled to stand, cradling his right arm.

Alexus turned to Stogie with anything but sympathy in her eyes.

"What happened?" she barked.

"He jumped me. I think he broke my arm." He held it out before him, obviously wanting her to understand that he had put up a fight.

She looked over at Mason.

"Why?"

Mason shrugged. "A prisoner tries to escape."

"But . . ." She shook images from her head. "It was a game, right? You were playing games with me."

There was no right answer, so he didn't offer one.

She turned to Coveralls.

"Take them both over to Rose Hill," she said, pointing to the cemetery across the street.

Coveralls grabbed the guard, and two other men grabbed Mason. Together, they pushed and dragged them across the street and up onto the large wooden stage in the center of the cemetery. The dead man who had been swinging from the gallows earlier in the day was no longer there. Instead, the empty noose floated in the night air beckoning its next victim.

Coveralls immediately pushed Stogie into position, securing his hands with a small leather strap and slipping the noose over his head.

"Please," the man begged, "it wasn't my fault. He jumped me."

"He's right," said Mason. "There's no need for this. He put up a hell of a fight."

Alexus stepped close to Mason.

"His blood is on your hands, not mine." She nodded to Coveralls, and he immediately hoisted the rope, lifting Stogie into the air about two feet. He tied it off on a metal peg that stuck out from the support post. The guard kicked and thrashed as he slowly suffocated.

"If you do this, you're all murderers," said Mason.

"You don't think I'm compassionate?" she asked, flashing him a wicked grin.

She walked over to the hanging man, wrapped both arms around his legs, and dropped downward, bouncing up and down with her full body weight until his neck snapped. When she was satisfied that he was dead, she got to her feet and turned to Mason.

"See?" she said. "My cup runneth over with compassion."

His eyes turned cold.

"You're a regular Mother Teresa."

Coveralls lowered Stogie, slipped the noose off his neck, and pushed the body off the stage.

"You're next, Cowboy."

Mason had been thinking about how to get himself out of the mess. His only chance was to convince Alexus that he had something she wanted more than revenge.

"If you kill me," he said, "you'll never get the gold."

Everyone turned to face him.

"What gold?" she said.

"Check my front pocket."

She stepped forward and slipped her hand in his pocket. When she pulled it out, she was holding the shiny gold coin. She held it up to the light of the moon.

"Where'd you get this?"

"It doesn't matter. What matters is that I have four hundred and ninety-nine more of them in safekeeping."

"You're lying." But even as she said the words, she seemed to be calculating the benefits of owning such a large cache of gold.

"I think you know that I'm not."

She studied the coin.

"It looks new."

"They're all new. And in pretty little cases too. Total size is about . . ." He held his hands out to roughly the size of the blue box. ". . . yay big."

"All right. Then you'd better tell me where the gold is right now."

Mason laughed. "Or what? You'll have me killed?"

"I could do a hell of a lot worse than that."

"You could," he said, meeting her stare. "But as a soldier who's seen his fair share of torture, I can tell you that it almost never gets you what you want."

Trying a different approach, she stepped very close and placed her hands on his chest.

"What do you want for the gold? Your freedom?"

"That. And my dog. And my truck. And anything else you took from me."

"That's it?"

"That's it."

She thought about his offer.

"If I let you go, I'll never see you or the gold again. Am I right?"

"I could offer you my word."

She laughed. "Not nearly good enough. Try harder. You're bargaining for your life."

"Send one of your best men with me," he said, glancing over at Coveralls. "When we get the gold, he can bring it to you, and Bowie and I will go on our way."

"Hmm," she said, rubbing her chin. "Still not good enough. You could get the jump on my man, and then I'm left with nothing. I tell you what. I'll keep your dog here with me. When you and my man both come back here with the gold, I'll give your dog back, and you can go on your way. If you don't, I'll gut your dog and hang his carcass right here for everyone in town to see."

Mason took a deep breath to keep his voice in check.

"If you hurt my dog, I'll come back and kill every last one of you." He looked around at the guards, studying their faces for any future hit list that he might have to make. Most of them looked away from his stare. Coveralls just grinned.

"Then we have an understanding," she said. "How far is the gold?"

"If we leave in the morning, we could be back by dusk."

She studied the coin again, rubbing it between her fingers. The metal had cast its spell over yet another greedy soul.

"Good," she said. "I've always wanted to be rich."

S amantha wiped the condensation from the Jeep's windows, hoping to see Tanner swagger around the corner like he didn't have a care in the world. The alley remained quiet and still, which, given the circumstances, wasn't so terrible either. Now that she was inside the Jeep, holding a loaded shotgun, she felt more tired than afraid. The one thing she was most afraid of was falling asleep and waking to find the mysterious creature staring in at her. Even the trusty shotgun might not be able to stop such a monster. More likely, it required a silver bullet or holy water. It usually did.

She wondered what time it was. She had never worn a watch because they pinched her wrist, but she decided that it was probably a good idea to get one. She might be in a situation like this again, and knowing how long she had been waiting would make her feel better. Next chance she got, she would ask Tanner to find her one. He didn't mind stealing things.

She wiped away a fresh layer of condensation and looked out again. *Where was he?*

&ev &

Tanner had an idea. The door to the underground shelter was very sturdy, but the black rubber seal around it was cracked and even missing in some places. Getting the occupants to open the door might not be as hard as he first thought.

With as much stealth as his two-hundred-and-fifty-pound frame would allow, he made his way back to the white 4Runner. Thankfully, there were still no signs of the infected. He unhooked the jerry can from the back of the vehicle and set it on the ground. It was heavy, which was good for what he had in mind. He unscrewed the cap and took a quick sniff. Gasoline. Perfect.

He hauled the can back through the recruiting station and set it down beside the bunker. He leaned down and put his ear to the door again. It was quiet inside. He smiled. It was going to get really noisy, really fast. Before the main attraction, however, there were a few things he had to get ready. He went back and collected several handfuls of broken glass, spreading the small shards between the bunker door and the recruiter's office. Then he moved the bodies and furniture around in the room so that nothing would look familiar.

When he was satisfied with the setup, he returned to the hatch. Hoisting the jerry can into the air, he began to slowly pour the fuel along the top of the hatch. The gasoline ran down the rubber seam, seeping in through the gaps. It worked even better than he had expected because the fuel started dissolving what was left of the rubber gasket. He estimated that the can contained three or four gallons of gasoline, and by the time he had emptied it, shouts were coming from inside the bunker.

He set the can aside and hurried back into the recruiter's office. There weren't really any great places to hide for an ambush, so, instead of hiding, Tanner simply lay face down on the floor. In the dark, he thought he could easily pass for one of the dead. He certainly smelled like a corpse.

After a few seconds, he heard the bunker door flop open with a heavy metal clang.

"Careful!" It was the voice of a young man.

There was a pause.

"No one's out here." The second man's voice was throaty, like he had spent a lifetime smoking Marlboros—the real ones, not the pansy-ass lights. "The gas can is here all right, but whoever did it isn't. You stay down there, Junior. If anyone other than me pokes his head in, you shoot it off."

"Don't worry. I'll shoot it off all right!"

Tanner heard footsteps crunching the broken glass as the man slowly approached. He was lying just inside and to the left of the back door, one arm splayed out above his head at an awkward angle, the other underneath him, holding the bat. The footsteps came very close and then stopped.

"No one's in here either," the man hollered back toward the bunker. "I'm going to check the street. You be ready!"

Footsteps continued past Tanner, and as they did, he tilted his head slightly to get a better look. The man was middle-aged, short, and stocky. He held a large revolver out in front of him with both hands. When he was about five feet away, Tanner sat up and swung the bat with everything he had.

The Brooklyn Crusher caught the man on the side of his right knee, and it not only canted inward, the femur actually broke away from the patella and tore through the flesh on the inside of his leg. As the man was falling, Tanner rolled up to one knee and brought the bat down on top of his head. The man's skull compressed downward against his spine, dislodging several vertebrae and severing his spinal cord. The gun fell from his hand, hitting the ground about the same time as his head.

Tanner shuffled closer and bent over him. The man's eyes were open, and blood bubbled from his mouth. He quickly searched the man's pockets, finding only a stainless Zippo lighter and a set of car keys. He took the lighter but left the keys.

"How many are inside?" he whispered.

One of the man's eyes stared at him while the other slowly swiveled up to look at the ceiling.

"Got it. You're in no mood to talk." Tanner picked up the revolver. It was a Smith and Wesson Model 29, chambered in .44 Magnum, the same model made famous by the *Dirty Harry* movies. He popped the cylinder and checked the shells. Six unfired rounds were inside. He snapped it shut and stood up, letting the bat fall to the ground. He had officially traded up.

Tanner walked back into the small outdoor break area. The bunker door was still open. A light shone from inside. He moved to stand about ten feet from the hatch.

"Hello, down there."

There was movement but no answer.

"I'm going to make you a proposition."

There was a brief pause, and then, "What'd you do to my pa?"

"He's here. My guess is he's busy asking Jesus for forgiveness."

"You kill him?" There was pain and anger in the young man's voice.

"He's alive," said Tanner. "For now, anyway."

"What do you want?"

"I'm here for the girl."

There was another pause.

"What girl?"

"How many you got down there?"

"We ain't got no girls down here."

"That's too bad, because, if I don't see a young woman walk out of your little love shack in the next thirty seconds, I'm going to toss a match down there."

"You wouldn't do that."

"The hell I wouldn't."

There was another brief pause.

"If I send her out, you'll go away and leave us be?"

"Unless I don't like what I see."

Tanner heard more movement from inside the shelter. The young man started talking to someone close by.

"I told pa you were nothing but trouble. Now you'd best get up the ladder. Do it now before I change my mind and shoot you in the eye. Ah hell, you don't know how to do nothin'. Here, put your hands on it. There. Now, get." There was the unmistakable sound of a hand smacking against flesh, followed by a small cry.

After a few seconds, footsteps sounded as someone began climbing the metal ladder leading out of the underground bunker. Tanner leveled the pistol at the open doorway. A woman in her early thirties stepped out. She had short, pixie-cut blonde hair and a petite frame. She was barefoot and blindfolded, and wearing white pants and a black t-shirt that were spattered with blood. Her hands were bound in front of her with bailing wire, and her shoulders slumped in defeat, as if being forced to walk the Bataan Death March.

"Step this way, dear," he said softly.

She didn't move.

"Over here," Tanner said a little louder. "I won't hurt you."

She still didn't move.

"She can't hear you," said the voice from down in the hatch, with a laugh. "She's a freakin' mute."

Careful not to get in the line of fire, Tanner leaned over and gently pulled the woman closer.

She trembled with his sudden touch, but stepped forward without complaining. He removed her blindfold. Bright blue eyes stared back at him. She pulled away, stumbling backward, nearly falling back down into the shaft.

"It's all right," he said. "I'm not going to hurt you."

She pointed at his clothes and made a disgusted face.

Tanner looked down at the blood, vomit, and crap covering his shirt.

"It was a rough night," he said with a grin. "Normally, I dress nicer when in the company of a lady."

She gave him a tentative little smile.

"Let me see your hands," he said.

She stepped closer and held them out without saying a word.

Keeping an eye on the bunker, he carefully unwound the wire. The metal had gouged the tender flesh, leaving thin bloody rings around both wrists. Tanner felt anger rising in his gut.

"You're okay now," he said, gently rubbing her hands to get the circulation back into them.

She reached out and touched his hands. It was a soft touch. A gentle thank you, perhaps.

"Did they hurt you?" he asked, still examining her hands.

She didn't answer.

He tipped his face up so that she could see his mouth.

"Did they hurt you?" he repeated.

She touched the side of her head.

He stepped around and looked carefully at the wound. It was a small cut, not too deep, but enough that the hair around it was covered in dried blood.

"We'll get that cleaned up."

"You got the woman," shouted the man in the bunker. "Now leave, so I can check on my pa."

"Why did you take her?" he shouted back.

"She was gonna be my wife. Pa said I needed a woman to keep our seed going forward. We didn't know she was a mute. How's she ever gonna teach our kids?"

"And you thought it was okay to kidnap a woman, kill her husband in cold blood, and make her carry your sorry offspring?"

"Pa says we have to live different now if we're gonna survive."

Tanner turned to the woman. He gestured toward the man he had brained with the bat.

"That one won't be bothering anyone again, but if you want me to end this seed they're so hell bent on spreading, I'll go down and ring the little bastard's neck. It's your call."

She put her hand on his chest and shook her head.

"You've got a bigger heart than mine," he said. Tanner turned back to the bunker. "Don't ask me why, but she's decided to let you live. I'd advise that you give us a good five minutes before poking your head out."

The young woman started walking carefully across the broken glass into the recruiting center. Tanner reached out and stopped her.

"Darlin', if you don't mind, I'll carry you for a bit."

She thought about it and then nodded, holding her arms out to make it easier for him to scoop her up.

He was amazed at how light she was. No more than a hundred pounds, for sure. He carried her into the recruiting station and placed her on one of the desks. Then he went over and pulled a pair of leather boots off one of the corpses. They were a couple of sizes too big, but he put them on her feet anyway and laced them up tight.

"I'm Tanner," he said, extending his hand.

She smiled and shook it softly. Then she formed one hand like she was holding a pencil and pretended to write on the other.

He nodded. "Got it. You want a pen and paper." He dug through the desk and came back with a small notepad and an ink pen with the words "Go Army" on the side.

She took it and began writing.

*Thank you for rescuing me. I'm Libby. I'm deaf.*

He studied her.

"How long have you been deaf?"

*Always.*

Her writing was slow and beautiful, like she was composing a love letter meant to be kept forever.

"You can read lips?"

She nodded and touched his lips. Her fingers were gentle and warm.

"You sure you want to let him live?" He gestured back toward the bunker. "He killed your husband."

She shook her head and started writing.

*I'm not married. They killed my neighbor. He was helping me to get out of the city.*

"Still, it wasn't called for."

*He was a good man. I don't think he would want blood spilled in his name.*

Tanner heard Samantha's voice in his head. *She's right you know. There's nothing to be gained from killing that young man.*

"Fine," he said to both of them.

He led her out of the recruiting station into the dark street. Libby rubbed the thin scabs surrounding her wrists, wincing from the pain. As hard as he tried, Tanner couldn't keep his anger from bubbling back up. They had murdered a good man and brutalized her. If he hadn't come along, they would have raped and killed her with no regard for her suffering.

"Just a second," he said. "I forgot something."

She nodded, studying her surroundings, obviously wondering where exactly she had been taken.

Tanner hurried back through the recruiting station and directly to the outdoor break area. The hatch was still open, and the young man had yet to come out. He took out the Zippo lighter and flicked it once. A tall flame sprang to life. It was a good lighter, he thought, and it needed to be used for a good purpose.

Without saying a word, he stepped a little closer and lobbed it into the bunker. A quick puff was followed by bright yellow flames licking out of the hatch. It quickly spread to the gas can, which melted into a pile of burning red plastic. There was no way out of the inferno, but just to be sure, Tanner waited until the screaming stopped.

As he walked back out to Libby, he heard Samantha's chiding. *That wasn't necessary. You should have forgiven him.*

"Hush child," he murmured. "You should know by now that I don't have a forgiving bone in my body."

ॐ ॐ

Tanner explained to Libby that they had to hurry back to his vehicle to check on Samantha. He told her that he had promised to get the eleven-year old home to her mother in Virginia, but he made no mention of her mother's position. He also explained that he and Samantha had been following the trail of her kidnappers for most of the day. He told her about his escape from the infected and his dumb luck in finding the white 4Runner. As he spoke, she watched his mouth carefully, nodding that she understood.

It took them the better part of an hour to make it back to the alley. Twice, they had to duck into buildings to avoid people on the street. Whether they were infected with the virus or just ordinary survivors braving the night, he didn't know or care. He couldn't chance another violent encounter with Libby in tow.

When they finally turned up the alley, Tanner was relieved to see the Jeep where he had left it. He half expected it to be gone. As they came up to the Jeep, he saw that Samantha was asleep on the driver's seat. His heart thundered with relief. The doors to the vehicle were locked, so he bumped lightly on the passenger side window. She spun around in her seat, whipping the shotgun toward him, and pulled hard on the trigger.

Tanner instinctively ducked, not that it would have made any difference. Fortunately, nothing happened. No explosion. No hail of pellets tearing through his flesh.

Samantha recovered from her panic and hastily set the shotgun down on the seat. She unlocked the driver's side door and fumbled with the latch. When she finally got it open, she jumped out of the Jeep and ran around to him. Before he knew it, she was hugging his waist with more strength than he thought possible.

"I figured you'd be mad at me for leaving you."

"I am mad," she said, never looking up.

He smiled. She would surely give him hell later. He turned so that she could see Libby, who stood a few feet away, watching them with tears in her eyes. Her beautiful face beamed with a warm heartfelt smile, the type that people have in airports when watching strangers returning to loved ones.

"Sam, this is Libby."

Without letting him go, she peeked around.

"Who?"

"Libby is the woman we've been trying to rescue."

She stepped away from him, a confused look on her face.

"How is it that you just happened upon the woman we've been tracking for miles and miles?"

"I live right, eat my vegetables, and help little old ladies cross the street," he said, grinning.

"Humph," she said, not buying any of it. She looked Libby over from top to bottom. "So you're okay, then?"

Libby nodded and stepped forward, extending her hand.

Samantha looked over at Tanner.

"That's weird, right?"

"She's deaf," he said. "Shake the woman's hand already."

"Oh." Samantha reached forward and shook Libby's hand. Then she looked back over at Tanner. "So she can't understand a word we're saying?"

"She seems to read lips pretty well."

Samantha cupped her hands in front of her mouth as if shouting to him.

"Got it. When we need to talk in private, we do it like this."

He sighed, shaking his head.

Samantha noticed the gore covering his clothes and began brushing off anything that had come into contact with him.

"What have you been doing?" she asked. "You look disgusting."

"You don't want to know," he said, setting the .44 Magnum on the Jeep's dashboard. He grabbed the shotgun and checked it. Then he picked up a couple of shells and called Samantha over. Libby followed closely behind.

"The reason it didn't fire is that you didn't move a shell up into the chamber." He showed her how to release the action to finish loading it. "Also, you had the safety on."

She nodded, lost in thought as she stared off at a large puddle near the Jeep.

"What?" he asked.

"You don't want to know," she said, mimicking his reply.

He shrugged. "Okay. Give me a minute, and we'll get out of here."

Tanner stepped to the back of the Jeep and pulled off his shirt and pants and tossed them away. He downed a bottle of water and used a second one to wash his face, hands, and chest. When he was satisfied, he dug around in the Jeep until he found a white undershirt and a pair of khaki pants. As he finished putting them on, he looked up and saw Samantha and Libby watching him.

"Better?" he asked.

They both nodded.

He walked over and picked up his pack and the Savage .22 rifle from where he had dropped them in the alley. He unloaded the rifle and handed the weapon to Samantha.

"This is going to be yours."

She looked at it like it was the vilest serpent ever to crawl the Earth.

"Uh, no."

"Uh, yes."

"No," she repeated, holding it out to him. "Besides, I don't know how to shoot."

He knelt down so they were looking at one another, face to face.

"While I was away, what did you do?"

"I hid under the Jeep like you said."

"And were you afraid?"

She glanced over at the puddle of urine slowly spreading into small streams crawling down the alley, like worms seeking a fresh grave.

"Of course."

"Sam, you need a way to protect yourself. I might not always be around. This rifle is something you can handle."

She looked at it again, this time with a little less revulsion. If she'd had it when the creature was there, perhaps she could have defended herself. No, she thought, such a weapon would not have killed that beast. Still, what he said made sense.

"All right," she conceded. "But I will almost certainly shoot you at some point."

Before she could change her mind, he stood back up and said, "Fine. Now, let's get started with your first lesson."

She shrugged. "It's your funeral."

"The rifle is too big for you to shoot comfortably while standing. You'll either need to take a knee or lie prone on the ground."

"How? Like this?" She squatted down and held up the rifle.

"That's good. Now put your lead elbow on your knee. It will help steady your aim."

She adjusted her stance.

"I feel like a minuteman from the Revolutionary War."

"Good," he said. "Now bring your cheek down to rest on the stock."

She did as he instructed.

"What do you see?" he asked.

"I see a hole in the back sight and a small circular ring on the front of the rifle."

"Line those up so that the ring is centered in the peephole. What you see at the center of the ring is where the bullet will hit."

"Oh, so it's like a looking glass."

He shrugged. "If you want to think of it that way."

She swung the rifle left and right as if playing a carnival shooter.

"All right," he said. "Now, let's learn to load and unload the weapon." He walked her through the process of loading bullets into the small magazine, seating it in the weapon, and cycling the bolt to chamber the first round. When it was ready to fire, he said, "Now get back into your shooting position."

She kneeled, looking up at him.

"Aim at the garbage can down there." He pointed down the alley. "When you get lined up, squeeze the trigger slowly to the rear. Don't snap it. Squeeze it."

She brought up the rifle and looked through the peep sight.

"Now?" she asked.

"I'm not getting any younger."

She squeezed the trigger and the rifle fired. The garbage can rang as the bullet punched a tiny hole in it. She looked up at him, smiling.

"That didn't hurt at all."

"The garbage can might beg to differ," he said. "Now, run the bolt and do it again."

She slid the bolt back and a small brass shell flew out. She pushed the bolt back forward, took aim, and fired. The garbage can rang again.

"Two for two. I guess I'm a natural."

He laughed. "I guess you are. Now let's get out of here before you have to shoot at something meaner than a garbage can."

# CHAPTER
# 15

Yumi Tanaka's heels clicked on the bunker's metal grating as she hurried to catch up with President Glass. She had only been Chief of Staff for two weeks but was already becoming widely respected as a highly organized and capable advisor.

"Madam President," she called, waving papers in the air. "A minute, please."

The president slowed her pace, as did the two Secret Service agents who were escorting her.

"What is it, Yumi?" she asked with a tired but friendly smile. "It's been a long day, and I was hoping to get a bit of rest. We're not all quite the Superwoman you are."

"Yes, ma'am, I understand. But before you retire for the night, I wanted you to know that we received word from the aerial patrols outside Atlanta."

"That was fast. Did they find anything?"

"Yes, ma'am. They located the emergency supplies that were captured from one of our relief convoys last week."

"They actually got a visual on the supplies?"

"That's right." She handed the president a glossy photo that showed a large tractor trailer with official markings on the side. "There's no mistake. It's one of ours."

"I see," she said, studying the faces of several men in the photo. "Do you know who these people are?"

"According to our intel, they're part of a group of convicts operating out of a country club on the northern outskirts of Atlanta."

"How many are there?"

Yumi looked down at the clipboard.

"Estimates put their number at about sixty."

"That many?"

She nodded.

"Do you know if anyone was hurt when they took the supplies?"

"I'm afraid so, ma'am. The four guards escorting the shipment were killed. The two drivers were allowed to leave unharmed, once they surrendered the payload."

The president shook her head, never looking away from the photograph.

"I understand people's desperation. I really do. But we can't let that sort of violence go unanswered."

"No, ma'am, I wouldn't think so."

"Do we have forces in the area?"

"General Carr said that two gunships are standing ready. He believes that they would be enough to disrupt the group and destroy any infrastructure they're building—a simple seek and destroy mission."

President Glass thought about the ramifications of such an action. By all accounts, the population already hated her government. Using military force, even against murderous thieves, might elicit more violence. Nevertheless, something had to be done. A government afraid to instill order was to be feared as much as one that ruled with an iron fist.

"Tell General Carr that the judicious use of force is authorized. Stress the word 'judicious.' Let's destroy this compound and the payload that they took. The goal is to send a clear message that there's nothing to be gained from stealing FEMA's supplies. But let's also remember that we're not at war. There's no need to hunt down and kill every last one of these bandits."

"Yes, ma'am, I'll tell him."

"Also, I want this kept quiet. Have him brief only those who need to know. Let's keep the circle small on this."

"Yes, ma'am."

President Glass looked at her watch.

"It's already late. Will they be able to conduct the mission while it's still dark?"

"The general indicated they would strike shortly after sunrise. He felt that the tactical advantage of darkness wasn't particularly important for this operation. I can ask him to move it up, if you like."

"No, no," she said. "General Carr and his men know what they're doing." She looked back at the photo one last time. "Wake me if something goes wrong."

ॐ ◌

Vice President Lincoln Pike shifted in his leather chair, staring at the piece of paper like it was the Last Will and Testament of a wealthy uncle. Yumi Tanaka stood behind him, her hands resting lightly on his shoulders.

"This is too good not to take advantage of," he said.

"I thought you might say that."

"If we could get video of this airstrike, it would be valuable propaganda."

"That's why the president wants to keep it contained."

"She knows that if things continue the way they are, it won't be long before people are in the street, burning effigies of her."

Yumi kneaded the muscles in his shoulders.

"What can I do to help?"

"For now, just stay close to her. General Hood already has men in the area hunting for the girl. I'm sure they can get the footage for me without drawing unwanted attention."

"The bloodier the video, the more likely it will serve your purpose."

"You know . . ." he said, thinking, "if I get a few rumors started about these bandits, the pilots might be inclined to take the fight to them with a bit more fervor."

She leaned in close, her mouth an inch from his ear.

"What kind of rumors?"

Her warm breath sent goosebumps down his entire back.

"Stories of horrible things they've done."

"Violent things?" she whispered.

"Yes."

"Degrading things?"

He swallowed. "Yes."

"Tell me," she whispered.

He took a deep breath, trying to collect himself.

"Later."

"Okay," she said, nibbling his ear. "But I won't let you forget."

He nodded, licking his lips.

"What about President Glass? Can you keep her from interfering?"

Yumi straightened up. "The old bag is asleep for the night. We're good for six or eight hours."

"Good. She's been a thorn in my side of late."

"She's a bitch, is what she is."

He laughed. "You're all wound up today."

"Seeing her in the meeting . . ." She squeezed his shoulders so hard that her nails pressed into his flesh. "It made me want to cut her eyes out."

He smiled nervously and reached up to touch her hand. One of the things he liked most about Yumi was her passion, both in and out of the bedroom. What he would never tell her, however, was that her cruel heart sometimes frightened him.

"Patience, my dear. Your access gives us opportunities like this one," he said, waving the paper. "It's an excellent chance to stoke the fire of discontent."

"I like the sound of that, Mr. Vice President. Stoking the fire is exactly what I had in mind." She reached around the chair and slid her hand down between his legs.

When he spoke, his voice was deep and raspy.

"Before long, everyone will see that she is incapable of leading us out of this nightmare. And then . . ." He let the words trail on, imagining Rosalyn Glass kneeling before a blood-stained guillotine.

"Then," she said, picking up where he left off, "it will be your turn to rise to the occasion." She squeezed with her hand.

He swiveled his chair and pulled her to him. When his lips pressed against hers, he felt the familiar heat in his loins, but there was something else. Something deeper and more troubling. Something that could only be described as love.

He didn't trust it, and he certainly didn't want it. Especially not with the likes of Yumi Tanaka. But he knew that it would be a mistake not to at least recognize it. Only a fool, he thought, hides from himself. One day he might very well have to put a bullet in Yumi's head, but for now, he would enjoy the ride.

Mason drove his truck north along Highway 161, flipping down the visor to block the early morning sun. Coveralls sat with his back against the passenger side door, the Supergrade leveled at Mason's gut. They had left the outskirts of York, and with every passing mile, Coveralls seemed to grow more irritated.

"It just isn't right," he mumbled under his breath.

Mason glanced over at him, not liking the tone of a man holding a gun on him.

"What's that?"

He leaned over and poked Mason in the ribs with the Supergrade.

"You getting a free pass like this."

"That rubs you raw?"

"You bet your ass it does."

Mason stared straight ahead, thinking about the situation and his limited options. Coveralls had just shown a weakness that could perhaps be exploited. He was angry, and angry people made mistakes. He glanced at the glove box, wondering if the Glock was still inside. He put the odds at better than even. If he could get Coveralls' attention on something else, there was a chance that he could have a pistol in his hand pretty quick.

"Why do you think Alexus let me go?" he asked.

"What kind of dumbass question is that?"

Mason shrugged. "You think it's just the gold then?"

Coveralls cocked his head, his interest clearly piqued.

"Why else?"

"No, you're right. That's probably it."

Coveralls leaned over and jabbed him again with the muzzle.

"Hey! There's no need for that."

"Why, then?"

"The truth is," said Mason, "I think she's a bit sweet on me."

"That's a damn lie."

"Okay, if you say so."

They sat quiet for a few seconds while Coveralls mulled things over.

Finally, he said, "What makes you say that?"

"You didn't hear about our little bedroom rendezvous last night? Forget it," Mason said, waving his hands. "I probably shouldn't have said anything."

"You and Alex? You two . . ."

Mason looked at Coveralls with a big toothy smile.

"That, and then some."

Coveralls' face flushed, and his hand tightened on the pistol.

"It doesn't matter anyway," he said under his breath. "She'll hang you when this is all over."

Mason shook his head slowly.

"I don't think so."

"Why not?"

"I think she wants me to step up and help run the militia."

"That doesn't make any sense. She's got me to do that."

Mason shrugged. "Beats me. Women can be pretty confusing. Don't worry about it. I'm sure she'll keep you on."

"Just shut up and drive," Coveralls said, turning to look out the window. "How much farther, anyway?"

"Not far at all. Maybe twelve miles."

"Twelve miles? You said it would take all day."

"Getting there won't take long," he said, "but retrieving the gold is going to be a pain."

Coverall squinted his eyes and studied Mason.

"There isn't any gold, is there?"

"You won't believe me until you see it, so I'm not going to waste my breath trying to convince you."

Coveralls jabbed him again.

"So help me, God," he said, "if you try to pull something, I'll put a bullet in your gut and leave you for the vultures to pick apart piece by piece."

"No, you won't."

"No?"

"No. You'll empty the entire magazine into me, and then stomp me with your boot until even my own mother wouldn't recognize me."

"Yeah," Coveralls said with a grin. "That sounds good too."

☙ ❧

As Mason came to the intersection of Highway 161 and Park Road, he saw a familiar green Camaro broken down along the side of the road. Steam billowed out from under the hood. Next to the car was the body of a man, lying face down in the road.

Mason smiled. It was an old trick, but one that worked more often than not.

"Slow up," said Coveralls. "Let me take a look."

Mason slowed the truck and pulled up alongside the body. Even from the cab of the truck, he could see that it was Cletus. Blood had soaked through the white bandage on his forearm, where Bowie had bitten him.

"You want to get out?" asked Mason, rolling down Coveralls' window.

Coveralls leaned out the window, trying to keep one eye on Mason while checking out the dead guy. Before he could make up his mind, Cletus suddenly sat up with a revolver in his hand. At that same moment, Blacksmith came hobbling from around the far side of the car, holding a Ruger Mini-14 rifle.

"Hands up!" yelled Cletus.

Mason put his hands up. Coveralls quickly shoved the Supergrade down between the seats and then raised his own hands.

"Out of the truck, ass-wipes," commanded Blacksmith.

Cletus stood to the side, jumping up and down, laughing and holding the pistol with both hands. He looked like he might wet himself—again.

Coveralls climbed out and stood with his hands raised. He left his door sitting open.

Mason walked slowly around to stand beside him.

"Lookie what we have here," said Blacksmith. He limped up to Mason. "I told you we'd meet again, Marshal."

"And I told you what would happen if we did."

Blacksmith pointed the rifle at his chest.

"What did you do with our gold?"

Coveralls looked over at Mason with genuine surprise on his face.

"You weren't lying."

"I'm honest, if nothing else."

Blacksmith stepped forward and nudged Mason with the muzzle of his rifle.

"I'm not going to ask again, Marshal. Where's the gold?"

"It's funny you should ask that."

"Why?"

"Because my partner and I were just on our way to get it," Mason said, glancing over at Coveralls.

Coveralls nodded. "That's right. It's hidden not far from here."

Blacksmith took a moment to pull his plan together. Then he gestured to Coveralls.

"You get in the back. Cletus, you get up there and watch him. The marshal and I are going to ride up front." Blacksmith turned back to Mason. "Where's your gun?"

"Lost it," Mason said, showing him his empty holster. He flicked his eyes over at the glove box.

Blacksmith caught the motion and smiled.

"Uh-huh," he said, waving Mason away with the rifle. He stepped up to the truck and popped open the glove box. The Glock G17 nearly fell out. "Thought you could get over on me?"

Mason shrugged. He hated giving up the Glock, but it added credibility to his story.

Blacksmith picked up the pistol and slung it down the highway.

"Now you don't got shit, Marshal."

Coveralls stared at Mason, clearly concerned that a gun had been so close at hand during their brief journey together.

They all loaded into the truck, with Blacksmith now taking Coveralls' place as Mason's captor. The man's leg obviously hurt from the gunshot wound, and he leaned awkwardly against the door as he tried to keep it straight.

Mason drove along Park Road, taking his time to let everything sink in. Despite now being surrounded by three people who all wanted him dead, things had actually improved. Coveralls was far more dangerous than Blacksmith and Cletus, and having him disarmed was a step in the right direction. Also, his newest captors were wounded and borderline stupid, a good combination for any prisoner. And, while the Glock had been found, the Supergrade was now hidden and within reach, making that situation a zero sum gain. Perhaps, what worked most in Mason's favor was that Blacksmith and Cletus had two people to worry about. And Coveralls didn't strike Mason as a man who would be able to contain his violence for long.

He drove them all the way to Lake Crawford and parked in the same location as the day before. Mason could hardly believe that it had been less than twenty-four hours since he'd hidden the gold. The brief time had been filled with more than one setback and certainly no lack of excitement. He had a feeling that things were only going to pick up further, as momentum continued to push the ball down the field.

With an idea slowly starting to form, Mason led them down the embankment toward the lake. The jon boat sat upside down on a muddy patch a few feet from the water.

"We'll need the boat," he said.

Everyone stopped and looked at him.

"Why's that?" asked Blacksmith.

"The gold's out in the lake."

"The hell it is."

"I figured the safest place for it was on the bottom of the lake."

"You gotta be freakin' kidding me."

Mason shook his head.

"If you want it, we'll have to go out in the boat. It's probably best if just you and I go out."

Blacksmith considered the offer.

"You'd like that, wouldn't you? One on one, and me injured, no less. No, we'll all go."

"Okay," Mason said, knowing it would actually be easier to execute his plan with four men in the boat. He needed two things. Weight and chaos.

Coveralls caught his eye and gave an almost imperceptible nod. Somehow he had picked up on Mason's plan and was indicating his willingness to participate.

They flipped the jon boat over and dragged it out into the water. Blacksmith had Cletus get in first, then Coveralls, Mason, and finally, he climbed in. Mason noticed that his leg was bleeding again.

"Okay, lawman, take us to the gold." Blacksmith pointed the Mini-14 at him, but they were in very tight quarters. It wouldn't take much for it to turn into a wrestling match for the rifle.

Mason rowed the boat to roughly the center of the small lake before coming to a stop about one hundred feet out from shore. Then he peered over the edge as if searching for their prize.

"It's around here somewhere," he said, glancing back over his shoulder. "I'm sure of it."

"You just dumped it?" said Blacksmith. "That's the dumbest—"

"Wait, is that it?"

Blacksmith and Cletus both leaned over to get a look. As their weight shifted, the boat canted to the side. Before anyone could react, Coveralls grabbed both sides and rolled the boat over.

As soon as Mason hit the cold water, he dove deeper. Only when he could no longer see the others behind him, did he snake sideways and swim in the direction that he sensed led back to shore. He glanced over his shoulder and saw a dark cloud swirling in the water above him. Blood. At first, he thought it might be from Blacksmith's leg, but then he saw Cletus slowly sinking down into the deep. His throat was cut so badly that his spine was the only thing keeping his head attached.

Mason held his breath for as long as he could, swimming in what he hoped was the right direction. When he finally came up for air, he was only about thirty feet from the shore and almost in line with where the boat had been docked. He sucked in a quick breath and dropped back below the surface. When the water became too shallow to swim, he stood and scrambled up the muddy bank. No gunfire erupted, so he continued running up the hill toward the truck at breakneck speed. He heard splashing behind him. Someone was hot on his heels.

He ran straight for the passenger side, tore open the door, and jammed his hand down between the seats. Footsteps thundered up the hill behind him. Mason gripped the Supergrade and pulled the weapon free. He spun around just as Coveralls lumbered to within a few steps of the truck, soaking wet and out of breath. He was holding Mason's hunting knife, which he must have grabbed when sitting in the back with Cletus.

Before either of them could react, Blacksmith hobbled up the bank carrying the Mini-14. As soon as he saw them, he stopped and brought the rifle up. Mason raised his Supergrade and put two in his chest, sending Blacksmith tumbling back down the muddy slope. Then he turned back to Coveralls.

"Did you kill Cletus?"

Coveralls nodded, still trying to catch his breath. He was only about eight feet away. Close enough to use the knife on Mason in less than a second. When it came to guns versus knives, anything inside ten feet could go either way.

Mason lowered the Supergrade so that it hung at his side, never removing his finger from the trigger. He watched Coveralls closely.

"You're a mean son of a bitch. Of that, I have no doubt. But you did your part to get us free, so I guess that means I owe you something."

Coveralls' eyes darted from side to side, deciding his next move. He remained slightly bent forward as if still trying to recover.

"If you start walking, I'll forget about the discomfort you've caused me. If you don't, I'll put you down on this gravel lot. The choice is yours."

Coveralls stood up straight. He was a big man, easily six inches taller and eighty pounds heavier than Mason.

"You let me go, and then what?"

"Then I'm going back to York to get my dog."

"And the gold?"

"I was never going to give you the gold."

Coveralls nodded. "I figured as much."

"So, what's it going to be?"

"If you go back, they'll kill you for sure."

Mason shrugged. "Maybe."

"Are you planning to kill Alex?"

He thought about her beautiful face and gorgeous body. He also thought about her dangling from Stogie's legs until his neck snapped.

"I don't know yet. She—"

Without warning, Coveralls lunged forward with the knife.

Mason tilted his wrist up and fired. He let the momentum of the recoil bring his arm up as he continued the zipper shot, opening five bloody holes that spanned from groin to nose.

# CHAPTER 17

Tanner had fully expected that driving out of Atlanta in the dark was going to be a slow and stressful experience. Most roads were blocked, and the trick was figuring out which ones still allowed passage. The infected were all over the city, and they seemed particularly busy now that night had fallen. He felt like a cat trying to sneak out of a junkyard that had "Beware of Dog" signs on every corner.

He ended up parking on a deserted street and waiting for morning, with the shotgun lying across his lap. Samantha sat beside him with the butt of her rifle resting on the floorboard. Libby was in the back with her eyes closed. Tanner wasn't sure if she was asleep, but he hoped so. She'd had a hell of a day, and some rest would do her good.

"You like her," Samantha said, catching him looking in the rear view mirror at Libby.

"What are you talking about?"

"Don't worry. She can't hear us." Samantha swung around to watch her. "She's pretty. Do you want to kiss her?"

"What's wrong with you?" he said, shaking his head.

"What? What did I say?"

"I'm going to sleep. You're on guard duty for a while."

"Okay," she said, shrugging.

He closed his eyes and leaned back against the seat.

In a voice barely above a whisper, she said, "If you weren't back by dawn, I was going to leave you."

"I know," he said without ever opening his eyes.

"I mean it."

"I believe you."

"You're not mad?"

He opened his eyes and looked over at her.

"If there comes a time when you need to leave me, leave me."

Tears formed in the corner of her eyes.

"Just like that?"

He nodded. "Just like that."

"I suppose you'll leave me too, if it comes to that."

He shook his head.

"No, Sam, I won't."

"You say that, but what if you had to choose between leaving me and, say, fighting a giant monster that likes to pee?"

He smiled and shook his head in utter bewilderment.

"Heavens, girl, what can I possibly say to that?"

ॐ ॐ

"Someone's hiding up there," she said, nudging Tanner's shoulder.

He opened his eyes. The morning sun was just beginning to peek between buildings.

"Where?"

Samantha pointed. "There, by the big orange car."

Tanner searched the street. She was right. At least two people were hiding behind an older model orange Ford parked about a block ahead of them. Two other cars had crashed in the center of the street, making it a great pinch point for an ambush.

"Now, that's something," he said.

"What?"

"The car. It's a '76 Gran Torino. You know, like from *Starsky and Hutch*."

"Who?"

He sighed. "Before your time."

"Did I mention that people are hiding behind the car? People who probably want to eat us?"

He smiled. "Still . . . a '76 Torino."

"Are you done?"

"Almost." He took one last look at the vintage automobile. "All right, done."

"Are we going to get out of here? Like now?"

Tanner looked over his shoulder. Backing up wouldn't be easy with all the cars and junk filling the street. Trying to do so would likely result in him hitting something, or, worse, puncturing a tire. He could try to turn the Jeep around, but that would be a slow process and put them in a precarious position.

Libby opened her eyes and sat forward. She immediately pointed toward the men hiding behind the car.

Tanner nodded. "We see them."

Samantha tightened her grip on her rifle.

"What are we going to do?"

"You two stay here," he said. "I'm going to introduce myself."

"Don't leave again," Samantha said, putting her hand on his arm.

"I'm not leaving. I'll be right up there. Besides," he said, patting his shotgun, "this will keep me safe unless there's a whole gang—"

"Horde," she corrected. "Zombies travel in hordes."

"Fine. Unless there's a whole horde of them, I should be able to hold my own." He turned to face Libby. "Can you drive?" Even as he asked the question, he realized that it was probably very insulting. "What I mean is, are you comfortable driving this Jeep?"

She nodded and smiled with more understanding than he deserved.

He stepped out, and Libby quickly climbed forward to sit in the driver's seat. She studied the controls, pushing the brakes and moving the blinkers and wiper levers up and down. As Tanner started down the street, Samantha cupped her hands around her mouth and hollered out of Libby's window.

"Don't get killed. I think she lied about knowing how to drive."

He ignored her and kept walking, his shotgun held at the ready. He traveled along a zigzag pattern in order to keep at least one car between him and the ambushers. As he got to within about ten yards of the Torino, one of the men who had been hiding suddenly stood up and stepped out. Tanner whipped the shotgun up.

"Sorry, friend," the man said, "I didn't mean to scare you." He was holding a shiny silver .45 semi-automatic in one hand, but it was pointed down at the ground. The man was short, but as stout as a bull shark. Homemade tattoos covered both forearms, and his ears looked like cauliflower, no doubt from years of wrestling or mixed martial arts.

Tanner saw that another man was still crouching behind the car.

"He might as well come out too," he said, gesturing toward him with the shotgun.

The first man motioned for his partner to show himself. He reluctantly stood up but kept the car between him and Tanner. The height and build of the two men were remarkably similar, and it was clear from their distinctive Filipino facial features that they were related.

"I'm Angelo," the first man said, sliding the .45 into his waistband. "That's my brother, Dani." He stepped forward with his hand extended.

"I'm Tanner," he said, shaking a hand that was half the size of his own. "Where'd you boys do your time?"

"Over in Jesup. You?"

"Talladega."

Neither asked why the other was incarcerated. A convict was a convict.

"That your ride?" asked Tanner, pointing to the Torino.

"It is now," he said with a laugh. "The world's become like Grand Theft Auto. You can pretty much drive anything you like if you're willing to look for it."

Tanner thought of his own selection of vehicles, which had included a minivan, a yellow Volkswagen Bug, a Ford Taurus, and, his newest, the Jeep Wrangler. He made a mental note to be a little more selective when car shopping.

"Excuse the scare," said Angelo. "We're trying to bag us a few of those pus-infested monsters."

Tanner nodded. "We spent most of the night running from them ourselves."

"I'm surprised you're still in one piece. It gets like *Night of the Living Dead* around here after dark. We tend to hunt mostly at dawn and dusk, when their numbers are fewer."

"And you're doing this why? Out of the goodness of your heart?"

"We're cleaning up our backyard. That's all."

"I see," said Tanner. "And are you winning the war?"

"Not really. For every one we kill, two more show up."

"Then what's the point?"

"I got no love for killing, but I've seen these things tear bodies apart like crazed animals. They're bringing my people down in a big way."

"Fair enough."

Angelo swept his arms left and right.

"We're hoping to create a safe zone. Some place that we can live without having to fear for our lives every night."

"How many of you are there?"

"Nearly a hundred now, and growing every day," he said with pride.

"All convicts?"

"Not all. We started that way. Probably no different than gangs all across the country. We took what we wanted. Killed a few people who probably didn't deserve it. Just thugs on the loose, you know?"

Tanner didn't say anything, wondering if Angelo and his brother were going to be trouble. While they both looked seasoned, he figured he could bench press the two of them with one arm.

"That's when Dani and I decided things had to change. We helped our brothers and sisters to see that acting like that would only get us killed. We got everyone to agree to a few basic rules. Don't kill each other. Don't rape the women. No freeloading. Stuff you shouldn't have to tell people."

"But you do."

Angelo nodded. "It's best not to assume that people who've spent their whole lives behind bars know how to play nice with others. Many of us are just now figuring out that working together is where it's at." He flashed a wry grin. "We've taken an evolutionary step, my friend."

"It sounds like you're setting up your own mini-government."

"No way. That's the beauty of it. There's no government at all. No one owns anything. No one tells anyone else what to do. Other than our Golden Rules, we just do our own thing. It's perfection, man."

"Sounds like a giant Woodstock commune to me."

"We just call it living free."

Dani bumped his brother's shoulder.

"We got company." He pointed down the street.

Tanner and Angelo turned to look. Four figures were approaching the Jeep.

Without saying a word, Tanner bolted toward them. Angelo and Dani quickly followed. At about that same instant, Samantha and Libby saw the creatures and started frantically honking the Jeep's horn.

By the time Tanner arrived, the four infected men were already at the Jeep. One of them grabbed the top of Samantha's window, splintering it into thousands of tiny shards. She screamed and scrambled to bring up her rifle.

Tanner didn't dare shoot the shotgun for fear that a stray pellet might hit one of the girls. Instead, he plowed ahead into the two men who were attacking the right side of the vehicle. He hit the first one head-on, knocking him off his feet. He only winged the second man, but it was enough to send him stumbling backward. Angelo and Dani engaged the two on the other side of the Jeep.

While the infected man on the ground scrambled to get back up, the second one charged ahead, screaming with bloodthirsty fury. Tanner swung the butt of the shotgun sideways, aiming for his head. The man managed to get a hand between his face and the rifle, but it made little difference. Wood met bone, splitting the skin behind his ear and sending a huge spray of blood across Libby's window.

The incredible blow sent the man spinning, but somehow he managed to remain standing. He used the momentum to whirl around and lunge forward again, this time latching onto the shotgun. Tanner jerked the gun sideways, hoping to pull it free. No matter how hard he tugged, he was unable to break the man's grip. As Tanner struggled for the weapon, his attacker lunged forward with his mouth open, biting at the flesh on his face and neck. Twisting the gun clockwise, Tanner finally managed to jam the barrel under the man's jaw. Before he could push it away, Tanner used his thumb to squeeze the trigger. The entire payload of triple-aught pellets blasted up into the man's brain cavity. The pressure was so great that his eyeballs popped out of their sockets like bloody marshmallows.

Before Tanner could wrestle the shotgun free, the second man barreled forward, catching him in the gut with a meaty shoulder. He drove Tanner back like a defensive lineman, smashing him into the side of a commercial carpet cleaning van. The blow was incredibly solid, and Tanner fought to keep from losing consciousness.

With nowhere left to push, the infected man took a step back and then jumped in again, aiming for Tanner's ribs. Tanner brought up a knee and caught him under the chin. While it wasn't strong enough to do much damage, it did redirect most of his forward momentum. Still winded, Tanner grabbed him by his hair and slung him sideways, hoping to buy himself a few seconds to recover.

The man shrieked and hurled himself forward, swinging his right fist with uncontrolled rage. Tanner ducked, planted his right foot, and fired a powerful uppercut. The blow caught the man squarely under the jaw, and his teeth slammed together, completely severing his tongue. He screamed in pain, and a shower of warm droplets sprayed across Tanner's face.

Tanner hit him with a jab and then a cross, breaking his nose and spilling even more blood. The man latched onto his face, trying to drive both thumbs into his eyes. Tanner slammed the top of his head forward. The blow hit his attacker in the mouth, knocking teeth free and cutting open Tanner's forehead. He leaned back and bashed his head forward again, this time hitting him on the bridge of the nose. The infected man's hands fell away as he wavered from side to side. Tanner stepped forward and smashed an elbow against the side of his head, sending him to the pavement.

Before he could recover, Tanner kicked and stomped his head until there was little left but blood and bone. When he was satisfied that the fight was over, he went over and retrieved his shotgun. Angelo had dispatched his opponent with a knife, and Dani had managed to put three 9-mm rounds into the chest of the fourth infected man. Both brothers were battered and bloody from their fights, but neither looked seriously injured. Tanner leaned against the Jeep and took several deep breaths.

Samantha opened the door and leaned out. Libby peeked out over her shoulder.

"You're bleeding again," Samantha said, her voice shaking. "Kind of bad this time."

Tanner felt blood running down his face. He looked in the Jeep's side mirror and saw a two-inch gash in the middle of his forehead.

"Are you going to be okay?" she asked.

"I'm fine," he grumbled.

She cringed, unable to look away.

He managed a small smile.

"I'll let you in on a secret."

"What?"

"The older you get, the less things hurt. I can barely even feel this."

"Really?" she asked, squinting at him.

"Really."

"Still, I think you're going to need stitches."

Angelo stepped around the Jeep, looking at Tanner's face.

"She's right," he said. "That's not going to heal right if you don't sew it up."

Libby slipped out the other side of the Jeep and came hurrying around to him. She was carrying a wet t-shirt. She carefully wiped the blood from his face and held the cloth tightly against the wound. She gestured for him to hold it there.

"I was about to do that," muttered Samantha.

Tanner turned to Angelo.

"You have anyone who could stitch me up?"

"Betty could," offered Dani.

Angelo nodded. "Betty was a veterinarian before all this. Definitely a crabby old witch, but she's got a steady hand and doesn't mind the sight of blood."

"I hope she was a large animal vet," Samantha said with a nervous laugh.

Tanner cut his eyes at her.

"I thought you were worried about me."

She pressed her lips together.

"You said you were okay."

Tanner turned back to Angelo.

"Do I have your word that the ladies will be safe at your compound?"

Angelo nodded. "Course you do, man." He glanced over at the bloody mess that Tanner had left on the street. "Besides, nobody's going to want to cross you."

৵ ๛

The compound was little more than two city blocks that Angelo's group had cordoned off in an upper class neighborhood in northern Atlanta. The area was only about four miles from where Tanner had previously hooked up with Janice, a mom desperate to find a strong man willing to protect her and her family. In the end, they had parted with a warm kiss, and he couldn't help but wonder how she had fared. Wondering was one thing; going back was something different. Janice was not someone who could be trusted, and according to Samantha, her oldest boy was one step away from torturing kittens.

He turned his attention back to the matter at hand, following Angelo's Gran Torino around a huge water fountain to a sprawling three-story brick building that resembled a small university. The brass plate on the front of the building identified it as the Dunwoody Country Club. Two men stood guard, holding rifles. When they saw Angelo pull up, they shook their weapons in the air like gladiators saluting.

Everyone gathered in front of the enormous building as Angelo introduced them to the two guards. Both men were Hispanic and covered in gang tattoos. They offered warm street handshakes to everyone, but their eyes never left Libby. Tanner inserted himself, and they seemed to get the message.

"Come on," said Angelo. "Let's get inside and see the doc. You're going to like her."

The inside of the building, which had once boasted shiny waxed floors and polished trophies, was now strewn with trash. The occasional stain of a cadaver island was enough to remind everyone that the Superpox-99 virus had not discriminated between beggar and socialite.

Angelo escorted them up to the second floor and into a small room that resembled a nurse's office in an elementary school. Two twin-size mattresses sat on the floor, with a cart of medical supplies and a rolling stool between them. The room's windows were wide open, and the chatter of people talking could be heard coming from outside. An elderly woman sat in a large La-Z-Boy recliner working a book of crossword puzzles. She looked up and grumbled as they entered.

Angelo motioned to Tanner.

"My man, Tanner, took some teeth to the forehead. Probably needs a few stitches."

"And you're a doctor now?" she snapped, reaching over and pumping a squirt of sanitizer onto her palm.

"No, ma'am," he said.

"Well, neither am I," she said, standing up and waving Tanner over. "So what the hell do we know?"

As Tanner approached, she pointed to the La-Z-Boy.

"Well, go on, have a seat."

He lowered himself into the chair, not at all confident that he was about to receive real medical care.

"Comfortable, right?" she asked, while inspecting his wound.

He shifted around. "Not bad."

"Don't get used to it," she said, pointing an accusatory finger. "I had that brought in special."

"No . . . ma'am."

She pinched the jagged cut closed.

"That hurt?"

"Only when you do that," he answered, grimacing.

"Great," she said. "We've got a wise acre." She slid the metal cart over and retrieved a small pair of scissors, a needle, and a spool of monofilament line. She pulled out about twelve inches of the line and clipped it off.

"Is that fishing line?"

She squirted a glob of sanitizer onto her palm and smeared it over the needle and line.

"String is string," she said, threading he needle. "So, let's hear it. How'd it happen? Tell an old woman a story already."

"Head butt," he said simply.

"Uh-huh." She poked the needle through his skin and started pulling the thread through.

He winced but said nothing.

"You want some pain medicine?" she asked.

"You got any?"

She laughed. "Nope."

"Figured."

Seemingly, for the first time, she noticed Samantha and Libby standing quietly by the door.

"Are you two traveling with this brute?"

"Yes, ma'am," said Samantha.

"Even if he could find someone to mate with, which I doubt, you're too young to be his daughter. Granddaughter then?"

"No, ma'am. We're . . . friends." She looked at Tanner, and he nodded slightly.

Betty let the needle hang from the string down in front of his face. Then she walked over and gently touched Samantha's cheek.

"You're pretty. I remember my daughter being your age." She shook her head. "That was a long time ago." She turned to Libby. "And who are you? Not his wife, I hope."

Libby smiled and held out her hand.

"She's deaf," said Samantha. "She can't speak either. We rescued her yesterday."

Betty squinted her eyes, studying Libby for several seconds.

"I don't like her. Too damn quiet."

The old woman spun around and returned to Tanner. She picked back up the needle and continued stitching, like her brief departure was all perfectly normal.

"What's a brute like you doing traveling with two sweet young ladies?"

"I ask myself that all the time."

She squatted down and stared into his eyes.

"Uh-huh," she said, standing back up.

"What?"

"I was looking for that darkness that I sometimes see in men. It wouldn't do for you to have it in you. Not with them two around, anyway."

"And did you see it?"

"No," she answered. Then, when he thought she might leave it at that, she added, "You've got something different in you. Dangerous and just plain mean. You're like a cranky dog that someone woke up from its nap."

He thought about arguing the point but realized her assessment was spot-on.

"Still," she continued, "there are times when a cranky dog is exactly what's needed." She pulled hard on the last suture to snug it up. "All done."

"Ouch."

"Have one of your lady friends cut out the sutures in about a week."

He nodded, scrunching up his forehead a few times.

She reached over and grabbed a small plastic bottle shaped like a bear.

"Honey?" said Tanner. "Exactly what kind of doctor are you?"

She squirted a little onto her fingers and rubbed it on his wound.

"It isn't going to make you any sweeter, but it might help with infection. If the wound starts to fill with pus, find antibiotics or a shovel."

"A shovel?"

"To dig your grave with, of course."

**M**ason stood beside his truck, drying off and taking stock of his situation. The knife, Supergrade, and Mini-14 were laid out on the seat. Beside them were three magazines for the Supergrade and two for the Mini-14. The bullets had gotten wet when everyone had gone into the drink, and he took a few minutes to unload the magazines and dry and inspect each round. When he was finished, he discarded only two that looked suspect. Total round count was seventeen for the Supergrade and fifty-four for the Mini-14. That was enough to do some damage but not enough to wage war on a small army.

He started with the Mini-14, loading two of the 20-shot magazines to capacity, and the third with the remaining bullets. Next, he topped off the Supergrade and slid it into the holster. Fully loaded, the weapon weighed only about forty-five ounces, but even the weight of Thor's hammer couldn't have been more reassuring. He put the spare magazines in the leather carrier on the other side of his belt, one fully loaded with eight rounds, and the other empty. The ever-trusty hunting knife topped off his waistband arsenal. It felt good to be armed and in control of his own destiny again.

While Alexus and a few of her militia were on his short list of people he wouldn't mind bringing to justice, Mason would have been willing to walk away. Even with her forced detention, it really wasn't personal. The problem, of course, was that they had made a huge mistake. They had kept Bowie. Not only did they have him, but she had threatened to kill the dog if he didn't return with the gold by nightfall. Given her past actions, he had no reason to believe that she was making an idle threat. The situation with Bowie dictated that he would have to return to York and settle accounts.

The question was what kind of entrance to make. As a sworn lawman, Mason faced an all too familiar problem. He had to go against an enemy who was willing to kill him without hesitation, but until they demonstrated such aggression, he felt obliged to show some measure of restraint. Killing townspeople who were just trying to pick up the pieces didn't fit with the oath he had taken when becoming a marshal. His only option was to try to get in and out with as little collateral damage as possible. If bullets started to fly, however, he would have no choice but to shift from noble lawman to ruthless soldier. If they forced a war, he would give them one they would never forget.

Alexus had boasted that her militia numbered around forty. Even if that count was exaggerated, it meant that he was significantly outnumbered. Overcoming an enemy of that size required three things: surprise, confusion, and fear.

Confusion and fear were like on-the-job accidents and personal injury lawyers. If you had one, the other could be counted on to show up in short order. Surprise was the hardest of the three to achieve. Alexus would know there was a very real chance that Mason would overpower Coveralls and return looking for a little payback. She would have put into place safeguards to prepare for that scenario. At a minimum, all the major roads going in and out of York would be guarded.

Mason pulled the atlas from his glove box and studied a map of the surrounding area. He counted at least twenty roads leading into York. The larger ones, like Highway 321, would be best protected. Also, those on the north side would likely be on high alert since that was the direction from which he and Coveralls had departed. But York was not a military compound. There were simply too many entry points to protect them all with anything more than a single sentry.

The Ross Branch waterway wound its way in through the southwest corner of York. If followed long enough, it eventually merged into the Upper York Reservoir. It flowed directly under Liberty Street, York's central thoroughfare. The intersection between the waterway and street was less than a quarter mile from the courthouse and only a hair more than that from Rose Hill Cemetery. Ground zero for where he anticipated the action would eventually take place.

He folded up the map and finished readying his weapons. In less than an hour, he would be knocking on their back door.

Charcoal grills had been set up on the tennis courts directly behind the clubhouse, and several dozen people stood around talking and eating from paper plates.

"Are you guys hungry?" asked Angelo.

Tanner, Libby, and Samantha all nodded. No one had eaten for more than twelve hours, and the smoky smell of barbecued meat was as luring as chum to a shark.

Angelo ushered them to the front of the line, ensuring that each got a plate of boiled potatoes and something that looked like pork, although no one dared to ask. Then he took them around and introduced them to various members of the group. Tanner was pretty certain that most of them were convicts, not so much by their faces or even their tattoos, but more by the look of newfound freedom still shining in their eyes.

Despite the questionable background of nearly everyone in the group, none seemed particularly dangerous. They were no different than a gang of Hells Angels. With Angelo's introduction, the three were adopted into their band, and harming them would be viewed as sourly as beating up one's own grandmother.

But Tanner was no fool. Men of all statures could be dangerous if given the opportunity. His job was to keep that opportunity from ever presenting itself. So, while all three mingled, shook hands, and got to know the group, he was careful never to let the girls out of his sight. Libby and Samantha eventually migrated to a small corner of the tennis court, where several other women were socializing.

"What do you think?" asked Angelo. "Pretty cool, right?"

Tanner looked around, nodding at a few of the people he had met.

"Keep them from killing one another for long enough, and you might have something here."

"My thoughts exactly. The more families that join, especially those with kids, the more likely it is we'll become a community where people look out for one another."

"Where are you getting your supplies, food, water, that sort of stuff?"

Angelo glanced around, as if someone might be listening in.

"That, my friend, is something I'll have to show you."

Tanner looked back at Samantha and Libby, unwilling to leave them. They had found lawn chairs and were now sitting at the edge of the tennis court, enjoying the early morning meal.

Sensing his apprehension, Angelo called to his brother.

"Dani, watch the girls for a few."

"All right," he said, getting up and starting off their direction.

"Hey," said Tanner.

Dani looked over his shoulder.

"Something happens, I'm holding you responsible."

"Don't worry, big man. I got 'em."

Angelo led Tanner around to the back of the country club. Parked side by side were two large tractor-trailer trucks with official government markings painted on the side. The back doors of both trucks were shut, and a guard stood nearby smoking a cigarette, his rifle slung over his shoulder.

He nodded to Angelo.

"What's up?"

"Give us a few."

The guard shrugged. "No problem. I need to pee anyway." He headed off, disappearing around the corner of the building.

Angelo stepped to the back of one of the trucks and pulled hard on a metal handle, swinging open the door. Inside were hundreds of boxes, drums, and crates, most still tightly wrapped in cellophane.

"We captured these trucks about a week ago. FEMA was trying to get them into Atlanta. There's everything in here—MREs, bottled water, blankets, candles, paper goods. This will keep us going for a while."

"It looks like quite a haul. What happened to the truckers?"

Angelo hesitated. "We let the drivers go free."

Tanner stared at him with doubt in his eyes.

"The guards didn't give up so easy."

"What about the folks in the city? The ones who they were taking the supplies to?"

"You saw what happens after dark. How many uninfected people do you think are still alive?"

Tanner shrugged. "A few maybe. Some would have banded together, just like you did."

"What can I say? We saw ours as the greater need." He patted the side of the truck. "Convicts aren't at the top of the government's relief efforts, but we got to eat too, you know? As far as I'm concerned, the government is our enemy. Anyone who works for them is an enemy . . . what's it called?"

"Combatant."

"Exactly," he said, snapping his fingers. "The government has everything and gives out nothing. While we starve and fight monsters off our children, they sit in their ivory castles, drinking lattes. We can't let that stand. You with me on this?" Angelo's voice was rising.

"I understand where you're coming from," Tanner answered, dodging the question.

"While we work to make peace with our unfortunate brothers and sisters around the country, we're going to wage a little war on the empire that put us here. Some might call us unpatriotic, but the truth is we're freedom fighters."

Tanner nodded again, unwilling to voice support but equally unwilling to make a stand against him. He didn't give a crap about Angelo's politics either way. Let them fight their little war.

"The reason I showed you this is that we'd love for you and the ladies to stick around. Like I said, families are our future."

Tanner pretended to give his offer the consideration that Angelo would have expected.

"I don't have any love for the government," he said, "but we'll be moving on."

Angelo tipped his head forward as a sign of surrender.

"I had to ask, you know? We could use a man like you. But we're all about freedom and liberties, so I can respect you choosing your own path. I only hope that one day we're not on opposite sides."

"You do what you need to do in order to survive," said Tanner. "As long as it doesn't interfere with me or mine, I won't have a beef with you."

"That's exactly the sort of attitude we're after. Let us be, and we'll let you be. When we're big enough, we'll spread that way of thinking to anyone who will listen." Angelo smiled and extended his hand. "Friends?"

Tanner grabbed his hand and patted him on the shoulder. "You were good enough to doctor and feed us. And for that, I'm thankful."

"One day, maybe—"

Tanner held his hand up, silencing Angelo. A soft rhythmic thumping sounded in the distance, as powerful blades cut through the air. Without saying another word, he turned and ran toward the tennis court.

≈◦ ◦≈

As Tanner reached Samantha and Libby, a phosphorous orange light flashed in the eastern sky. He grabbed both of them and dove behind a metal hot dog cart that had been used to serve food. An instant later, an explosion rocked the tennis court. It was as if a volcano had suddenly erupted from under the feet of would-be partygoers, tearing off legs, splitting flesh from bone, and decapitating in every direction.

Tanner's ears rang from the thunderous shock wave, but he was otherwise unhurt. Samantha and Libby also seemed to be free of any serious injury. Shifting the shotgun to one hand, he scooped Samantha into his arms and motioned for Libby to follow. The scene was one of complete pandemonium. People pushed and shoved, desperately trying to get through the swinging metal gate leading out of the tennis court. A few peeled away and began climbing the ten-foot chain link fence. People fell under the stampede, blindly trampled by those more fleet of foot.

Tanner ran for a man-sized hole that had been blown in the far side of the fence. He slipped and skidded across blood and gore, like he was trying to make his way across a melting ice skating rink. Samantha refused to look up, instead, burying her face against his shoulder. Libby had a quiet calm about her, a resignation that she was still trapped in a nightmare.

As they cleared the fence, a second explosion hit. This one struck the gate to the tennis court, and the bloody mayhem was as bad as if the victims had been collectively tossed into a wood chipper. Pieces of bone, flaps of scalp, and buckets of blood rained down on those who remained alive. Even at more than sixty yards away, the resultant shock wave knocked Tanner and Libby to their knees. Tanner was sure that people were screaming, but he heard nothing. It was as if someone had simply dialed down the world's volume knob.

He scrambled to his feet, pulled Samantha back into his arms, and ran through knee-deep grass that had once been part of the golf course. His only thought was to get clear of the target area. A third blast hit the clubhouse. Bricks and splinters of furniture shot up into the air, landing on the fairway hundreds of yards away.

Tanner ran down a steep slope that led to a small man-made water trap.

He whipped left and raced along the water's edge, stumbling over bushes and unkept vegetation. Libby followed close behind, riding in his wake.

The universe suddenly found its volume knob again, and sounds of horror erupted from behind him. People screamed in excruciating pain. Debris crashed into the ground. The *tat-tat-tat* of automatic gunfire sounded from the sky. Tanner knew that if they were to have any chance of surviving, he needed to put hard obstacles between them and the helicopters.

He ducked behind a small garden shed used for storing grounds maintenance equipment and paused to catch his breath. The small sheet metal building offered little protection, but it did, at least, take them out of their attackers' lines of sight. He set Samantha on the ground and motioned for Libby to take cover. She moved close to the building and squatted down, breathing heavily.

"You okay?" he asked Samantha. His voice sounded strange to his ears, like he was talking into a coffee can.

She looked up at him, tears running down her face. At the moment, she was as incapable of speech as Libby.

He pulled her close.

"I won't let them get you, Sam."

"Y-you can't promise that," she said, her voice shaking uncontrollably. "Don't they know I'm only eleven? People are supposed to live longer than eleven years. I'm just a—"

Tanner covered her mouth with his hand.

She kept talking for a moment, but finally quieted.

"You done?" he asked.

She narrowed her eyes and nodded.

He slowly removed his hand.

"I don't want to hear you talk like that again. You're better than that."

Another explosion thundered from the direction of the clubhouse, but neither of them broke eye contact.

"When you're dead, you're dead," he said. "Until then, we fight with everything we've got."

Her face tightened like she might argue with him, but then it softened.

"Take a deep breath," he said.

She inhaled and let it out slowly. Her body shook as she exhaled, but when she was finished, she seemed steadier.

"Okay," she said.

"Okay what?"

"Okay, you're right."

"Of course, I'm right."

She smiled and squeezed his hand.

"My mom says that even a watched clock is right twice a day."

Tanner wrinkled his brow, thinking that her words didn't sound quite right but unable to figure out why.

"She says that?"

Samantha nodded. "I told you. She's very smart."

"Obviously." He looked over at Libby. "How about you? You okay?"

She nodded and held up a tiny defiant fist.

He smiled. In one sense, Tanner thought it was probably easier on Libby. She couldn't hear the explosions or the screaming. Maybe it felt like a silent movie, something that she could ignore by simply closing her eyes.

"What are we going to do?" asked Samantha.

"We're going to get out of here."

"I don't get it. Why would Agent Sparks kill so many people just to get to me?"

"Why doesn't matter right now," he said, standing up and taking a quick glance around the corner of the shed.

Two helicopters buzzed over the clubhouse, flashes of tracer fire streaking from their underbellies to strike those running for cover. A fiery explosion licked up into the sky as a car burst into flames. Not surprisingly, none of Angelo's men had yet to return fire. It had all happened too quickly. Everyone was just trying to escape the death raining down from the sky.

The shed they were hiding behind was small and certainly unable to withstand the firepower the helicopters were putting out, but Tanner didn't know where else to run. Behind them was a sprawling golf course, which, other than a few trees, would leave them exposed and in the open—the proverbial fish in a barrel.

The only other option was to get them the hell out of there, and that required wheels. He peeked around the shed again. Through the smoke, he saw the Jeep still parked out in front of the clubhouse. If he could get to it—and if they didn't blow him to smithereens on his way back— they could make a run for it. Not great odds, but it was better than waiting around to be turned into chili con carne.

"You two stay here," he said, setting the shotgun on the ground beside them.

"Where are you going?" Samantha asked, clearly not liking the idea of him leaving them alone.

"Just be ready to move. And if anyone sticks their head around this corner who isn't as pretty as me, shoot them."

She leveled her varmint rifle in both hands.

He bent down and kissed her on the forehead. Before he could stand up, Libby wrapped her arms around his neck and kissed him on the cheek. Tanner reached around and pulled them both into a bear hug, wondering if it would be the last time he would ever see them.

As he turned to leave, he said, "Keep an eye on one another. Right now, you're all you've got."

Libby and Sam both looked at him and then to each other. Without clarifying further, Tanner darted around the corner and ran. Rather than jigging from side to side in hopes of being a harder target, he made a bee-line for the Jeep. He figured that it was all about time of exposure. The fewer seconds he was in the red zone, the better.

The tennis court was barely recognizable. The expensive clay surface couldn't have looked worse if it had been dug up with a backhoe in search of Jimmy Hoffa. Nothing remained of the net except for a few white strings still fluttering from the metal poles. Blood and body parts were everywhere. Tanner tore past, never breaking stride.

He saw one helicopter directly ahead and heard a second one off to his left. They appeared to be circling the area, picking off those who had escaped the initial bloodletting. Fortunately, at the moment, their attention was not in his direction. That, however, he knew could change with the simple twist of a pilot's head.

Coming up on the wrong side of the Jeep, Tanner hopped on the hood, slid across, and landed in front of the driver's side door. He tore it open and scrambled inside. A quick turn of the keys, and the car was alive. He popped it into four-wheel drive and took off the way he had come, bouncing over bodies, bricks, and the occasional severed leg. He raced the engine in low gear, and it screamed almost as loud as the victims trying to hold in their guts. There was still a scattering of people running for cover and even a few who were now trying to return fire. Tanner hoped it was enough to keep the pilots' attention off one lone Jeep racing down the grassy hill. If not, with the squeeze of a finger, they would cut the vehicle in half.

It only took him about twenty seconds to reach the small utility building, and in that time, not a single bullet hit the Jeep. He locked the brakes and slid around the corner, hoping to partially hide it from view of the patrolling gunships.

"Let's go, let's go!" he shouted, frantically waving for them to get in.

They hopped into the Jeep, and he floored it. Bumping over rocks and debris, they raced across the golf course heading for the tree line. Peaking out at fifty miles an hour, the vehicle got air more than once. Tanner knew the general direction to get to Ball Mill Road, but he had no idea exactly where he would come out of the golf course. When he saw an opening in the trees to the left, he jerked the wheel, sending everyone slamming into the side of the Jeep.

"Maybe I should drive," Samantha yelled, bracing against the roll bar.

"You look out the window," he shouted back. "Tell me what the choppers are doing."

She rolled down the window and leaned her head out.

"I only see one."

"What's he doing?"

She looked back at Tanner, biting her lip.

"He's coming our way."

かわ ぬり

The Jeep bumped off the curb and onto a deserted suburb street. Expensive stucco houses with slate tile roofs lined one side, and a thick row of golf course pines bordered the other. Finally finding an open stretch of road, Tanner popped the Jeep from low into drive, never removing his foot from the gas pedal. The Jeep barked its tires and fishtailed slightly before he brought it back under control, barreling down the two-lane road.

The powerful vibration of helicopter blades grew louder and louder as it beat the air around them, rocking the Jeep from side to side.

Still looking out the window, Samantha's teeth rattled as she shouted, "They're almost directly over us!"

Tanner glanced back. It didn't figure. They could have taken the Jeep out without risking getting so close. Were they going to try to grab Samantha? If so, that was good news. That meant they still had a fighting chance. Running was pointless. Escaping a helicopter in a car was all but impossible, especially when there was no one else on the road.

He turned sharply up a driveway, crashed through a metal gate, and screeched to a stop in front of a home that looked like it had been modeled after the mansion in Graceland.

"Inside!" he shouted. "Go!"

Samantha grabbed her rifle and backpack as she and Libby bailed out and ran for a set of French doors. Tanner snatched his shotgun, backpack, and the .44 Magnum from the dash before racing after them.

The helicopter hovered over the street, tipping its nose down like a giant insect studying them. It unleashed a long string of machine gun fire, tearing hundreds of holes in the Jeep and sending the hood flying through the air. A few seconds later, the car burst into flames with a soft *whoosh*.

The front doors of the mansion were locked, and Libby and Samantha frantically pulled and pushed on the handles. Without breaking stride, Tanner charged ahead and smashed shoulder first into one of the doors. Two hundred and fifty pounds of angry violent offender were enough to tear the striker plate out of the support beam between the doors. He stumbled in, and the others quickly followed, slamming the door behind them.

The house was hot and stale inside. Sunlight spilled in through a large window at the back of the open living area.

"Why aren't they shooting us?" asked Samantha.

He glanced out a small panel of windows beside the door.

"They must want you alive."

Libby instinctively put her arms around Samantha, only to get a confused look from the girl.

"Can we fight them?" she asked.

Tanner looked at Samantha and grinned.

"What do you think?"

She put on a brave smile.

"We're not dead yet."

"Not yet." He looked back out the window. "They'll hit us with flashbangs and CS gas." He turned to Libby. "Go to the kitchen and gather a few small towels. Soak them in either lemon juice or vinegar, something acidic. That will help with the smoke."

"Sam, you go up to the bedrooms and look for earplugs. If you can't find anything else, round up a pack of cigarettes."

"Cigarettes?"

"Worse comes to worst," he said, "we can use the filters as makeshift earplugs."

"Oh," she said. "Hey, that's pretty smart."

"Go!"

Samantha turned and bolted up the winding staircase. In less than a minute, she returned, racing back down and tossing him a partially used pack of Basic cigarettes. A book of matches had been placed inside the cellophane wrapper.

He shook his head, studying the pack.

"Living in a million-dollar house and smoking generics. What's the world come to?" He shook a cigarette out, stuck it between his lips, and lit it with a match. It had been more than ten years since his last cigarette, and might be ten more before his next. Assuming he lived that long.

"Really?" Samantha said, completely exasperated. "You do know that smoking can kill you in, like, a thousand different ways?"

Tanner looked at her, wondering if she would see the absurdity of her concern. She didn't. Right was right. Wrong was wrong. He took one final drag and snubbed it out against the doorframe.

The sound of the helicopter started to change, and he turned to look out the window, expecting to see it lowering to the ground to deposit an elite group of commandos. To his surprise, the gunship was lifting higher into the air. When it cleared the trees, it turned east and sped away.

Tanner stood, scratching his chin and staring off into the distance, wondering what exactly had just happened.

&#x6df; &#x6cf;

Within minutes of the helicopter's unexpected departure, Tanner, Samantha, and Libby were on the move. He found keys to a black Cadillac Escalade parked in the garage, and they were now racing down the side streets of northern Atlanta.

"I don't get it," Samantha said, digging through her backpack for a bottle of water. "Why didn't they come in after us?"

"We're not sticking around to find out."

Libby was riding in the back seat, carefully watching their mouths as they spoke. She scribbled a note and passed it up to him.

"Libby says that she thinks God spared us," he said.

Samantha thought about it for a moment. She had never really thought that God did much of anything. Not for little people, anyway. Maybe for that pastor on television who helped people walk, but not someone like her. She didn't even pray except for when she wanted something really bad. Like when she was lying under the Jeep. Had he heard her then? The monster had left without finding her. Maybe Libby was right. Maybe God was watching over them.

"What do you think? Could He," she said, pointing upward, "really be on our side?"

"As a Buddhist, I've never bought into the divine intervention thing. Good or bad, we make our own lunches."

"How else would you explain what just happened?"

He thought about it before answering.

"You ever heard of Miyamoto Musashi?"

"Is that the knife that cuts through cans?"

He smiled. "Musashi was reputed to be the greatest samurai who ever lived. The story goes that, one day, he came to a narrow bridge crossing a long river. At the other side of the bridge was a much younger samurai. The two stared at one another for several minutes. The proper thing to do would be for the younger samurai to step aside and let Musashi pass, or dare risk disrespecting the great master. Instead, the young samurai strode directly onto the bridge toward Musashi." He stopped to let the story build.

"So what happened?" she asked. "Musashi cut him in half, right?"

"No. Musashi stepped aside and let him pass."

"What? Why? You said he was the greatest samurai ever."

"Ah, yes," Tanner said, holding up a finger. "Many asked that same question. Musashi's only answer was that, when he looked into the other man's eyes, he saw his own defeat."

Samantha wrinkled her brow.

"What does that have to do with the helicopter?"

"Perhaps," Tanner said without the slightest hint of a smile, "when the soldiers looked into my eyes, they saw their own defeat."

Libby laughed from the back seat and patted him on the shoulder like he had just told a doozy.

"That's-that's ridiculous," stammered Samantha. "Are you saying that a battalion of soldiers in a helicopter took one look at you and ran for their lives?"

"It's just a working theory."

She made a funny face at him before turning to Libby.

"I think you might be right about God helping us," she said with a loud, exaggerated movement.

"Why are you talking like that?" he asked. "She still can't hear you."

"I know that," she said out of the corner of her mouth. "I just figured I'd make it easier for her to read my lips."

He shook his head.

"Where are we going, anyway?" she asked.

"Right now, we need distance between us and them. Whether it was divine intervention or battlefield prowess, I'd rather not have them pick up your signal again."

"We're heading to Virginia?"

"Not yet. We've lost nearly all of our supplies. We need to get someplace safe where we can restock and regroup."

"And where's that exactly?"

He smiled. "We're going to my house."

To Mason's disappointment, the Ross Branch waterway was little more than a stream in early spring. He had expected it to be large enough, and, more important, loud enough to mask his approach. As it was, he could literally step across it at some points. The waterway was, however, recessed about twenty feet from ground level and lined with a thin barricade of birch trees on both sides. He hoped that the channel would offer enough concealment for him to make his way into the town undetected.

He carried the Mini-14 and had his Supergrade holstered at his side. Even though he didn't have enough firepower or ammunition for the task at hand, it felt good to be armed and free.

From where he had parked his truck, the walk along the waterway to Liberty Street was only about half a mile. He moved slowly, keeping a careful eye out for anyone who might take notice of his approach.

His first encounter was with an old woman washing clothes in the stream. Like countless pioneers before her, she knelt beside the waterway, first dipping the clothes and then scrubbing them against a smooth rock. She had a box of detergent sitting beside her that she occasionally sprinkled onto the clothes.

Mason got to within a few steps before she even noticed him. The sight of an armed man approaching startled her, and she fell back. He hurried forward and helped her to her feet.

"It's okay, dear," he said.

"You scared me," she said, hanging onto his arm to steady herself.

"I'm sorry. Alex has me out on patrol. You haven't seen anyone unusual, have you?"

"Just you," she said, looking down at the basket of laundry that had fallen over.

Mason squatted down and picked up the clothes, placing them back in the basket.

"There you go," he said. "All better?"

"I wish you boys would put away all those guns and get some water running through the pipes. That's what we really need."

"Yes, ma'am. I'll suggest that to Alex the next time I see her."

The woman squatted back down at the water's edge.

"Don't tell her where it came from. We don't want any trouble." She studied her clothes to see what required the most attention.

"Of course not," he said, slowly walking away.

When Mason was sure that she wasn't actually a clever spy about to run up and sound the alarm, he continued his hike into York. He didn't see another person until he got all the way to the intersection with Liberty Street. A young man, barely out of his teens, stood on the small bridge that passed over the waterway. He was holding a rifle, and his attention was clearly on the road.

Mason worked his way to the edge of the bridge and crouched in its shadow. He doubted that he could get any closer without the guard spotting him. Picking him off with a single shot to the head would be easy enough, but he remained unwilling to use deadly force without just cause. That meant he would either have to rush up and take the man out in close quarters, something he felt uneasy about after his botched encounter with Stogie, or wait for him to step away from his post. Reminding himself that a patient man has the advantage of selecting the battlefield, he decided to wait.

Mason shuffled under the bridge and sat down. He didn't think it would take long. A man standing guard on a bridge over a steady stream of trickling water was bound to need a pee break.

In less than thirty minutes, he heard footsteps trudging down the steep embankment. The guard was whistling Bobby McFerrin's "Don't Worry, Be Happy," obviously unaware that death might only be seconds away. He stepped down onto the driest part of a little dirt landing at the water's edge, set his rifle on the ground, and unzipped his trousers. Mason waited until he finished and started to zip up before rushing him. Such courtesy had been paid him in the past, and it seemed only fair play.

He came up from behind, cupping the man's mouth with one hand and bringing the knife around to his throat with the other. He felt the soft stubble under his palm of what were perhaps the young man's first whiskers. Before the youth could react, Mason swept his feet out from under him, guiding him to the ground with the press of the knife. Once he was flat on his back, Mason stepped over and straddled his chest. The man's eyes were as wide as saucers, and his heart pounded so violently that Mason could see the carotid artery in his neck pulsing with every beat.

"Keep quiet if you want to live," he said.

The man swallowed and nodded.

Mason slowly removed his hand from the man's mouth.

"Please! Please!" he whispered. "Don't kill me."

Mason patted him down with his free hand. He didn't find any weapons and only a handful of bullets in his shirt pocket.

"Give me a reason not to gut you like a fish."

The man's eyes darted left and right, searching for anything with which to negotiate.

"I . . . I know where your dog is."

"I'm listening."

"Alex brought him to the cemetery. She says that she's going to hang him for everyone to see unless you come back with the gold."

Mason pushed the knife against the man's throat.

"I know that already. What else?"

"I can get him for you," he said, feeling out the words. "Yes, yes, that's it. I'll bring him here. You won't even have to go into town. I'll do it for you."

Mason considered the man's offer.

"How do I know I can trust you?"

Tears formed in his eyes.

"Look, you're sparing my life. I won't forget that. If you let me go, I'll bring the dog. You have my word. Swear to God."

Mason stood up and stepped back. He extended his hand and helped the young man to his feet.

"What's your name, son?"

"I'm Jimmy."

"Jimmy, this is the luckiest day of your life. I'm going to wait right here under this bridge for you to come back with my dog. Don't you disappoint me."

"No, sir," Jimmy said, shaking his head. "I'll bring your dog. You'll see."

Mason inspected the man's rifle. It was a bolt-action, .30-06, deer rifle, which packed a solid punch but was too slow to be of much good in a modern firefight. He removed the bolt and threw it into the water before handing the weapon back to Jimmy.

"Carry this, or they'll know something's up."

"Right," he said, looking at what was now a useless hunk of metal and wood.

"Well, what are you waiting on? Go get my dog."

"Right. Right," he said, turning and then scrambling up the hill. "Don't worry, I'll get him. You wait right here. I'll get him."

"Just hurry."

When Jimmy got to the top of the hill, he dusted himself off and began jogging east on Liberty Street.

Mason waited until he was out of sight and then took off at a dead run.

The vice president sat outside on a small balcony, finishing his lunch. General Hood sat opposite him, staring out at the plush green foliage of the Shenandoah Valley, which served as the backdrop to the Mount Weather Emergency Operations Center. Two Secret Service agents stood inside the room, conspicuously looking the other direction. A soundproof glass door separated them from Vice President Pike and General Hood.

"I'm assuming that the operation was a success."

General Hood nodded, settling back into the wicker chair.

"Yes, sir, highly successful."

"You seem pleased with yourself."

The general took a deep breath of fresh mountain air.

"And why shouldn't I be?"

"Did you get video of the strike?"

"Both from the gunships as well as from a cell phone on the ground. We're splicing the two together right now. It should be quite a show."

Vice President Pike took a small bite of his sandwich.

"Disseminate it to as many anti-government groups as possible—separatists, survivalists, militias, anarchists, anybody who harbors the slightest distrust of President Glass. Of course, do it discreetly. We want them thinking they've uncovered something controversial."

"Yes, sir."

"We need to spread the seeds of discontent wide enough to bring about change," he said, chewing his food.

"People are already attacking the remaining government outposts for food and supplies. This brutality will only make matters worse."

Vice President Pike nodded, his mind already mulling over other matters.

"Sir, if I might ask you an obvious question?"

"Yes?"

The general looked over at the agents guarding the vice president and then lowered his voice.

"If you're so determined to replace President Glass, why not just . . ." He hunted for the right words.

"Kill her?"

General Hood tipped his head.

"It wouldn't be too difficult. A single shooter, a drop of poison."

Vice President Pike offered an understanding smile.

"Her dying at the hands of an assassin is the last thing I want. No matter the circumstances, I would forever be viewed with suspicion. Even more important is that people wouldn't have had time to appreciate the need for change. If she goes down as a martyr, there will be a push to maintain the status quo by continuing her legacy."

"Ah, I see," said General Hood. "Before taking office, you want everyone to grow disillusioned with her."

"Not only her, but also her ideology and methods. We need for people to welcome a change. Hell, we need for them to demand it." Vice President Pike finished his lunch and set his fork and knife on the plate. "As a military man, you already know that a war must be fought on several fronts."

"Of course."

"That's what we're doing. If we can find Samantha, we'll use her to force the president to do our bidding. But we can't count on having that leverage. So, in the meantime, we'll make President Glass stumble and fall on a grand scale. Riots, violence, and chaos will eventually force law-abiding citizens to demand change."

General Hood smiled and nodded.

"Understood."

"General, do you ever think about why we're doing all this?"

The general looked concerned, as if he felt he was being tested.

"I know why we're doing this. We're trying to save our country."

"And that means taking out the trash, starting first with the people who were infected."

"Of course. They're a clear and present danger."

"And the violent separatists. They must be cleaned up as well."

"Anyone who would take up arms against the government must be suppressed. What's your point, sir?"

The vice president pushed his plate away and turned his chair to better face General Hood.

"My point, General, is that, when we began this journey, we agreed to rebuild a stronger nation by starting with a clean slate."

"And?"

"And to succeed on this incredibly noble mission, we will need to work both sides of this little war."

"Meaning?"

"Meaning that we must continue pressing the president to conduct improper or failed military actions so that she will be viewed as both violent and ineffective."

"Are you suggesting that we motivate her to conduct more raids like the one in Atlanta?"

"No," he said. "We have to up the ante."

"And how would you propose we do that?"

The vice president sat back in his chair.

"I have a new mission for you, General. It has two objectives. The first is to put weapons in the hands of people who are the most discontent."

General Hood couldn't hide his concern.

"Are you proposing that we arm the very people who would overthrow the government?"

"Don't get self-righteous on me, General. I'm talking about arming select groups that have the most inclination to take action. Let them do some damage. If the demand for change gets loud enough, the president will step down voluntarily. If she doesn't, the discontent will strengthen my call to have her removed."

"You should understand that even her removal would not placate these separatists."

"I'm sure that's true," he said. "Most of them feed on hatred."

"And if these same people don't stop their attacks when you take office?"

Vice President Pike waved the question away.

"Threats like those wouldn't last long under the hand of a strong leader." He paused, choosing his words carefully. "Tell me, where can we get, say, a few thousand rifles?"

"A few thousand?" Again, the general seemed unsure of the proposition.

"It needs to be enough to wage a small war. A few thousand disgruntled anarchists should do the trick. So?"

General Hood took a deep breath before answering.

"Military weaponry has been secured all across the nation. Breaking into any of these outposts would be a major endeavor."

"I don't need you to tell me what can't be done."

The general sat quietly considering options. After a moment, his face broke into a small smile.

"I may have something."

"Tell me."

"When Fort Benning was closed, one of their small arms caches was transferred to the Federal Law Enforcement Training Center in Glynco, Georgia. The US Marshals stepped forward and took possession of the weapons. The rifles were used to train infantry soldiers, so they're not new weapons, but they're still functional."

"The Marshals?"

"Yes, sir."

"How many officers remain at the law enforcement center?"

"After the pandemic, what remained of the Marshal Service was consolidated to Glynco. Total count is probably only a few hundred. But these are good men and women, very well trained. Still, with the proper distraction, the right group could probably get in and out without too much bloodshed."

"We'll need for whoever conducts the raid to be outside the main military—no traceability back to us."

"You're talking about mercenaries," said General Hood.

"Can you set that up?"

The general thought for a moment.

"I'm sure there are a few groups still active. The very best is run by a man named Nakai."

"That's an odd name," said Vice President Pike. "What makes him so special?"

An unmistakable gleam shone in the general's eyes as he started talking.

"Nakai is a full-blooded American Indian. He served with distinction in the Marine Corps' Force Recon. His specialty was deep reconnaissance missions, many times operating behind enemy lines. I served with him and can personally testify that he's truly one of the best."

"An effective killer?"

"I wouldn't want him coming after me."

"And for the right price, he'll do whatever we ask of him?"

"Anything but betray his own men."

The vice president nodded.

"How many serve under him?"

"Last time I checked, there were around fifty. All ex-military. All very hard men."

"Perfect." The vice president sat back and considered his plan. Nakai sounded like exactly the type of man he needed. "Meet with him to see if he's interested."

"Assuming that he's still alive, he'll do it for me. No need to even ask."

"That brings me to the second objective of our mission." He leaned forward. "I want this to be a different kind of operation. Something less surgical than what you've described."

"If you're suggesting that they conduct a frontal assault against the Marshals—"

"No, no, nothing like that," he said, holding up his hands. "I have something else in mind."

Now, it was Vice President Pike's turn to look around. He waved for the general to come closer.

"Some time ago," he said, his voice barely above a whisper, "I acquired a rather special weapon. I think this may be the right time to use it."

"What kind of weapon?"

"The kind that will make President Glass feel the fear of war."

# chapter 22

The drive from Atlanta to Tanner's cabin in North Carolina was about three hundred miles. What would normally have taken five hours, Tanner calculated, was now certain to take at least twice that. The hardest part was avoiding the congestion on major thorough-fares, especially near the larger cities. Tanner managed to navigate much of the trip on Highway 123, which paralleled I-85 but proved to be far less congested. The beginning of the drive went remarkably smooth. There were no gunships darkening the skies, and very few people even noticed their passing.

They sped through a host of small towns, including Toccoa, Westminster, and Seneca, each in varying states of despair. When they got near Greenville, they turned north, detouring around Table Rock State Park. It was nearing dusk as they entered the town of Hendersonville, North Carolina.

Hendersonville was a tourist town like many others dotting the Blue Ridge Mountains. Its only significant attraction had been the strip of his-torical buildings on Main Street, consisting mostly of antique shops, res-taurants, and boutiques. The sign coming into town proudly announced that the "City of Four Seasons" had a population of 13,517. By the look of things, however, that number was now grossly exaggerated.

The town had once measured six square miles, but the entire west side had recently caught fire and burned to the ground. A huge landscape of charred timbers and hollow brick frames stood as grim reminders of busi-nesses and churches that had once served as the lifeblood of the small community. The fire no longer burned, but the faintest wisps of white smoke still rose from small pockets of smoldering embers.

They cruised slowly through what was once Hendersonville's retail dis-trict. One side of the street was completely destroyed by the fire, but the other was relatively intact, save for missing windows and scorched walls.

"What do you think happened?" Samantha asked, looking out her win-dow with a mix of awe and sadness.

"Fire."

"I meant, why did they let it burn so much of the town?"

He shrugged. "The fire department probably wasn't up and running anymore. They're lucky it finally burned itself out."

Libby passed up a note.

*It looks like there was a war here.*

Tanner nodded to her and smiled.

"It stinks like smoke," Samantha said, checking to ensure her window was rolled all the way up.

"Smoky or not, we'll have to stop for the night. We need some rest."

"And water." She tipped the bottle up and shook the last few drops into her mouth.

"And water," he agreed, licking his lips.

Libby passed up another slip of paper.

*We can check the stores for water. Restaurants, too.*

Tanner nodded. "I'm sure we can find something, but let's figure out where to bunk first."

He turned east, moving deeper into what remained of the town. The Escalade bumped over an old set of train tracks and, before they could pick up speed again, a man darted out into the road. He was hunched over and clutching his stomach.

Tanner hit the brakes, sending everyone flying forward.

The man stumbled up to vehicle, leaning across the front of the Escalade. His face was twisted in agony. Before anyone could say a word, he collapsed onto the road, leaving large streaks of blood across the hood.

"Just drive around him," Samantha said, her voice shaking.

Tanner grabbed the shotgun and pulled the door handle.

"If we're in danger, I want to know it."

"At least be careful. No more stitches."

He grunted and stepped out with the shotgun at the ready. The man was lying on his side in front of the Escalade's wheels. The headlights illuminated the street, but the man was so close to the vehicle that he remained largely in shadows. Tanner stepped closer and nudged him with his boot.

He didn't move.

Tanner knelt down and held his hand a few inches above the man's mouth and nose. Nothing. He rolled him over, and intestines and diaphragm muscles spilled out through his open belly. The man looked to be approaching fifty and was dressed like he was preparing to go to church: dark gray suit, white shirt, and polished black leather shoes.

Unrolling her window and leaning out, Samantha asked, "Is he alive?"

"Nope," he said, standing back up.

"What happened to him?"

He walked back to the Escalade and climbed in.

"Gutted."

She cringed. "Ouch."

Libby passed him a note.

*Was he infected?*

He shook his head, studying the street for any sign of danger.

Samantha joined him in looking around.

"Who do you suppose stabbed him?" she asked.

"Don't know, don't care." He put the vehicle in drive. "Let's go find a place to sleep."

They drove another half-mile before entering a neighborhood filled with small single-story houses. Cars lined both sides of the street, their windshields covered in a thick layer of pollen.

He pulled up to the curb and pointed to a small blue house that still had its doors and windows intact.

"That one okay?"

Samantha shrugged.

Libby smiled and nodded with sleepy eyes.

Everyone grabbed their gear and approached the house like a party of weary adventurers. The shutters were drawn tight, but there was enough of a gap to see that it was dark inside.

"It looks clear, but let's be sure." He banged on the door a few times. No one answered; nor was there any movement inside. He tried the knob and found it unlocked. "We're in luck."

They stepped in and set their backpacks on the floor, letting out a collective sigh of relief.

"Do you smell that?" Samantha asked, tipping her head so that her nose was up in the air. "It smells like . . . food."

Libby rubbed her stomach, smiling.

They walked around the two-bedroom house, quickly searching every room, hoping to find a feast ready and waiting. Despite their noses telling them otherwise, they didn't find an obvious source for the odor.

Tanner did, however, find a doorway leading down a narrow set of stairs.

Samantha took a whiff.

"It's not coming from the basement," she said.

"No," he agreed. "But I'd like to see what's down there before it gets too dark."

Out of habit, he hit the light switch on the stairway wall. Nothing happened. He went back and retrieved the headlamp from his pack that he had taken from Outdoor World. Samantha slipped hers on too. Libby left them to wander the house for a second time, determined to find what smelled so good.

Tanner started down the stairs with his shotgun at the ready. The old wooden staircase creaked and moaned with every step he took. Samantha walked a few feet behind him, carrying her rifle.

"We're not going to surprise anyone unless you lose a little weight," she whispered.

He couldn't come up with a clever rejoinder, so he ignored her.

When they got to the bottom, he swung left, and she turned right. They swept their headlamps and weapons from side to side. On one side of the basement were stacks of boxes, small plastic barrels, and a giant green tank with a spigot on the front. The other side had been converted into an elaborate laboratory. Long metal tables were covered in beakers, glass tubes, and burners. Along its far wall was a huge built-in shelf, spanning from floor to ceiling and stuffed with hundreds of jars and canisters.

Tanner motioned for her to check the lab while he inspected the supplies.

"It looks like where a mad scientist would work," she said, walking slowly around the equipment. Despite her curiosity, she was careful not to touch anything for fear of setting off some kind of deadly chemical reaction.

Tanner shone his light on one of the small yellow barrels. The words "pinto beans" were written on the side in large black letters. He checked another one. Rice. The boxes also had labels: strawberries, potatoes, green beans.

"Forget the chemistry set. I've found food." He tapped the large green tank. It felt nearly full of liquid. "And beer."

"Beer?" she said, walking toward him. "Really?"

He laughed. "Okay, probably just water. Still, this is quite a find."

They heard a knocking sound coming from the top of the stairs.

"Come on," he said, wheeling around and hurrying back upstairs.

When they got to the top, Libby was standing at a sliding glass door that opened up to the backyard. She waved to them with excitement in her eyes.

As they hurried over, she slid the door open, and the unmistakable smell of grilled meat wafted into the room.

Stepping out, they saw a small charcoal grill sitting on a simple concrete slab that acted as the back porch. Tanner lifted the lid and found a pile of smoldering wood ashes. The grill was empty but still slick with grease and the unmistakable remnants of chicken fat. He picked up a small piece of crispy chicken skin and put it in his mouth, closing his eyes to savor the flavor.

"Where'd they get—" Samantha was interrupted by a loud *balk* coming from the rear of the yard.

They all turned to see a large coop, easily measuring fifteen feet on a side and eight feet in height. It was painted barn red and constructed from wood and wire mesh.

Libby hurried over and peeked in through the wire netting at the top. Once again, she gestured for them to come and see. Inside the coop were at least two dozen chickens roosting on straw nests. Even the sight of the birds was enough to cause everyone's mouths to water.

"Someone must still live here," said Samantha.

"Yep," Tanner said, unable to take his eyes off the chickens.

"Think they'd mind if we borrowed one or two?"

"Borrowed? As in with barbecue sauce?"

She shrugged.

"Would you, if they were your chickens?" he asked.

She mumbled something under her breath.

"What was that?"

"I said I was kind of hoping that you'd want to take them. You've never minded stealing anything else."

"I don't mind taking things from dead people or stores that have closed up. But someone's cared for these birds for a long time. If some knucklehead took my chickens, I'd knock a few of their teeth out. Besides, you told me that you'd never let me kill a sweet little animal. Remember?"

"They're chickens," she said. "They're supposed to be eaten."

"They might beg to differ."

She frowned at him.

"So you're not going to let us eat them?"

"Sorry Kiddo."

"What if I was starving? Would you let me die?"

"Are you starving?"

"Well, I'm hungry."

"I'm hungry too. And I'm sure that goes for Libby, too," he said, looking over at her. "But we won't steal another man's food. Not unless we have no other choice."

Libby was watching their exchange with great interest. She quickly wrote something on a slip of paper and handed it to Samantha.

After reading it, Samantha pressed her lips together and nodded to Libby. It was the first positive reaction he had seen her give their new addition.

"Okay," she said to him. "Let's go find something else."

He looked to Libby and then back to Samantha.

"What was that about?"

"Nothing," she said, stuffing the note in her pocket.

"Women and their secrets," he muttered, heading back toward the house.

The three of them went back in the house and gathered up their backpacks. As they opened the front door to leave, they saw a group of twenty or more people walking down the street. One by one, they slowly broke off and went into houses around the neighborhood. Most carried plates, pans, or other cooking supplies. It was like watching a group of union workers returning home with lunch pails in hand.

Tanner pushed everyone back into the house and stared out the front window. As the group neared the blue house, a man and a young girl, perhaps six years old, turned up the driveway. They seemed tired but relieved to be home.

Samantha stood next to Tanner, peeking out from the edge of the curtain.

"They're coming," she said. "Should we hide?"

"No. Just stay cool. They don't appear to be armed. Let's try to keep this friendly."

Tanner had Libby and Samantha stand behind the couch, with the kitchen and back door behind them. If they had to escape, it would take only a few seconds. He stood directly in front of the couch, the shotgun held across his body at waist level.

When the man opened the door, he was looking down at his daughter, and it took him a few seconds to realize that he had uninvited visitors. By the time he stopped, he was already three or four steps into the house. The front door stood wide open behind them.

For a moment no one said anything. The man looked concerned, and the child was nothing short of terrified.

"What are you doing in my house?" he demanded.

"Close the door behind you," Tanner said in a calm voice.

The man pushed it shut with his foot, never taking his eyes off him.

"Are you armed?"

The man shook his head. His daughter started to cry, and he quickly lifted her up into his arms.

Tanner lowered the shotgun.

"You have our apologies for breaking into your home. We thought it was empty."

The man and his daughter both looked at him with suspicion.

"He's telling the truth," Samantha said, stepping around from behind the couch. "We're just trying to get home, his home, and then mine. It's a long story."

Tanner put his hand on her shoulder. Libby slowly walked around to join them.

The man looked them over carefully before speaking.

"Who are you people?"

"I'm Tanner."

"I'm Samantha, and that's Libby. She's deaf."

Libby waved to the man's daughter who was studying her.

The girl gave a little smile and then tucked her face into her father's shoulder.

"I'm Professor Duncan Callaway. This is my daughter, Rachel."

"Professor," said Tanner, "if you could direct us to an empty house, we'll be on our way. Like I said, I don't go around breaking into other people's homes."

"That's true," Samantha said, glancing up at him. "He'll break into just about any other place—restaurants, grocery stores, hospitals—"

"Sam," he said, cutting his eyes at her.

"My point is that we aren't bad people. We didn't eat your chickens or anything."

Professor Callaway smiled. "Is she always this lively?"

"She's usually worse," Tanner said, sighing.

"You'd probably better wait until morning to move on," he said, setting his daughter down. "The soldiers would punish you if they found you out past curfew."

Tanner and Samantha both spoke in unison.

"What soldiers?"

"The VDC." When he saw the puzzled look on their faces, he continued.

"The Viral Defense Corps that was dispatched by the president to kill off the infected."

Tanner looked to Samantha, and she shrugged.

"We don't know anything about that," he said. "But even so, why would they care if we're out past curfew? We're not infected."

Duncan turned and looked out the window.

"Because," he said, "this particular unit is enforcing its own agenda."

"Which is?"

"Close as I can tell, it's to demand homage from the people of Hendersonville."

"What's homage?" Samantha asked, looking up at Tanner.

"Uh—" He turned back to Callaway. "Professor?"

"It simply means that they're demanding that we serve them in every sense of the word. That's where everyone was returning from tonight. We were delivering our daily food. I even had to kill one of my precious chickens for their fat-cat colonel."

"And if you don't meet their demands?"

"They beat us. Or worse. And it's not only food that they take." He glanced at Libby and Samantha. "If they find out they're here, they'll come for one or both of them, and there's nothing you'll be able to do to stop them."

Tanner tightened his grip on the shotgun.

"The hell there isn't."

&#x2767; &#x2619;

They spent the next two hours discussing the situation in Hendersonville. Professor Callaway gathered food from the basement, as well as a basket of fresh eggs, and everyone ate and drank their fill while sharing stories of life before and after the pandemic. Samantha stayed by Tanner's side, not wanting to miss out on anything the grownups were talking about. Libby, on the other hand, seemed content to entertain Rachel by playing games and helping her put together puzzles by candlelight.

Tanner learned that the soldiers had arrived a week earlier, and after cleaning up the few infected who remained in town, decided to stick around. They set up a small operating post at the Hendersonville Railroad Station, a landmark that dated all the way back to 1879.

Every evening, they required that residents deliver food and drink.

Those who resisted or questioned the order were either beaten or publicly executed. The man whom Tanner had found disemboweled was the soldiers' most recent victim. His crime was refusing to reveal the whereabouts of his fifteen-year-old daughter. The more Tanner heard, the more he thought that the VDC soldiers in Hendersonville were akin to the Nazis in occupied France. They took what they wanted, with little or no regard for the suffering of those around them. They had become occupiers in every sense of the word.

Having been raised on a farm in Alabama, Professor Callaway was a man who understood the importance of self-reliance. When he lost his wife to cancer two years earlier, he pledged to take his role as the sole provider to his daughter more seriously. He filled the basement with non-perishable food, installed a large polyethylene water tank, and bought an AR-15 rifle with enough ammunition to deter any who would do his family harm. Never did he suspect that his preparations would prove so useful so quickly.

Callaway had retired to Hendersonville after working for twenty years at the University of North Carolina as a chemistry professor. He confessed to being something of a legend, not because of his teaching prowess, but rather for creating concoctions that required his entire building to be evacuated.

While they spoke, Tanner repeatedly got up and went to the window to look out. He didn't want anyone showing up unannounced. When it was nearing nine in the evening, he spotted his first sign of trouble. A group of three soldiers stumbled down the street, clearly intoxicated and looking to blow off a little steam. He waved the professor over to the window.

"They're out looking for women," said Callaway.

"Will they force their way into homes?"

"Oh, yes." He instinctively glanced over at his own daughter. "If she were older, I'd probably already be dead."

"Do you think they'll come here?"

He shook his head.

"No, they have a few houses that they visit regularly. Sometimes, they'll drag the women out into the street to humiliate them. It's a horrible thing to see, but no one can stop it. Those who tried were the first to be killed."

Tanner nodded, staring out at the three men. He knew what needed to be done. Someone had to make an example out of them. He reminded himself that this wasn't his fight. If prison had taught him anything, it was to stay out of other people's troubles. He stood quietly and watched, gritting his teeth.

All three soldiers stopped directly in front of the professor's house and started urinating on his lawn, crisscrossing streams of piss, like Jedi masters dueling with their lightsabers. Their faces were alive with joyous revelry in anticipation of a night of torture and humiliation. Try as he might, it was not something Tanner could allow to go unpunished.

He turned to Samantha to deliver his usual warning.

"I know, I know," she said. "You want me to stay here."

He nodded.

"What are you going to do?"

"Make a point."

She looked worried but didn't question him further.

"And I don't want you to look out the window, either," he said.

"Why?"

"Just because."

"Because you're going to be mean, right?"

He nodded again.

"Okay," she said. "But don't get killed. I don't want to be stuck here." She looked over at the professor. "No offense."

Tanner went to the front door and took one last look out the side window. The soldiers were tiddling their names on the professor's overgrown lawn. Tanner swung the door open and rushed out, the shotgun raised at shoulder level.

"Hands where I can see them!"

All three soldiers panicked, frantically trying to put away their peckers while looking around for the rifles they had haphazardly set aside.

He fired the shotgun into the ground by their feet, quickly chambering another shell.

"Hands!" he yelled.

The three soldiers stumbled back into the street with their hands up. Tanner maintained a safe distance so they wouldn't be tempted to go for his shotgun.

"Don't shoot," one of them slurred. He wore an Atlanta Braves baseball cap in place of his official military fatigue hat.

The second soldier was a big man with a lazy eye. He said nothing, but his face was twisted in anger. The third man was much shorter, and his head was cleanly shaven, reminding Tanner of Telly Savalas in the '70s TV show, *Kojak*.

He trained the shotgun on the man standing in the center of the group, ready to swivel his point of aim if anyone decided to get frisky. Despite what people thought, the pellets of a triple-aught shell only spread about the span of a hand at twenty feet.

"I hear you boys are out looking for a little fun."

Lazy Eye slowly brought his hands down and spit off to the side.

"What's it to you—"

Tanner raised the shotgun and shot him in the face. Lazy Eye's entire head disintegrated in an explosion of blood and bone.

The other two soldiers jumped back and screamed.

"Shut it," he said, turning the shotgun their direction.

"We-we're not even armed," stammered Braves.

"And the women you rape? Are they armed?"

He didn't answer.

"What do you want?" asked Kojak.

"I don't want a damn thing."

"Listen, mister—" started Braves.

Kojak reached over and put his hand his buddy's shoulder.

"Save it. It's not going to make a bit of difference."

Tanner smiled. "I see you're the smart one." He noticed that several people had stepped out on their porches to see what was happening. "You're absolutely right. There's going to be no negotiation. No fast talking or promises of payoff." He tossed the shotgun over by the men's rifles. "We're gonna fight."

Kojak and Braves were both shocked by his decision to give up his weapon.

"You shouldn't have done that," Kojak said, raising his fists like a classic pugilist. "I was a Golden Gloves champion for two years in a row."

"Good for you," said Tanner.

Kojak shuffled forward in a traditional boxer's stance, jabbing with his left hand as soon as he got to within striking distance. Braves seemed less sure of himself and hung back, eyeing the rifles lying on the ground.

The jab hit Tanner's nose about the same time that his shin kick slammed into Kojak's thigh. Of the two, the kick was far more devastating, and the man stumbled back, hopping on his rear leg.

"Sonofabitch!" he cried, leaning back to ease the pain from the huge hematoma now forming on his leg.

Tanner used the back of his hand to wipe the blood that oozed from his nose. He smiled. It wasn't even broken.

"And you call yourself a boxer?" he scoffed, licking the blood off his hand. "I've been hit harder by girlfriends when I reached for their goodies."

Braves suddenly charged, head down and screaming. Tanner stepped back with one foot and struck out sideways with a hammerfist to the man's temple. The blow spun him away like a billiard ball. Braves staggered, trying to get his bearings as the world continued to spin. Tanner stepped forward and kicked up into his groin from behind. The instep of Tanner's foot hit him so hard that it ruptured one of his testicles. Braves' eyes rolled back, and he fell forward, his scalp gashing open as he smacked headfirst into the curb.

Before Tanner could turn back, Kojak came in fast, leaping off his good leg and swinging a powerful superman punch. Tanner shuffled in close, bringing up an arm up to block the strike and a knee to the man's gut. Kojak doubled over, grabbing his stomach as he fought for air. Tanner snaked an arm around the man's neck and hoisted upward, like he was heaving a giant catfish out of the water. The man's cervical vertebrae separated and then snapped. Tanner jerked violently to one side, breaking Kojak's neck. He held him for a few seconds while the body twitched and spasmed. Then he dropped the lifeless hunk of meat to the ground.

He walked back over and retrieved his shotgun. Several people who had witnessed the violence shouted cheers of support from their porches. Most stopped cheering, however, when Tanner walked back over to Braves' limp form and repeatedly smashed his head with the butt of the shotgun.

꿍 ꩜

"You shouldn't have done that," said Professor Callaway, wringing his hands. "They'll come looking for them. Even if we hide the bodies, someone will tell them what happened here. You've put us all in danger." The more he spoke, the more his voice trembled.

"Don't worry. They won't miss a few drunken soldiers."

"Maybe not now, but they will by morning."

"Then we'll have to give them something bigger to worry about."

The professor furrowed his brow.

"Like what?"

"We need to bring the fight to them."

"We don't have the manpower to fight twenty or more professional soldiers."

"Listen, Professor, you and your daughter are living on borrowed time. Men who can do whatever they want only grow more violent. We are all wolves. Fight or be eaten. There is no other way."

Callaway sat back in his chair.

"It's not that I disagree," he said in a defeated voice. "I just don't see how you expect us to fight a small army. I'd be lucky to find three people who would stand and fight."

"Three would be enough for what I have in mind."

Samantha had been listening intently.

"You have a plan?" she asked.

"When don't I have a plan?"

"Are you kidding?" she scoffed. "What about when—"

He held up his hand and turned back to face Callaway.

"I'll need your help with this, Professor. In fact, everything depends on you."

"I'm not a great shot. I haven't been to the range in more than a year."

"That's not the kind of help I'm talking about."

"What, then?"

Tanner hesitated, searching for the right delivery. When he couldn't find one, he just blurted it out.

"I want you to make a bomb."

"*What?*" The professor jumped to his feet. "Why?"

"Why do you think? To blow them to hell and back."

"But—"

"But, nothing. Can you make a bomb or not?"

Callaway hesitated. "We'd only have one chance at this. If we didn't kill them all, they'd slaughter the entire town, my daughter, Rachel, included."

"So, we kill every last one of them."

"Are you going to build an atom bomb?" asked Samantha.

"That's a little bigger than I had in mind," said Tanner.

"You're thinking of a fertilizer bomb," said Callaway.

He nodded. "What would we need?"

The professor rubbed his chin.

"Not much really. Fertilizer, a fuel, and a simple detonator."

"That sounds easy enough."

"Hardly. The fertilizer has to be pure, no additives, and the detonator must be powerful enough to generate sufficient energy to start vaporizing the ammonium nitrate."

"And can we get those?"

"I know we can get the fertilizer from the old agricultural plant across town. As for the fuel, we have our choice. We could use gasoline, jet fuel, or fuel oil." He chuckled nervously. "For that matter, we could even use sugar."

"Sugar?" Samantha stared at him.

"Sugar can be used to create dimethylfuran." When he saw the blank look, he added, "It's similar to ethanol, like you get at the pump. But it would take a lot of work, and we don't really have time. We'll be better off with traditional fuels." He turned to Tanner. "You know, I had a friend who lived over on Gypsum Street who used to race cars. I'd bet you anything that he still has a tank of high-octane fuel in his garage."

"Sounds perfect."

"Once we have the fertilizer and fuel, the trick will be to mix it in the right ratio."

"And what about the detonator?" asked Tanner. "Where would we get that?"

"The best way to do that is with a piece of detonating cord."

"Detcord? Like the stuff that the military uses to blast through doors?"

"Exactly."

"Any chance that you have some of that lying around?"

The professor shook his head.

"Of course not. But . . ."

"Yes?"

"I might be able to make some. Detcord is nothing more than a thin plastic tube filled with pentaerythritol tetranitrate. I think I can improvise something with the supplies I have in my lab."

"Am I hearing you right, Professor? Are you telling me that you can build us a bomb?"

The professor nodded. "I suppose I am."

"And will you?" asked Tanner.

"You haven't really given me any choice now, have you?"

M ason figured that a man with a knife at his throat would say absolutely anything to get it removed. Before the knife's impression had even faded from the skin, however, rational thought would begin to take over. If he hadn't already, Jimmy would soon realize that tossing his lot in with a single outlaw was a surefire way to find himself dangling from Alex's rope. And once he came to that obvious conclusion, he would rat Mason out faster than wiseguy Joe "The Ear" Massino.

That didn't mean that Jimmy couldn't be useful, however. On the contrary, he would almost certainly draw Alex's forces to the bridge, hopefully giving Mason time to get in and out before they realized that they had been played.

He sprinted southeast, paralleling Liberty Street. Most of the area was heavily wooded and undeveloped, and he saw only the occasional small house. He ran for about a third of a mile before coming to a large thoroughfare. He couldn't remember the name of the road but knew that if he turned north, he would run directly into the courthouse. The cemetery was only a couple of blocks from there.

If Jimmy had been telling the truth, Bowie would be at the cemetery, perhaps allowing Mason to do a quick grab and run. If he had lied, or if things had unexpectedly changed, there would almost certainly be a good deal of bloodshed. While Mason had no desire to kill the men and women who had picked up arms in the name of their town's militia, he would not hesitate to do so if his or Bowie's life were in danger.

Mason turned and ran north until he saw the familiar yellow brick of the courthouse building. He hid behind a large oak tree and watched as six armed men raced out of the back of the courthouse, heading west. Jimmy was at the front of the pack, waving them on. Mason figured that he had about twenty minutes before they realized he had intentionally drawn them out. As soon as they were out of sight, he hurried east.

After two blocks, he turned back north. The cemetery was dead ahead. Even before crossing Liberty Street, he could make out the image of a large dog lying on the hangman's stage. It was Bowie. A man stood beside him, holding a rope that was being used as a makeshift leash. Neither of them noticed Mason until he came sprinting up along the edge of the cemetery, rifle held tightly against his shoulder.

Bowie scrambled to his feet and pulled hard on the leash. The man struggled to keep him under control while simultaneously trying to yank a revolver out of his belt. Mason stopped, steadied himself, and fired a single shot from the Mini-14. It made a high-pitched crack, and the man fell back, clutching his throat.

Bowie pulled free and launched himself off the stage. He leaped the small wrought iron fence and bounded high into the air, apparently hoping that Mason would catch him in his arms. Barreling into him with more than one hundred and forty pounds, the dog knocked Mason to the ground as effortlessly as if he were a child.

"Take it easy," Mason said, wrestling the ecstatic dog off him.

Bowie pressed in tightly, licking and scrubbing against him.

"That's a good boy," he said, holding him close and slipping the rope from his neck. "I've got you."

Bowie whined and lay against Mason, his tongue snaking in and out of his mouth in anticipation of more affection.

"We'll have time for that later. Right now, we've got to get out of here." He stood up and surveyed the area. The single shot from the .223 rifle hadn't drawn much attention. A woman across the street was peering out her open window, but she seemed more curious than threatening.

"Stay close," he warned.

Bowie's ears tipped back as they always did when he realized that danger was near. Then he raised his nose into the air and sniffed, attempting to sort friend from foe.

Mason led them back the way he had come, hurrying across Liberty Street. He had only made it halfway across the street before realizing that getting out was not going to be as easy as getting in. Alexus and six of her deputies rushed out from the courthouse, barely two blocks way. They turned and started walking his direction, uncertain of exactly what they were witnessing.

Mason squatted down and brought the rifle up. Two blocks was not particularly far, but shooting while unsupported at moving targets was a challenge. He took his time and fired three shots. The first shot hit the lead man in the chest, sending him to the ground. The next two missed their marks as Alexus and her henchmen raced for cover.

Engaging in a firefight against multiple attackers from the middle of the street was not something Mason could hope to win. He ducked down and darted the rest of the way across the street with Bowie now leading the way. Rather than retreat into one of the buildings, he hurried around it, running into a small alley that snaked between buildings.

A man suddenly popped around the far corner of the alley holding a .50 caliber, Desert Eagle, semi-automatic pistol. Without even bothering to aim, he began firing. With each squeeze of the trigger, the weapon belched flame and a thunderous *boom* sounded. A garbage can next to Bowie exploded as a huge slug punched a hole through it.

Mason ran towards him, shooting the Mini-14 from the shoulder. The distance was close enough that the first bullet found its mark. The man fell back, clutching his gut, the Desert Eagle dropping from his grip.

Bowie raced ahead to tear into him, but Mason called him off.

"Come on! No time!"

They ran across an empty parking lot toward a thick wooded area. A barrage of gunfire sounded from behind them, the air whistling as bullets sliced through the air. As they ducked into the trees, a volley of jacketed lead splintered tree trunks and snapped branches. Mason wheeled around and dropped prone, pulling Bowie down with him.

He looked back across the parking lot to see eight men clustered together on the other side, roughly two hundred yards away. They hurried forward, obviously figuring they had their prey on the run. Mason took careful aim with the Mini-14 carbine and squeezed the trigger. The first bullet dropped the man spearheading the attack, striking him in the center of his chest. Unlike Hollywood action movies that show people flying off their feet, the 55 grain .223 slug barely moved him at all. He simply stumbled and then pitched forward, as the bullet pierced his lung and right coronary artery.

For a moment, the other seven men seemed unsure how to react. Mason helped them make up their minds by firing two more bullets, hitting one man in the head, and a third in the shoulder. Both were out of the fight. That left five men, all of whom were now hugging the pavement.

Bowie growled and tried to stand up. Mason reached over to calm him. Like the feudal samurai battling the advent of gunpowder, the dog wouldn't last long in any kind of ranged fight. Up close and personal, he was more than any one man could handle, but he was no match for an opponent with a rifle and fifty yards between them.

"It's okay," he said in a soothing voice, petting the dog. "You'll get your chance later. Easy, boy."

Bowie slinked over and started licking the side of his face.

Mason lay there for several minutes, enjoying the dog's affection while watching the parking lot. The men on the ground slowly got their courage back, first rising to their haunches and finally to a standing position. Two of them broke off to the left, running toward Liberty Street, probably going for reinforcements. The other three continued ahead, staying close together as if that somehow ensured their safety.

Mason waited until they had taken about ten steps before popping off six more rounds. All three men fell on the ground, moaning and crying.

ॐ ॐ

Rather than continue his retreat to the southeast, Mason skirted the parking lot and ran west. He figured that Alexus would try to get her men ahead of him. By reversing direction, he hoped to once again evade the bulk of her forces.

He made it as far as the courthouse before running into trouble. As he stepped around the corner, he nearly bumped right into Alexus and four of her lieutenants. She was busy giving them instructions on where to position their men. The entire group was standing in a circle not more than twenty-five feet from him, but they were so engaged in the hunt that no one had yet to notice that their prey was standing right behind them.

Mason was pretty sure he could have ducked right back around the corner without being detected, but he stood his ground. He had done enough running. Instead, he pushed his jacket back off his shoulders and let it fall to the ground behind him. Then he set the Mini-14 down and placed his hand on butt of the Supergrade—a weapon that he had truly mastered. Bowie peeled away and began circling to their right, tail tucked and teeth bared.

The sound of Bowie's growl caused everyone to spin and face them. Two men held rifles, and the other two had long guns slung across their backs. Realizing that they would never get to them in time, they brought their hands to hover over holstered M&P 9 mm pistols. Alexus didn't have a firearm, but she wore a full-size Marine Corps Ka-bar knife on her belt. She rested her hand on the pommel, with the air of an Amazon hunter about to quarter her prey.

"Marshal," she said with a big smile, "I was beginning to think that you had outsmarted all of us."

Mason nodded to her.

"I had hoped to avoid this bloodshed, but we are where we are."

The group started to spread out as everyone sidestepped into the center of Liberty Street. People stared out windows and doors like patrons at an old western saloon.

"I suppose you're planning to shoot all five of us," she mocked.

"That depends."

"On?"

"On whether anyone wants to surrender."

Alexus snickered, and several of her men laughed, looking to one another to make sure they were all in on the joke.

"Not hardly."

"Then, yes, I'm planning to shoot all of you."

"You're a ballsy fella. I'll give you that." She cocked an eyebrow. "I wonder if you're really as good as you think you are."

"It shouldn't matter to you whether I'm that good or not."

"Why's that?"

"Because I'm going to shoot you first. Those who survive can talk about what happened next. You won't be in on the conversation."

"You're not going to shoot me," she said in a seductive voice. "You're too noble for that. I don't even have a gun." She tugged at the knife to emphasize the point.

The four men spread about five feet apart, two on either side of her. Mason played through the draw, sequencing from left to right. He would hit the two on the left, skip Alexus unless her blade was out, and then come back to pick her up as needed. Two seconds for all five tops. Another second to double up on any who needed it.

While three seconds was amazingly fast, it was also a long time to keep from getting hit in a gunfight. Mason took a deep breath and let it out slowly, calming his heart and steadying his hands. He was horribly outnumbered, but he had one distinct advantage. He wouldn't hesitate. All he needed was something to give him even the slightest edge on the draw.

"I want you men to understand something," he said.

They stared at him, each working hard to keep their hands from shaking.

"I do this for a living. I figure I've drawn a pistol more than ten thousand times." He let the words sink in. "I'm guessing that's about nine thousand more times than all of you put together."

The men exchanged glances, uncertainty beginning to shine in their eyes.

Mason continued. "I shoot 230-grain jacketed hollow-points. The good news is that, once they enter your body, they'll stay in one piece. The bad news is that the tips will mushroom until they're about the size of a dime. Given the current state of medical care, the chances of your surviving a bullet wound to the chest or abdomen are close to zero."

They looked to each other again. This time the uncertainty had been replaced by raw fear. Their questions were obvious, even if unspoken. How could he be so confident? Was he really that fast? Who would he shoot first? Were they going to die in the next few seconds?

The man furthest to the right shifted nervously, sweat trickling down his face.

"Y-you should just give up," he said, his voice shaking almost as badly as his hands.

Sensing his partner's fear, the man next to him reached over and patted him on the shoulder.

"Get it together—"

Mason pulled.

The first shot hit the man on the left directly through the heart. He never even had a chance to raise his rifle. Mason sidestepped to the left, shifted his aim, and fired at the next man over. The man was just starting to pull the M&P from its holster when the bullet tore through his liver and lodged in his right kidney. Mason skipped Alexus because, although she was drawing the knife, her feet remained fixed in place. At twenty-five feet, she would still require a little time to close the gap.

By the time he adjusted his aim, the third man had swung his rifle forward and was squeezing the trigger. Unfortunately, in the stress of the moment, he had forgotten to remove the thumb safety. He was frantically squeezing the trigger when Mason's third bullet punched out the back of his head. Mason pedaled backwards, hoping the movement and extra distance would disrupt the final man's aim. An instant before the man pulled the trigger on his M&P, Bowie's mouth latched onto his arm. The bullet chipped out a piece of asphalt, and the gun flew out of his hand as Bowie slung him to the ground.

The dog bit into the man's forearm, and he screamed as he tried to beat the animal off. With a powerful jerk of his head, Bowie shook the man's arm so hard that it dislocated both his elbow and shoulder. He screamed even louder and draped his working arm across his face, hoping to protect himself. Bowie never let up, shifting his attack from the man's arm to his throat. They wrestled for several seconds, but it was clear from the beginning that the man would not be getting back up.

Alexus stepped toward Bowie, raising her knife into the air.

Mason shifted his aim and shot her in the butt. She teetered sideways and then fell back, moaning as the knife clattered to the ground.

She rolled over and stared at him, her eyes flashing with hate.

"Why?" she cried. "You could have had everything! The town, the militia—even me!" Her voice softened, and tears leaked from her eyes. "Why?"

"Isn't it clear by now?" he said. "I never wanted anything you had to offer."

She squeezed her eyes closed, trying to shut out everything around her.

The man who had been shot through the liver cried out as he struggled to hold back the flow of dark blood.

"Help me," he moaned.

There was no help for him, only suffering. Mason brought his pistol up and shot him in the head.

"Now, what?" asked Alexus, as she used both hands to try to stem the flow of blood from her own wound. "Are you going to kill me, too?"

Bowie had finished off his opponent and was turning his attention to Alexus. The fur around his mouth was soaked with blood, and his dark eyes fixed on her without a hint of mercy. Mason whistled, motioning for him to let her be. Bowie reluctantly returned to stand at his side, never taking his eyes off Alexus.

Shouts could be heard coming from down the street. Mason turned and saw at least a dozen people coming his way. Some were part of the militia. Most were just townspeople who had witnessed the shooting. He dropped the spent magazine from his Supergrade and slapped a fresh one in place. Then he walked over to Alexus and pulled her to her feet.

"Hey," she cried, "I'm shot!"

"You'll live." He turned her to face the oncoming crowd.

They approached cautiously, unsure if the violence was over.

"Someone shoot him!" Alexus shrieked. "Shoot him, or, I swear to God, you'll hang."

"Let her go," said one of the men carrying a rifle.

Mason gestured to the badge on his belt.

"This says that I'm an official lawman for the United States of America. Which of you can say the same?"

A few people looked to one another. No one spoke.

Mason pointed to a large man in the crowd who was holding a double-barreled shotgun.

"Before all this, what did you do for a living?"

"I ran the movie theater," he said.

Mason moved on to the woman beside him.

"And you?"

"I sold houses."

He pointed to an older man next to her.

"I worked over at Old Pete's body shop," he said.

"And look where this woman has taken you," Mason said, pointing to the gallows in the adjacent cemetery. "Is that what the people of York hold dear? A hangman's noose?"

Several people began to murmur about things that had happened.

"He's right," a woman said, stepping forward. "We're not murderers. For the love of God, we shouldn't be doing this. We should be holding onto one another, rejoicing that we're even alive."

Several people nodded and nearly every weapon lowered.

"While I understand your desire to instill order," continued Mason, "it can never come at the expense of justice. Take your weapons home. Secure them in case they should ever be needed. Now is the time to build something better."

Alexus struggled free of Mason's grip and stumbled toward the crowd. A steady trickle of blood ran down her leg.

"Somebody shoot this bastard. I mean it!"

A deafening blast rang out, lifting Alexus off her feet. A huge red spray puffed out behind her. The owner of the movie theater had discharged both barrels into her. He looked around defiantly at the horrified faces in the crowd.

"She hung my son-in-law for stealing food. That boy was nineteen years old, may he rest in peace." He turned to face Mason. "I'll go quietly if you want to arrest me, Marshal."

Mason stared down at what was left of Alexus and shook his head.

"No," he said quietly. "She had it coming."

❧ ❦

By the time Mason retrieved his M4 rifle as well as the cans of ammunition that the militia had taken, nearly the entire town of York had gathered in front of Rose Hill Cemetery. The gallows had been dismantled in a move as symbolic as the tearing down of the Berlin Wall. People took turns standing on what remained of the stage, addressing the crowd. Promises of better access to food and water supplies and of a more just society were common themes.

Mason stood beside his truck and watched the event with a sense of pride. Unlike the town of Boone, which had been threatened from outsiders, York had fallen prey to predators from within. With Alexus's iron fist now broken, they were rethinking their path forward. Where they would end up, he couldn't say. Perhaps they had learned a hard lesson about imparting too much power to any one individual. If nothing else, he hoped they now understood that freedoms were easy to surrender but hard to reclaim.

Bowie leaned out the passenger side window, apparently afraid to let Mason out of his sight.

"Are you about ready to get out of here?"

The dog paced back and forth across the cab of the truck, anticipating their departure.

Mason swung the door open and climbed in.

"Let's see if we can get to Glynco without any more bloodshed."

President Glass carefully read the two-page report as she spread a collection of photos across her desk like a photo shoot for the swimsuit edition of *Sports Illustrated*. These photos, however, were not of voluptuous women in G-string bathing suits. Instead, they showed scenes of bloody carnage that could only be stomached when presented in black and white. General Carr was standing in front of the desk, his face red and his brow damp with sweat.

"What the hell happened?" she demanded.

"I honestly don't know," he said. "I gave orders to minimize casualties. Somehow those orders were either misunderstood or simply disregarded."

"Disregarded?"

"Apparently, there were rumors circulating that this group had been responsible for several brutal attacks on US service men and women."

"And was that true?"

"I don't think so."

"This was supposed to be about delivering a message. This," she shoved some of the photos across the desk toward him, "is not a message. It's a goddamn massacre!"

"Yes, ma'am."

"How many did they kill?"

"Battle assessments indicate at least fifty dead."

She closed her eyes.

"Women and children, too?"

"Women, yes. No children."

She took a deep breath and let it out slowly, piling the papers back into a neat stack.

"I want these photos destroyed. No copies kept anywhere. Are we clear?"

"Yes, ma'am."

She waited, but the general didn't turn to leave.

"Do you have something else?"

He considered his words carefully before speaking.

"As you know, the relief supplies were tagged with RF identifiers."

"Of course. That's how we located these people in the first place. Oh, God, don't tell me there was a mistake." Her gut twisted into a knot.

"No, ma'am. There was no mistake. We positively identified that the stolen supplies were onsite."

"What then?"

"While pursuing the enemy, the soldiers in one of the gunships picked up an unusual RF signal."

She looked at him, waiting for the point.

"Ma'am, I want to be clear that there's a chance that this could simply be an anomaly in the technology. We're double-checking that now."

"What are you talking about, General? Get to it."

"They inadvertently picked up the distinct RF signature of someone who we thought was dead."

"Who?"

He took a deep breath.

"Your daughter, Madam President."

"*What!*" She leapt to her feet, her reading glasses falling to the desk.

"I have no other explanation. The RF signature was uniquely coded to her transponder."

President Glass's eyes filled with tears.

"It must be a mistake. It has to be. They told me—"

"Yes, ma'am, I'm aware of the crash reports. But the aircrew sat for several minutes confirming the signal. I don't see how it could be a mistake."

"Could—" she started, choking on the words. "Could someone have gotten the chip, or . . . her body?"

"That was my first thought as well. But the soldiers reported seeing a young girl fleeing the battle."

President Glass slowly sat back down, suddenly feeling lightheaded.

"Was she alone?"

"No, ma'am. She was with two other people, a man and a woman."

"She was their prisoner?" The implications of such imprisonment were too painful for her to even consider.

"I can't say for sure, but I don't think so."

"Why not?"

"It appears that Samantha was armed."

President Glass shook her head in disbelief.

"That's impossible," she said with a nervous smile. When he didn't offer anything more, she said, "Armed?"

"Yes, ma'am, with a rifle of some sort."

General Carr reached into his jacket and pulled out a single photo. He laid it on the desk before her. It showed a woman and a young girl struggling to open the front door of a large house. The girl's face was angled away from the camera, but her height and build were about right for Samantha.

President Glass stared at the photo for a long time, tipping it from side to side as if that might help her to get a better view. Then she gently touched the young girl's face with her fingertips.

"It's her, isn't it?" she said.

"I think so, yes."

As impossible as it seemed, Samantha was alive. Not only had she lived through the helicopter crash two weeks earlier, she had survived the horrific massacre initiated by her own mother's hand. President Glass closed her eyes, and tears spilled out the corners.

"We have to find her," she whispered.

"Yes, ma'am. I've already pulled together an elite team of operatives. They'll take to the air within the hour. Assuming that she hasn't moved, they should have her in hand shortly."

She took a deep breath, trying to steady her voice. But as the words started to come out, she couldn't keep from crying.

"General, do whatever it takes. You find my baby girl."

The night air was warm and sticky, leaving Tanner covered with a thin layer of sweat even before he stepped out into the darkness. Four frightened men watched as he climbed down from the brown United Parcel Service delivery truck.

"Let's go over it again," he said, looking at Callaway.

The professor nodded. "Bob and I are going to use ladders to climb onto the roof of the furniture store. We'll wait until exactly midnight to start firing."

"That's when Joe and I will light up the cars," said another man.

"And once they're on fire?" asked Tanner.

"I'll run to the south end of the rail station. Joe will go to the north. We'll do our best to shoot at them as we move."

"Remember," cautioned Tanner, "it doesn't matter whether you hit anything. We just need for the soldiers to hunker down and focus on the street." He patted one of the large UPS truck tires. "I'll come in by the railroad, lights out, and as quiet as this beast will allow. Then I'll set the fuse and run like hell. Keep in mind that, when Timothy McVeigh blew a bomb this size, it collapsed most of a large federal building. If you're within a couple hundred yards when this thing goes off, you won't walk away from it."

Everyone looked at him, shifting their feet around as they struggled to rein in nerves.

"Why are we doing this horrible thing?" asked Tanner.

For a moment no one said anything. Then the professor spoke up.

"To protect our children."

"And our wives," added Bob.

"And to punish them for what they've done," said Joe.

"People are going to die tonight," said Tanner. "But, by God, they deserve it. Don't you forget that when you have those bastards in your sights."

❧ ❧

Tanner tilted his watch so that the moonlight illuminated the face. It was less than a minute until midnight. He climbed into the UPS truck and waited. There were countless things that could go wrong with his plan. For one, the bomb might simply not go off. The professor wasn't an explosives expert, and as he had pointed out, there were countless subtleties that could cause it not to work. The soldiers might also see or hear Tanner coming and riddle the truck with bullets before he could get close enough. Or, even if everything went according to plan, the soldiers might decide to go on the offensive and move away from the railway station before the bomb detonated.

He took a breath. There was nothing new here. Victory or defeat waited on the other side of every fight.

A shot rang out. And then another.

It had begun.

He popped the truck into low gear and eased it forward, straddling the railroad tracks. The night was dark, but the moonlight lit the tracks well enough to keep the truck centered. The few times he drifted too far one way or the other, the tires scrubbed against the track, telling him to correct his position.

Two bright explosions flashed several hundred feet to the right, as cars burst into flames. So far, so good. The gunfire became more rapid—soldiers returning fire on the professor's position. A fifty-caliber machine gun began spiting heavy rounds, reverberating through the night like a sledge hammer pounding on a cement slab. He and Bob wouldn't last long on the roof. Hell, the roof wouldn't last long. More small arms fire sounded, coming from nearly every direction now. Tanner hoped that it was from his team getting into position, not from soldiers who had ventured out on the hunt.

The long structure of the railway station came into view as he crept around the bend. Spotlights from vehicles shone out onto the street and toward the various points of attack, but none faced back onto the tracks. It was too far away for him to see if soldiers had set up defensive positions behind the building. If they had, he would know it soon enough.

Like a lone caboose, the UPS truck slowly inched up behind the train station. When he was in position, Tanner killed the engine and tossed the keys into the weeds. Then he climbed out with his shotgun in hand and crept around to the back of the truck. The rear of the station was dark, but it sounded like all hell was breaking loose out front. Loud explosions shook nearby buildings as soldiers cut loose with rocket-propelled grenades.

He shoved open the back door and inspected the bomb. It consisted of four parts: the fertilizer-fuel mixture, which stunk to high heaven, a three-foot length of homemade detcord, a shotgun shell that had been configured to act as a blasting cap, and a roll of epoxy-coated twine.

The professor had said that the idea was simple enough. The twine would bring the flame, which would set off the blasting cap. That, in turn, would ignite the detcord. The resultant shock wave, from which, would get the fertilizer mixture to explode. Yeah, thought Tanner, simple.

He gave a short salute to the bomb.

"Don't you fail me."

He picked up the roll of twine and routed it through the handle of the back door to secure it in place. Then he started unspooling it as he slowly backed down the train tracks. When he got about fifty feet away, he knelt down, cut the twine, and lit the poor man's fuse. The epoxy sizzled for a moment and then ignited. The flame slowly spread down the length of twine. Tanner had no idea how long it would take for the fire to reach the truck, or whether it would even make it there at all. All he knew for sure was that, if it made it, and if the professor's calculations were right, there was going to be one hell of an explosion.

With nothing left to do, he turned and ran.

❧ ❧

When nothing happened for four whole minutes, Tanner became convinced that something had gone wrong. There had been no explosion, not even a simple gasoline fire. That could only mean that the fuse had burned out somewhere along the way. Gunfire still sounded from the direction of the train station, but it was slowly tapering off. The only option left was to gather the girls and get out of town as quickly as possible.

He had just rounded the corner to Professor Callaway's street when the explosion finally went off. Even from nearly a quarter of a mile away, the blast was powerful enough to blow out nearby windows and knock him off balance. He looked back and saw a huge orange fireball swell up into the sky, surrounded by a plume of smoke and dust. Bits and pieces of the train station, trees, and cars flew through the air, only to rain back down all across town.

Tanner ducked behind a large pickup truck, waiting for the hailstorm of debris to subside. The burnt and twisted shape of an engine block skittered down the street toward him, as chunks of painted yellow boards smashed into roofs and cars. When it finally quieted, he stood up and looked in the direction of the train station. All he could see was a faint orange glow lighting up the sky.

He needed to witness the destruction firsthand to know whether the fight was over or just beginning. Darting across the closest yard, he jumped over a small chain-link fence and ran into the alley beyond. He turned north, racing in the direction of the train station.

Before he had even gone two blocks, Professor Callaway came hobbling down the alley toward him, his face covered in a layer of dirt and gunpowder. His pants had a large hole in them, and blood was soaking the fabric from the knee down. He was barely recognizable as the mild-mannered father whom they had met only hours earlier.

"Well?" asked Tanner. "Is it done?"

The professor carefully lowered himself to sit on the ground.

"I've never seen anything like that."

"Yeah, but did it take out the train station?"

"That and more. The only thing left of the station is that old engine the tourists used to come to see."

"It's over then? The soldiers are dead." The last part was more of a statement than a question.

He nodded. "God rest their souls."

Tanner put his hand on Professor Callaway's shoulder.

"We fight to win. There's no other way."

"I know," he said, looking back at the column of rising smoke. "My worry now is the fire. Without running water, we'll have to resort to bucket brigades and portable water trucks. We don't want to lose the other half of our town."

"Don't worry, Professor. Unlike a gun battle, I suspect you won't have any trouble finding volunteers willing to save their homes."

❧ ❧

A cloud of thick white smoke still engulfed most of Hendersonville as Tanner loaded up the Escalade. Professor Callaway had been gracious enough to provide him with a few days' supply of food and water. If all went well, they would be at Tanner's cabin within hours and wouldn't need to use it. But as they were learning, the path between points A and B was not always a direct one.

Tanner knew what was coming even before Libby stepped out of the house with her paper and pen in hand. As she approached, he nodded to her.

"You're staying, right?"

She smiled and scribbled on the paper.

*It's okay?*

"Of course," he said. "I think the professor and his daughter will be lucky to have you here."

*Rachel is a wonderful little girl. She needs a mother. And the professor is injured.*

"Darlin', you do what you need to. Sam and I will push on."

*You saved my life.* Tears welled up in her eyes. *I don't know how to say thank you.* She underlined "thank you" several times.

Tanner leaned over and kissed her on the cheek.

"Given the life I lead, it's good that I had the chance to balance out my karma a little. It doesn't put me in the black, but maybe it moves me a little closer to being out of the red."

Libby leaned in and cupped his face with both hands.

"Thank you." She struggled to voice the words, and they were distorted and throaty. Then she leaned in and kissed him on the lips, a long, warm kiss that said thank you in ways that words or paper could not.

Tanner enjoyed the soft press of her lips, but they were gone all too soon. The sight of Samantha hurrying out the door with her backpack brought him back to reality. Libby wasn't his. She never had been. But he had his own family, of sorts.

Samantha tossed her pack into the backseat of the Escalade, but before she could climb in, Libby ran around the vehicle and embraced her.

"Okay, then," Samantha said, leaning away. "We'll be seeing you."

Libby kissed her on the forehead and then reluctantly let her go. Samantha quickly hopped into the Escalade and closed the door. She didn't roll down the window.

Tanner looked over and saw Professor Callaway and his daughter standing in the doorway of their home. The lower half of his leg was wrapped in a long white bandage. Tanner nodded to them and climbed into the SUV.

As he started the engine, he looked over at Samantha.

"It's just you and me again, kid. You cool with that?"

She tilted her head as if giving the question serious consideration.

"Yeah," she said, "I'm cool with that."

Mason drove south on Highway 321 for more than a hundred and fifty miles. The route was a bit off the beaten path, but it allowed him to bypass all of the major cities, including Columbia and Savannah. It also kept him off the interstates, which were both heavily congested and becoming more dangerous by the day. He passed through an endless string of small South Carolina towns, including Chester, Winesboro, and Denmark. Unlike the town of York, the other small communities had yet to organize and provide any services to their survivors.

As he got closer to the Georgia border, he switched over to Highway 301 outside the town of Allendale. The community had been in decline for more than a decade, and even before the pandemic, only boasted a population of four thousand. The entire town, end to end, was no more than a single mile wide and that counted a few houses that had long since been abandoned to four-legged critters.

The sun was high in the sky when Mason slowly rolled into Allendale, like a gunslinger wandering the badlands. Bowie was sleeping in the truck bed, completely disinterested in yet another lifeless town. A large sign for the Executive Inn pointed off to the right. The rotting corpse of a man lay draped around the base of the pole, like he was waiting for a bus that would never come. An eighteen-wheeled tractor-trailer was parked in the middle of Dorr's Ferry Highway, a two-lane road that acted as the town's single thoroughfare. The truck's rear doors were swung open wide, and the only thing left in the back was a push broom leaning against the wall.

Mason steered his truck around the tractor-trailer to see if anyone was in the cab. It was empty, but the driver's door was ajar, like he had just stepped away and planned to return. The truck was parked directly in front of an old white cinderblock building. A rusty neon sign, like that of a vintage movie theater, stood by the road featuring a large red anchor and a lobster with a top hat and monocle. Perhaps, many years before, it had been a local favorite for those with a taste for seafood. Now, however, it appeared lifeless and rundown, like countless other small town businesses that suffered when tourists migrated to the interstates.

An ice machine and a black cast iron smoker sat out front. Soft white smoke puffed out from the smoker. Mason pulled into the driveway and stepped out of his truck. Despite something cooking only a few feet away, the stench of decomposing bodies eclipsed any odor of the food. The putrid smell of death and decay were ever-present nearly all across the country. It was like living with a giant industrial paper plant as a next-door neighbor. Mason guessed that it would take months for bodies to degrade enough to fully release all their noxious fluids and gases. Until then, every corner of the planet would stink of mankind's demise.

Bowie sat up and looked over the edge of the truck bed, yawning.

"Go check it out," Mason said, gesturing toward the defunct restaurant.

Bowie climbed down and slowly walked toward the building, his head hung low as if being forced to plow a farmer's field. Mason followed behind him, his hand on the Supergrade. Both were equally startled when an old woman suddenly appeared on the other side of the screen door to the restaurant.

The woman was short and squat, and had more wrinkles than Iron Eyes Cody. She wore a plain denim apron, an old pair of house shoes, and dark-rimmed glasses.

"What have we here?" she said.

"Afternoon, ma'am."

Still unnerved by her sudden appearance, Bowie backed away, growling lightly.

"That's a fine dog you got there."

Mason motioned for him to stop growling. Bowie quieted but never fully relaxed.

"Are you here by yourself?" he asked.

She eyed him suspiciously.

"Who wants to know?"

He showed her his badge.

"I'm one of the good guys."

"A lawman?"

"Yes, ma'am."

She snorted. "My boys will be home soon enough. Until then, you might as well come on in outta the sun." She held open the screen door.

He walked toward her, glancing over at the smoker.

"Cooking up some lunch?"

"Sure am," she said with a broad smile. "We had a trucker roll in with some fresh meat two days ago."

"And he just left the truck?" he asked, looking back at the eighteen-wheeler.

"We traded for everything he had. Next thing we knew, he done took off in that little sports car that used to belong to Doc Perkins."

He nodded. "Do you want some help moving it out of the road?"

"Nah," she said. "We figure it gives people a reason to stop and say hello. You're welcome to stick around and enjoy some lunch, if you like."

He nodded his appreciation. Most of Mason's meals came from cans or pouches, and the thought of a freshly cooked meal was enough to start his mouth watering.

As he stepped through the door, Mason found that the inside of the restaurant had been converted to a residence, and it looked like the transformation had occurred a long time ago. The living room opened up into a large kitchen that still had a commercial stainless steel dishwasher, a ten-burner gas stove, and an old Philco refrigerator that may well have been purchased to protect its owner from an atomic bomb.

"I'm Flo," the old woman said, walking back into the kitchen where she had been busy chopping carrots on a cutting board. She pulled down a couple of drinking glasses.

"I'm Mason, and that's Bowie."

Bowie stared through the screen door, whining to come in.

"Make yourself comfortable," she said, motioning for Mason to take a seat on an old couch.

The couch was covered with stains and cigarette burns, but he sat anyway. Southerners prided themselves on their hospitality, and recipients were expected to play a part in that dance as well.

"Where you headed?"

"Marshal center in Brunswick. Have you and your boys lived here long?"

"Better part of thirty years. Bought this place for a nickel on the dollar—"

A man suddenly screamed from a back room.

Mason jumped to his feet, his hand going to the grip of his pistol.

Flo didn't even look up.

"Quiet down, you ol' fool!" she hollered. Before Mason could ask, she said, "My husband. He's got the pox. Sufferin' real bad. But knowin' my luck, he's gonna make it."

The man's scream turned into a plea for mercy.

"Just kill me!" he yelled. "Kill me!"

Flo handed Mason a glass half-full of a dark orange liquid.

"What is it?" he asked, still unsettled by the sudden outburst.

"Just the best darn mash you've ever tasted."

He sniffed it.

"It smells like peaches."

She laughed. "That's cause it's made with peaches right outta the back-yard. Go on, give it a go."

He took a sip. It had a little bite, but as far as moonshine went, it was right up there. He drank a little more.

"Good enough for a Yankee?" she asked with a warm smile.

He nodded, taking another sip.

She picked up the butcher knife and continued chopping carrots.

"We got nothin' else to do 'round here but make the mash."

The screaming from the back room subsided, replaced by a soft sobbing.

"Shouldn't you check on him?" he asked.

"My boys and I, we keep him clean and fed. Can't nothin' else be done. You're welcome to look in on him if you like. Just gotta watch the pox, is all."

Mason shook his head.

"I don't know what I could do for him."

"Ain't nothin' you can do. Either he'll live or he won't."

Mason took another drink and returned to the couch. Bowie suddenly started barking as he moved away from the door to let two men enter the house. They were both well over six feet tall and probably weighed six hundred pounds all told. One wore military fatigues that were a size too small, and the other, a pair of white painter's pants and a black AC/DC t-shirt. Given their sizes and striking resemblance, they reminded Mason of Tweedledee and Tweedledum from *Alice in Wonderland*.

They seemed alarmed to see him in the house. One raised a hatchet that was already in hand, and the other reached for a large knife hanging on his belt.

"Unh-unh," said Flo. "No need for that, boys. This here's Mason. He's just passin' through. Show him a little hospitality, already."

Mason had already gotten to his feet, but he kept his hand clear of his weapon. This was their home after all. Bowie was back at the screen door, giving a deep warning growl to the two men.

Tweedledee turned to his mother.

"You give him some of the good mash?"

"I did," she said, smiling. "We ain't gonna be selfish with our guests."

Her words were slow and slurred, like they were being played back at half speed. Mason swayed to his left and then his right, unable to maintain his balance. Flo and her two sons smiled and stared at him, their faces swelling and shrinking like reflections in a fun house mirror.

"You okay, Marshal?" Tweedledum said with a chuckle. His voice was slow and deep.

Mason knew that he was about to fall. As he felt himself teeter forward and then back, he drew his Supergrade and began firing. He saw the first bullet blow the top of Tweedledum's head off. The next four bullets were all shot blind, as he fell into the darkness.

&#8190; &#8190;

Mason woke to find himself lying on the couch, with Bowie's huge sticky tongue sliding across his face. He tried to push the dog away, but his arms refused to move.

"I'm okay," he mumbled, unable to get his mouth to fully form the words.

The dog didn't slow its incessant licking.

Mason tried to sit up. All he managed to do was tip over on the couch so that his face was pressed into the dirty cushion. It did, at least, stop Bowie from continuing the tongue bath. Mason rotated his head and blinked a few times. The room spun counterclockwise in a slow, circling motion. When it finally stopped, he saw the body of Flo's youngest son lying halfway out the front door. The top of his head was completely missing, and blood was splattered across the screen like someone had thrown out a jar of spaghetti sauce.

His older brother lay to his left in a huge puddle of blood. He had a bullet hole in his left shoulder, but that was clearly not the cause of death. The man's left leg had been chewed almost completely off. From the tremendous amount of blood, Mason could only guess that his femoral artery had been severed. As for Flo, he didn't see her anywhere.

He tried to sit back up and, with a great deal of effort, managed to slowly right himself. Bowie moved to sit across his lap, spanning the entire length of the couch. Over the next ten minutes, Mason slowly regained control of his limbs. It started with the major muscles first and slowly extended all the way to fingers and toes. He sat there for several more minutes letting his vision clear, petting Bowie. The dog's tongue licked in and out of his mouth, and his hind leg bounced up and down as he relished in the attention.

When Mason finally went to push him off so that he could stand, Bowie whined in pain. He pulled his hand back to find bright red blood on his fingertips. Mason gently slid Bowie off his lap, making him lie on his side so that he could get a better look. There was a gash on the dog's right rear leg.

"Stay here," he said. "I'll be back."

Mason struggled to his feet. The world was no longer spinning, but he still felt like he'd had one too many pints of Dogfish Head ale. He carefully leaned down and picked up his Supergrade off the floor, replacing the partially spent magazine with a fresh one. Keeping an eye on his surroundings in case Flo or someone else decided to show up, he went back out to the truck and retrieved his first aid kit. When he came back into the restaurant, Bowie was stretched out on the couch with his eyes closed.

Mason poured hydrogen peroxide over his hands and shook them dry. Then he flushed Bowie's wound, washing away the blood and soaking the fur around it. The cut was clean and didn't appear to have sliced into the muscle. It looked painful to be sure, but not in any way debilitating. The biggest risk was infection. He blew on the wound until the hydrogen peroxide evaporated. Then he withdrew a needle and small roll of black suture from his kit, coating both with the peroxide.

"This is going to hurt," he said, threading the needle.

Bowie's injured leg twitched as if he knew what was coming.

Mason pinched the wound together and began stitching. Bowie whined a little, but he never once growled. When Mason was finished, he smeared a thick layer of antibiotic ointment over the area. Then he laid a non-adhesive pad over the wound and wrapped it with a gauze roll, taping down the end.

"You'll live," he said, leaning over and kissing Bowie on his head. Mason couldn't help but feel emotion swelling up inside him. If it weren't for Bowie, he would almost certainly be dead. "Did you get the old broad, too?" he choked out.

Bowie stared at him, tilting his head sideways.

He sighed. "One day, I'm going to have to teach you how to talk."

Mason stood and made his way toward the kitchen. Even before he entered the room, he saw Flo lying on the tile floor, her face resting in a pool of blood. She looked as dead as her sons, but just to be sure, he put a bullet in the back of her head.

The man in the back room screamed again.

Bowie crawled off the couch and hobbled over to Mason, keeping his rear leg raised a few inches off the floor. He tugged on Mason's pant leg, trying to lead him out of the restaurant.

"Not yet," he said, patting the dog on its side. "Let's see what this is all about."

Bowie released him but started whining in protest. Mason walked slowly to the bedroom door, twisted the knob, and pushed it in.

A man was lying on an old brass bed. One arm and one leg were tied to the bedposts with electrical cords. The other two limbs were missing. The leg had been cut off at the knee. A bloody sheet was wrapped around the stump and strapped tight with a belt. The man's arm had been removed at the elbow, and it, too, was wrapped in bloody bed linen and bound by a makeshift tourniquet. Strips of the man's face had been sliced off, as had sections of his scalp and shoulders. One of his eyes was missing, the vacant socket stuffed with an old dishrag.

For a full five seconds, Mason stood in the doorway, unable to move or even look away. Blood rushed to his face, and he fought to keep from vomiting as the horror threatened to overwhelm him.

The man was conscious and staring at Mason with his one remaining eye.

"Please," he begged. "Please kill me."

Mason felt like he was moving in slow motion as he drew his pistol and fired.

ॐ ॐ

Having served in two wars as an Army Ranger, Mason had been exposed to several forms of torture, including the military's current favorite, waterboarding. He didn't know whether covering a man's face with rags and pouring water over them was as effective as using a car battery to hotwire his testicles, but what he did know was that, once witnessed, torture was not something easily forgotten. The image of the man lying on the bed in Flo's home, like a pig on the cutting block, was something that threatened to haunt him for the rest of his life.

He had seen countless horrors on the battlefield, but none worse than cannibalism. When he was just a young soldier, his commander had told him that the way to keep from being overwhelmed by the horror was to remember that life was experienced in moments, some comforting and some terrifying. The good ones, he said, were worth reminiscing over, but others needed to be spit upon and buried in dark graves. Such was the case with Flo's hungry house of horrors. He would lock the memory away so deep that it would never again be allowed to touch his spirit. If ever he did find himself dwelling upon it, he would remind himself that Flo and her boys had been put down like the animals they were. While a fitting end was not enough to right the wrongs, it was sometimes all that could be achieved.

Satisfied with his place in the world once again, he reached over and rubbed Bowie's belly. The dog gave a high-pitched yawn as it sprawled out on the seat beside him. The bandage on his leg was still white, which meant that the knife wound had already stopped bleeding. With a little care, he would be fine.

"I guess I owe you my life," he said, patting the dog's side.

Bowie stared up at Mason with one eye open, as if weighing whether his praise warranted opening the other one.

"I never told you this. But when I found you in that convenience store, I had this feeling that you'd been waiting for me, that our futures were somehow connected. Crazy, right?"

Bowie slid his massive frame closer and raised his head to rest it on Mason's lap. He had made his decision. Both eyes were now closed.

"Anyway, I'm glad we found one another. I saved you from the gallows, and you saved me from the dinner plate. When we do finally fall, I suspect we'll do so with empty magazines and the taste of blood in our mouths."

"Not to be rude," Samantha said, wrinkling her nose, "but you stink."

"You're no bed of roses yourself, Sunshine."

She sniffed of her shirt.

"We need to get cleaned up. If my mom saw me like this, she wouldn't even recognize me."

"We can take showers at the cabin," said Tanner. "It will be like a five-star hotel compared to what we've had lately."

She looked out the window. The hills were slowly growing in size as they pushed closer to the Blue Ridge Mountains.

"How much farther?"

"A couple of hours. It's a straight shot from here." As if on cue, a light started flashing on the Escalade's dashboard. "Looks like we're going to need fuel before then. That means we'll have to stop in Boone either to find gas or switch to another car."

"No more stops, please."

"I suppose we could walk the rest of the way."

She sighed. "Fine. We can find gas, but let's keep this car." She patted the seat. "It's pretty nice."

Tanner ran his fingers across the smooth leather steering wheel.

"Agreed."

"What do you think happened to the people who bought it?"

He shrugged. "My guess is they discovered new priorities. Instead of spa treatments and Gucci handbags, they're probably out looking for cans of beans and bottles of water. Assuming they're not dead, of course."

She turned to look back out her window and up into the sky.

"At least we seem to have lost the helicopters."

"For now, maybe. But with that bug in your arm, they'll eventually find us. We'll have to figure out some way to cut it out."

The concerned expression on her face said more than words ever could.

"Did you say 'cut it out?'"

"Just a figure of speech."

"Cut it out is not a figure of speech. It's something people say when they're going to cut something out."

Tanner started laughing and couldn't stop. He wasn't sure if it was Samantha's dead pan delivery or just the right time to let go of the truck-load of stress he had been carrying around. Either way, it felt good. He finally rolled down the window and let the fresh air calm him.

"You okay?" she asked, eyeing him warily.

He smiled and patted her on the leg.

"Just enjoying the journey."

"Do you mean that for real? Or is that some kind of Buddhist thing?"

"A little of both."

She studied him for a moment.

"What?" he said.

"I was just thinking that we're doing all right—you know."

"We're not dead yet, and it isn't for lack of trying. I guess that's something."

"Do you remember when you asked what Libby wrote on her note to me?"

"Yeah, I remember."

She pulled it out of her pocket and handed it to him.

He read it quietly to himself.

*Trust him. He's earned it.*

Tanner smiled and handed it back to her.

She put it back in her pocket and turned to look out the window, pondering things she couldn't put into words. Samantha never knew it, but the smile never left Tanner's face as he watched her reflection in the window.

༄ ❧

By the time Boone came into view, it was nearly three in the afternoon. The sun was hot and the sky nearly cloudless. They drove in from the south on Highway 321, and one of the first things they saw was a sign for the Watauga County Hospital.

"I wonder . . ." he said.

"What?"

"Do you think they're up and running?"

"Why would we need a hospital?"

"No reason," he said, glancing down at her. "But let's check it out anyway."

She cut her eyes at him with suspicion.

He turned the Escalade up Deerfield Road toward the hospital. They passed a woman and two young boys holding hands, walking toward the hospital like they didn't have a care in the world.

"Did you see that?" asked Samantha. "There are people out walking. Not running or hiding, but actually walking."

He nodded. "They seem to be doing a little better here."

"Are you kidding? The last town we were in had people sacrificing chickens."

"Good point," he said, turning into the parking lot. He grabbed the shotgun and quickly checked it.

"Do you really think you'll need that here?" she asked.

"Would you rather we go in unarmed?"

She thought about it for a moment.

"No," she said, grabbing her own rifle. "We should be careful."

He smiled. His padawan was learning.

As they stepped from the Escalade, a heavyset man wearing priest's vestments came out of the hospital. He had a jovial face, with puffy red cheeks and a white ring of hair around his scalp, like a halo that had been cut one size too large. He eyed Tanner warily.

"Hello," he said, extending a hand, "I'm Father Paul. I'm not sure that we've met."

"I'm Tanner," he said, shaking the man's hand. "This is Sam."

The priest smiled and bent over to look at her.

"And how are you, young lady?"

"I stink, but not as bad as him," she answered.

"I see," he said, standing back up. "Well then, I have some good news."

"What's that?" asked Tanner.

"We have running water here in Boone. A bit of a rarity, I think."

Both Tanner and Samantha were genuinely surprised. Boone was the first place they had been to that had running water.

"You guys must not have been hit as hard as the rest of the country," said Tanner.

"On the contrary," he said. "Just days ago, we were fighting for our lives. Gunfire, explosions, the whole nine yards. It was all very hairy indeed."

Tanner looked around. Everything seemed peaceful enough now.

"Well, it looks like you won," he said, starting past the man.

"That we did, thanks to Marshal Raines."

Tanner stopped in his tracks and spun back to face the priest.

"What did you just say?"

Alarmed by his sudden change in tone, Father Paul took a step back.

"I said that we won our town back with the help of Marshal Raines."

"Isn't that—" started Samantha, looking up at Tanner.

A broad smile came over his face.

"You know the marshal then?" the priest said, obviously uncertain if he was in the company of friend or foe. "I should tell you that he's become a bit of a folk hero around here."

Tanner extended his hand again.

"Let's start over, Father. I'm Tanner. Tanner Raines."

❧ ❦

Once it became clear that Tanner was Mason's father, the priest immediately ushered them into the hospital to meet Ava, Mason's girlfriend and one of the town's few remaining doctors. They spent the next hour talking about Mason, the town's battle against Rommel, and how the city council had helped to get Boone back up and running.

The town now had two huge storage tanks full of water, a soup kitchen that offered evening meals, and a single gas station that provided fuel to verified residents. The gasoline was tightly rationed to prevent abuse, but it allowed people to transport supplies and conduct rudimentary business. The police force was operational as well, led by two brave deputies who had fought in the big gunfight. Retired Police Chief Blue was no longer on the force, but there was talk of electing him as mayor of the small community.

The only part of the conversation that alarmed Tanner was when Ava mentioned that some of the people infected with the virus had also come to the aid of the town during the firefight.

"You must have a different breed than the ones we've seen," he said. "Every single one we've encountered was mean as hell."

Samantha nodded vigorously. "It's true. They just about ate Tanner in the JC Penney."

"As big as you are," Ava said, patting him on the arm, "that would have taken the better part of a week, I imagine."

Tanner grinned. Ava was not only beautiful; she was fun.

"If you don't mind," she said, gathering up supplies, "I'd like to take a look at the cuts on your face. Was that from fighting with them?"

He touched the stitches on his forehead and the scab on the side of his face.

"More or less."

Samantha leaned forward, eager to explain.

"The first cut happened when he jumped into the slime water. The second one was from the teeth of a zombie. But don't worry, he won't turn into one. We've been through that already."

Ava nodded, carefully cleaning the wounds with gauze and Betadine.

"It sounds like you two have had quite the adventure."

"Everything from secret agents to wild dogs," Samantha said with an air of pride.

"Wow, that does sound exciting." Ava finished by smearing a little antibiotic salve on Tanner's cuts. Then she turned to face Samantha. "What about you, young lady? Any injuries to report?"

Samantha looked herself over but didn't find anything more than a few scrapes.

"To be honest," she said, "I think I'm more careful than him."

"There is one thing you might be able to help us with," said Tanner, looking over at Samantha.

She shot a warning look at him, obviously hoping that he wouldn't say it.

"Sam here has a tracker embedded under her skin." He turned to her. "Show her, Sam."

She reluctantly held out her arm and rubbed her fingers over the small bump on her skin. Ava and Father Paul both studied it.

"What in the world is that?" asked the priest.

"Like I said, it's some kind of radio tracker. It allows people to find her, people that we'd rather avoid."

"I've see things like this in animals, but never people," said Ava. "Why would anyone put this in a child?"

Tanner looked over at Samantha.

"Want to tell them?"

She shrugged. "I guess."

"We don't have to," he said, sensing her reluctance.

"No, no, it's okay." She looked up at Ava. "My mom's the President."

"President of . . . ?"

"You know . . . bum bum babum bum babum babum babum bum."

"Was that supposed to be 'Hail to the Chief'?" Tanner asked, laughing.

"You try it. It's not that easy."

"Wait, wait," Ava said, holding up her hands. "Are you saying that you're the daughter of the President of the United States?"

Samantha nodded. "You'd probably recognize me if I wasn't so dirty. Before I met him, my mom made me take baths every day, sometimes twice."

"My word," said Father Paul, clapping his hands together. "Tanner, the Lord has really placed a great responsibility on your shoulders."

"Father, you have no idea."

"Hey, I got that!" Samantha said, pushing him lightly.

Tanner turned back to Ava.

"What do you think about the tracker? Can you remove it?"

"Well, sure." She pinched the skin around it. "It's just a subdermal implant. It wouldn't take but a minute to remove." She looked at Samantha. "What do you think? Should we take it out?"

Samantha wrung her hands together as she considered the question. "Will it hurt?"

"Not much. I have a local anesthesia that I can give you. The shot will pinch a little, but only for a second. Then I'll make a tiny cut, and it should pop right out. After that, I'll use a drop of Dermabond to glue your skin back together."

Samantha perked up. "No stitches?"

"I don't think they'd be necessary. In a few weeks, you won't even know it was ever there."

"And you could do it? I mean, you have real credentials and all. You're not a horse doctor or something?"

Ava laughed. "Do you want to see my license to practice medicine?"

Samantha thought about it for a moment before answering.

"Yes," she said, nodding. "I think I would."

స్త్రీ శ్రీ

Tanner felt powerful emotions stir as he turned up the dirt driveway to his cabin. He hadn't been home since before his incarceration, and memories of times gone by with his ex-wife and son nearly overwhelmed him. Good times. Bad times. Life's moments that were not to be forgotten.

He pulled through the metal gate and proceeded on up toward the cabin. The first thing he noticed was a bright red Hummer sitting out front. For a fleeting moment, he wondered if Mason might have returned from Glynco. Or perhaps someone else had discovered the cabin and taken refuge. He parked the Escalade about fifty yards away and grabbed his shotgun.

"Sit tight while I check it out."

Samantha picked up her rifle, careful not to disturb the small bandage that Ava had put over the incision on her arm.

"I'll come too," she said.

"Suit yourself."

They stepped out and slowly approached the cabin. It was dark, and there were no sounds of movement coming from inside. A large blood-stain covered the bottom stair of the porch.

"You circle right," he whispered, "and I'll go left."

She nodded.

Tanner walked around the left side, peeking into the kitchen window as he passed. The cabin appeared to be empty. When he got to the back, he saw a large contraption consisting of a burn chamber, turbine, and a maze of metal piping. A thick bundle of electrical wires routed out one side and into the cabin's junction box.

"That's new," he mumbled to himself.

Samantha tiptoed around the other corner, holding her rifle like Elmer Fudd out hunting wabbits.

"See anyone?" he asked.

"Nope."

"All right then. Let's go inside and get cleaned up."

"I can hardly wait for a hot shower," she said with a dreamy smile.

"Who said anything about hot?"

"You want us to take cold showers?"

"Not necessarily. But if you want it hot, we'll have to fire up the burn box."

"And what's that exactly?"

He pointed to a large iron box built into the back of the cabin.

"We put wood in that box, and it heats water in the boiler."

"Did you make that?"

"I did," he said, swinging open the heavy door and looking inside.

"Can it heat the house too?"

Tanner was surprised by her question.

"Is there some sort of punch line coming?"

"What?" she said. "Can't I be curious?"

He tilted his head, suspicious of her motives.

"The box," he explained, "is surrounded by masonry that goes inside the cabin. The wood burns in the box, and the masonry warms up to radiate heat into the home. It basically acts as a kachelofen."

"You made that word up," she said, laughing.

"Call it a masonry heater if you want. The only difference is that I burn the wood out here rather than inside. It can heat the cabin for hours, and like I said, it also provides heat to the boiler."

"Which will give us hot showers."

"Exactly."

She eyed him with a new measure of respect.

"That's pretty cool."

"You want to go inside and rest while I get it ready?"

She shook her head.

"No, I can help."

"Who are you and what have you done with Samantha?" he said, chuckling.

She shrugged. "I was just thinking that I should help out more. We're a team, right?"

"Since the day we met."

"That means that you're depending on me as much as I'm depending on you. Besides," she said, turning toward the woodpile, "it might be awhile before we get to my home. I don't want you getting tired of me."

"Too late," he said, chuckling again. "I wake up every morning wondering if I should leave you somewhere."

"No, you don't," she said. "Even with all your talk, I know that you love me."

Tanner stood there for a moment, watching Samantha walk away with the rifle slung over her shoulder. He replayed the violence and struggles of the past days, the close calls they had shared, the fear and horror that had always brought them back together.

He didn't have any idea what would happen next. The only thing he could say for sure was that she was absolutely right. He did love her.

# CHAPTER
## 28

The Federal Law Enforcement Training Center in Brunswick, Georgia, was a sprawling complex spread across nearly a full square mile. Before becoming a training center in 1970, it had been a Naval Air Station, and many of the buildings, hangers, and runways still looked the part. Since its inception, it had grown into a huge interagency training center for ninety different government agencies, including the US Marshals. The compound consisted of large office buildings, dormitories, shooting ranges, several driving tracks, and full-size mockups of homes and businesses that allowed realistic urban warfare training. Adjacent to the north side of the training center was the Brunswick Golden Isles Airport, which dated back to the 1940s when it had served as an operational base for blimps.

By the time Mason arrived at the main gate on FLETC Avenue, the sun was just beginning to dip behind the thick western tree line. The gate allowed for four lanes of traffic to enter and exit the facility and had a large guardhouse centered between the lanes. He pulled up to it and gave the horn a short honk. No one came out. He hadn't really known what to expect, but he was hoping that the center had somehow survived the pandemic. Apparently, it had not. If they no longer maintained even basic perimeter security, it could only mean that the center had been evacuated.

He put the truck in park and stepped out. Bowie rested on the seat, looking out at him. He still seemed tired from his fight back in Allendale.

"Just take it easy," he said. "You're good."

The dog yawned and laid its head back down.

Mason approached the guardhouse with a hand on his pistol.

"Deputy Marshal. Anyone in there?"

No one stepped out to challenge him.

The doors to the guardhouse were constructed of tinted bulletproof glass, and he couldn't make out anything except the blurry shapes of furniture inside. He pulled on the handle and was surprised when the door swung open.

Inside, two men were lying on the floor. Unlike the countless decomposing corpses that now littered the planet, these men looked more like they were taking an afternoon siesta. He stepped in and let the door swing closed behind him. Neither man moved. Both wore black fatigues, bulletproof vests with US Marshal insignias, and gun belts with Glock 22s, handcuffs, and pepper spray. Wet stains covered the crotch area of each man, and the room stunk of urine and feces. The rest of the room looked completely undisturbed, with clipboards, radios, and pens all sitting ready to be used.

Mason stepped over the closest guard and squatted down to take a look. The man's mouth was wide open, and his lips were blue, like someone had smothered him with a pillow. Both hands clutched at his throat. Rigor mortis had started to set in but hadn't yet peaked, which meant that he'd been dead for less than twelve hours.

Using his thumb and forefinger, Mason pried open one of the man's eyes. The pupil was constricted, and the white of the eye was laced with a cobweb of burst blood vessels. Asphyxiation appeared to be the likely cause of death, but what actually suffocated him was not obvious. The Superpox-99 virus certainly hadn't killed these men. Nor were there any signs of forced entry or a violent struggle.

Mason rolled the man over, unhooked his bulletproof vest, and removed his gun belt. He did the same to the second man and carried all of the equipment to the door. When he stepped out, he was surprised to see Bowie standing a few feet away. He was resting weight on the injured leg, which Mason took to be a good sign. The dog was also no longer yawning or sleepy-eyed. His full attention seemed to be on their surroundings.

"You sense it, too. Something's not right."

The dog sniffed him a few times, as if detecting a new odor, and then went back and climbed into the truck. Mason followed after him. He stowed the gun belts and body armor in the back of the truck.

The bulletproof vests in particular would come in handy. It was only a matter of time before an enemy's bullet found its mark. Wearing a vest could mean the difference between lying in a pool of blood or living to fight another day. They were a bit too hot and heavy to wear around the clock, but he could slip one on quickly enough before a gunfight. Using paracord, he thought he might even be able to string together a harness to protect Bowie. That, however, was a project for another day.

Looking over the top of the steering wheel into FLETC and then back at the guardhouse, Mason paused, unsure how to proceed. His inner voice warned him not to enter the facility, but raw curiosity beckoned him to go in and check it out.

He glanced at Bowie.

"We've come a long way. We should see this through, right?"

The dog sniffed him again and then sneezed violently, trying to clear the smell from its nose. Mason leaned down and smelled his shirt. He didn't detect anything unusual. That wasn't too surprising, given that a dog's sense of smell could be up to ten million times more sensitive than a human's. There was no way he would ever understand the world of odors in which Bowie lived. And that, he thought, might be as much a blessing as a limitation.

"Let's go take a look," he said, making up his mind. "I want to know just how bad this is." He started the truck and proceeded slowly into the training center.

Glynco was a huge compound, but Mason figured that, if anyone were still alive, they would be at the Registration Center. The three-story building abutted a long row of dorms that would enable survivors to bunk within close proximity of one another. Fortunately, it was only about a quarter of a mile inside the main gate.

He slowly cruised past several unmarked cars, the radio antennas on their trunks giving away their use in law enforcement. The driver and front passenger doors of one of the cars hung open, and two men lay dead on the pavement. Both men had marshal badges hanging from chains around their necks. Mason eased up next to the bodies. Like the two guards, neither had any visible signs of injury. A large puddle of vomit sat beside the driver's face, and both men's clothes were soiled where they had lost control of their most basic bodily functions.

Mason continued on without getting out of his truck. As soon as he turned onto Registration Road, he was forced to brake to a stop. The road ahead had collapsed into a small crater, as if a sinkhole had opened up and swallowed a ten-foot section of the asphalt. There was no way to get the truck across or around it without taking the chance of becoming stuck.

He and Bowie both climbed out and cautiously approached the crater. All around the hole were small pieces of sheet metal panels and remnants of electronic assemblies. There was nothing at the bottom of the crater, except for a white cone with four brass plugs that had once held it to something larger.

He rubbed his chin and studied it. There was something familiar about the shape of the cone and the color of the paint, but it had been too long

ago to pull from memory. Bowie walked around sniffing the pieces of metal housing, sneezing every few seconds as if he had suddenly developed an allergy to aluminum. Mason followed behind, finally reaching down and picking up a panel that had writing stamped on the inside. There were several block numbers that looked like some kind of serial number. They meant nothing to him. He flipped the panel over and saw a single word that caused the breath to catch in his throat. *Weteye*.

He tossed the panel away like it had just bitten his hand.

"Get to the truck!" he shouted. *"Go!"*

The dog was confused by the sudden outburst and stood motionless, staring at his master. Without waiting for him, Mason turned and ran for the truck. Bowie gave a short *woof* and raced after him.

They scrambled into the truck, and Mason threw it in reverse, fishtailing to the side before righting himself on the small road. He punched the gas and raced back down FLETC Avenue, speeding as fast as he dared. He flew past the main gate and out onto Chapel Crossing Road. Unable to free himself of the panic, he frantically dodged abandoned cars and roadway debris for five long miles before finally coming to a stop on a small overpass.

He shut the truck off and took a deep cleansing breath like that a yogi might take to enter a higher state of awareness. His palms were still damp, but his heart was beginning to find its normal slow rhythm.

Mason had spent six long years in the Army. For the bulk of that time, he had been part of an elite group within the 75th Ranger Regiment. He had done tours in both Iraq and Afghanistan, and during those deployments, he had heard the word *Weteye* only once. It was during the pre-briefing for an early morning raid that the rangers were to conduct on a weapons supply depot. The Iraqis had reportedly acquired a US-made Mk-116 bomb, which dated all the way back to the 1960s. *Weteye* was the fitting nickname for the Mk-116. What made the Mk-116 terrifying was not the fact that it carried up to 500 pounds of payload, but that its thin aluminum body, weighted nose, and internal baffles were designed for one purpose; to deliver chemical weapons.

The *Weteye* bomb was specifically configured to carry sarin, a nerve gas five hundred times more deadly than cyanide. Sarin had stepped on the world stage in 1995, when the Japanese religious cult, Aum Shinrikyo, used it to poison more than five thousand people in the subways of Tokyo. It popped its ugly head up again in 2013 when Syrian President Bashar al-Assad killed more than fourteen hundred civilians with the deadly gas.

Sarin was colorless and odorless, making it impossible for those being affected to detect. Early symptoms included a runny nose, tightness in the chest, and constriction of the pupils. Within minutes, it caused nausea, drooling, and difficulty breathing. Eventually, victims lost control of their bodily functions and motor control, twitching and jerking until they died by asphyxia. Death by nerve agent was not on anyone's list of preferred ways to go.

For a reason Mason couldn't fathom, someone had bombed Glynco with sarin gas. He could think of only three possible scenarios that might have led to such a horrific event. The first was some kind of accident. Perhaps a plane loaded with the bombs had been attempting to land at the Brunswick Airport as part of a weapons relocation action. That same plane could have experienced problems and inadvertently dropped its payload.

The second possibility was that terrorists, whether religious zealots, separatists, or anarchists, had used a small aircraft, either fixed or rotary wing, to drop the bombs. Mason had no idea how hard it would be for a group to get their hands on the weapon itself, but flying over the training center wouldn't have been terribly difficult, given the complete shutdown of the air transportation system.

The final possibility was the most terrifying. It suggested that the US government had intentionally used the vilest of its military assets to attack one of the nation's most renowned law enforcement facilities. That option made even less sense than the other two. Mason could think of no sequence of events that would pit the officers at Glynco against their own country's military.

Of the three, a terrorist attack seemed the most likely. The big question was why. In a time when people were literally digging through dumpsters for food, why would anyone go to the trouble to attack the infrastructure of an already defeated nation? Their motivations couldn't be to frighten the masses. There simply weren't any masses left alive. So, what could they be after?

He opened the door to his truck and stepped out, staring off at the western sky. Bowie moved up behind him, standing in the cab and resting his chin on Mason's shoulder. The sun was beginning to set, and the last rays of sunlight cast a beautiful pink glow across the Georgian sky. Mason took a deep breath and let it out slow and easy.

"What are we going to do now?"

Bowie licked his lips like he was expecting a treat.

"They're all dead."

As he put words to his despair, Mason suddenly felt like a boat adrift at sea. The Marshals had provided him with the first real sense of community since his time in the Rangers. They were more than coworkers; they were part of his identity. His existence as a lawman was now in question. Was the Marshal Service even still viable? Was he the last of their kind? Did his badge even mean anything anymore?

He reached over and laid a hand on the side of Bowie's enormous head. The dog pressed its wet nose up against Mason's cheek. He couldn't help but feel steadied by Bowie's unconditional affection.

"We can't let this stand," he said softly. "I don't know how we're going to find them, but I won't rest until I figure out who did this. I'm going to find them, and, by God, I'm going to kill them."

Mason leaned back against the truck, folding his arms across his chest. He felt the press of the harmonica in his jacket pocket. With all the running and fighting over the past two days, he was surprised that it had managed to stay with him. He slipped the instrument from his pocket and studied it. It was a beautiful silver Hohner, and he imagined Ernest T.'s family sitting around on rocking chairs, listening to him play late into the night.

And while Mason certainly didn't consider himself an expert, he had learned to play well enough to carry a tune. The harmonica was one of the few musical instruments both small enough and rugged enough to be carried into the field.

Bowie leaned over and gave it a sniff. Apparently satisfied that it smelled like a harmonica should, he laid his head back down on Mason's shoulder.

Mason blew a single note, and Bowie's ears perked up in surprise.

"Do you want me to play something?"

Bowie stared at him with excitement in his eyes.

Mason thought for a moment.

"I've got one that seems to fit."

He brought it to his lips and played the beginning of Neil Young's *Long May You Run*. The song's melody had a cool western sound, like something a cowboy might play when out on the open trail. He heard Young's nasal-inflected voice in his head.

*We've been through some things together*
*With trunks of memories still to come*
*We found things to do in stormy weather*
*Long may you run*

Mason pulled the harmonica away from his mouth, closed his eyes, and let the last rays of sunlight wash over him. The hint of a smile touched his lips as he thought of his mother and father, of his girlfriend Ava, and of the yet indistinguishable faces of evil men whose appointment with justice was not far off.

## ONLINE INFO

For information on my books and practical disaster preparedness, see:

### http://disasterpreparer.com

## CONTACT ME

If you enjoyed this book and are looking forward to the sequel, send me a short note (*arthur@disasterpreparer.com*). Like most authors, I enjoy hearing from my readers. Also, if you have time, perhaps you would be kind enough to post a positive review on Amazon.com.

I frequently travel the world giving disaster preparedness seminars. If you are a member of a church, business, or civic organization and would like to sponsor a disaster preparedness event, please keep me in mind.

### *Best wishes to you and your family!*

## FREE NEWSLETTER

To sign up for the *Practical Prepper Newsletter*, send an email to:

### newsletter@disasterpreparer.com

# Do you have a Plan?

Ninety-nine percent of the time the world spins like a top, the skies are clear, and your refrigerator is full of milk and cheese. But know with certainty that the world is a dangerous place. Storms rage, fires burn, and diseases spread. No one is ever completely safe. We all live as part of a very complex ecosystem that is unpredictable and willing to kill us without remorse or pause.

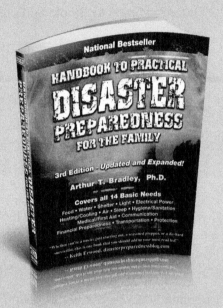

This handbook will help you to establish a practical disaster preparedness plan for your entire family. The 3rd Edition has been expanded to cover every important topic, including food storage, water purification, electricity generation, backup heating, firearms, communication systems, disaster preparedness networks, evacuations, life-saving first aid, and much more. Working through the steps identified in this book will prepare your family for nearly any disaster, whether it be natural disasters making the news daily (e.g., earthquakes, tornadoes, hurricanes, floods, and tsunamis), or high-impact global events, such as electromagnetic pulse attacks, radiological emergencies, solar storms, or our country's impending financial collapse. The new larger 8" x 10" format includes easy-to-copy worksheets to help organize your family's preparedness plans.

**Available at Disasterpreparer.com and online retailers**

# Learn to Become a PREPPER

If your community were hit with a major disaster, such as an earthquake, flood, hurricane, or radiological release, how would you handle it? Would you be forced to fall into line with hundreds of thousands of others who are so woefully unprepared? Or do you possess the knowledge and supplies to adapt and survive? Do you have a carefully stocked pantry, a method to retrieve and purify water, a source for generating electricity, and the means to protect your family from desperate criminals? In short, are you a *prepper*?

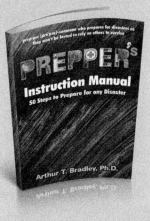

This book comprises fifty of the most important steps that any individual or family can take to prepare for a wide range of disasters. Every step is complete, clearly described, and actionable. They cover every aspect of disaster preparedness, including assessing the threats, making a plan, storing food, shoring up your home, administering first aid, creating a safe room, gathering important papers, learning to shoot, generating electricity, burying the dead, tying knots, keeping warm, and much more.

Recent events have reminded us that our world is a dangerous place, whether it is a deadly tsunami, a nuclear meltdown, or a stock market collapse. Our lifestyle, and even our very existence, is forever uncertain. Join the quickly growing community of individuals and families determined to stand ready.

# Are you Prepared for the Worst?

What would happen if terrorists detonated a nuclear device high above the United States? What about if the Sun emitted a large coronal mass ejection that resulted in a damaging geomagnetic storm? In either case, electrical power could be lost for months. Shortages would quickly ensue—food, water, and fuel would disappear within days. Widespread panic and suffering would be unavoidable. Are you prepared for these large-scale disasters?

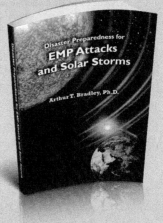

This book will help you to prepare for two end-of-the-world-as-we-know-it (TEOTWAWKI) events: the EMP attack and the solar storm. Each threat is carefully studied with analyses of its likelihood and potential impacts on our nation's critical infrastructures. Practical preparations are outlined, including steps to meet the fourteen basic needs in the absence of modern utilities, and the use of Faraday cages and uninterruptible power supplies to protect personal electronics.

Several techniques for constructing ad-hoc Faraday cages are presented. The shielding effectiveness of homemade Faraday cages is measured and compared, including metal garbage cans, foil-wrapped boxes, fire safes, static bags, ammo cans, and microwave ovens. Finally, a low-cost method of constructing a room-sized Faraday cage is presented.

**Find at Disasterpreparer.com and online retailers**

CPSIA information can be obtained
at www.ICGtesting.com
Printed in the USA
LVOW04s1439271015

459955LV00022B/1051/P